I0630264

QUEST FOR NAMAI

Quest for Namai

Marie Q Rogers

Namai Press

Copyright © 2021 Marie Q Rogers

The moral right of the author has been asserted.

All rights reserved.

No part of this publication may be reproduced, stored in a retrieval system, or transmitted, in any form or by any means, without the prior permission in writing of the publisher, nor be otherwise circulated in any form of binding or cover other than that in which it is published and without a similar condition including this condition being imposed on the subsequent purchaser. This is a work of fiction. Names, characters, places, and incidents are products of the author's imagination or are used fictitiously and are not to be construed as real. Any resemblance to actual events, locales, or persons, living or dead, is entirely coincidental.

Published by Namai Press

ISBN 978-1-7342413-2-7

Typesetting services by BOOKOW.COM

To my Grandchildren

My biggest fans

ACKNOWLEDGMENTS

I am most indebted to the Writers Alliance of Gainesville, whose members provided support and guidance through this labor of love, especially my writing pod who gave me invaluable criticism: Ken Campbell, Allison Durham, Richard Gartee, and Bonnie Ogle, as well as others who have inspired me.

Other novels by Marie Q Rogers
Trials by Fire
Season of the Dove
Notebooks Hidden in an Abandoned House

As a Contributor:
Local Lives in a Global Pandemic: Tales from North Central Florida

CONTENTS

CHAPTER 1
EVACUATION

The day of the volcano eruption played out in Fern's mind. The morning had begun innocently enough, but when she touched the water in the creek, it nearly scalded her. She called her sister Tira, who summoned Rina, Fern's adopted mother, who checked the water and looked upstream. A column of steam rose among the trees. That meant one thing—magma forcing its way to the surface—a new volcano emerging —dangerously close to home.

No time to waste! Everyone in the village had prepared for possible evacuation. Now disaster was upon them. Fern stuffed her few possessions into her backpack and everybody ran.

The mountain behind them exploded. A volley of molten rocks fell, setting fires in the forest. In terror, they sheltered under a cliff until the bombardment ceased. Then they threaded their way among the fires, rushing to safety. By some miracle, no one was hurt, but the home they'd left behind had been destroyed. Taran, Fern's adopted father, said they would go to the village of their cousins who lived by the sea and stay with them until they could rebuild.

That first night, a red glow remained visible in the western sky. Although dimmer than what had loomed over the village during those nights of watchfulness before the eruption, it was enough to disturb Fern's sleep. By the second night, they'd put more distance behind them. Now only the moons and stars lit the night sky.

Since then, they'd been walking for three days. Fern couldn't remember how many mountain ridges they'd crossed. It had been a hard forced march, but the lives of nearly one hundred people, babies to great-grandparents, depended on it. Their pace slowed only when they reached relative safety.

For the second time in her short life, Fern had been forced to flee from fire. She and her mother had come to this strange new world a year and a half ago, Earth reckoning, by wrashiru, a teleportation method she'd never imagined existed. It was a miracle, the only way they could escape from their burning house back on Earth. But no one on her new world understood how they'd managed to wrashiru without training, and they hadn't been able to return home.

Shortly after their arrival, Fern's mother died and Taran's family adopted her. She had struggled to adapt to their customs but still hadn't mastered Human Talk, their very alien language.

* * *

Fern stopped to take off her moccasins. They were woven of tough cord, and she'd mended them every night, but by now they were worn beyond repair. With a sigh, she tossed them into the woods. Simbi, the toddler accompanying her, looked up quizzically. Fern shook her head and said, "No good."

The child nodded. Simbi's parents had discarded her worn-out moccasins the day before. Simbi's mother was very pregnant and her father carried the family's belongings. To help the family, Fern had been put in charge of Simbi, so the little girl walked with her.

Fern removed her hat to smooth back the strands of blonde hair that kept creeping into her face. Then she put it back on at an angle to shade her fair skin. She'd given up on getting Simbi to wear a hat, but at least the child's darker complexion was less vulnerable to sunburn. Taking Simbi's hand, they resumed walking.

Fern didn't notice the leaf-covered rock in her path and stubbed her toe. "Ow!" She scrunched her eyes to stop the tears. She was used to rambling barefoot through the forest, but not for days on end. She examined her foot. Only a little scrape, but she wanted to scream out in fatigue, frustration, and pain. She drew a deep breath and stopped herself. If little Simbi could bear the ordeal, so could she.

She counted things to be grateful for—they were still alive, walking was easier in the river valley than in the mountain heights, and her backpack was lighter because the food she carried was half gone. But they still had days to go before they reached the sea.

The river valley narrowed to a gorge with steep rocky sides. Fern regarded it with dismay. The water churned over slippery rocks, too hazardous to wade through. Doran, her other father, started to climb the wooded hillside beside the gulley. The rest of the villagers began to follow him. Fern looked up the steep grade and groaned. "I wish there was a path through the ravine."

Taran heard her. "There is a path, a narrow one, but some of us have an uneasy feeling, so we're being cautious. If a flash flood came, we'd be trapped."

Fern didn't argue. When these people had a premonition, it was wise to obey. She adjusted her hat, grasped Simbi's hand, and set foot on the hill. In the distance, thunder rumbled.

Although Doran had chosen the easiest part of the incline, it was still so steep in many places that Fern needed her hands to grasp rocks, roots, saplings—anything—to pull herself up. More than once, she lost her footing. Simbi also struggled.

Halfway up, Simbi wrapped her arms around a small tree and sat down. "Simbi tired."

"We have to keep going," Fern said in English, because she didn't know the correct words in Human Talk. "I'll carry your backpack for you." Even though she didn't have a free hand to carry it! Somewhat roughly, she pulled the toddler to her feet. "Come on. We can rest at the top."

"No." Simbi squirmed away and ran toward her parents. Her mother was creeping up the hill on all fours. Her father struggled under his burden.

Fern threw Simbi's backpack to the ground. "I can't do this anymore!"
Then Simbi tripped and skidded down the hillside, screaming.

"Oh, no!" Fern was helpless to stop Simbi, but she inched down the
slope toward her. One of Simbi's grandfathers, who was walking behind
them, caught the child. Simbi cried as though in pain.

Taran, also in the rear, shouted to Fern, "Go on up. Get Andli."

Andli, Fern's other mother, was a healer. If Taran thought she was
needed, Simbi must be injured. I shouldn't have been so cross with her,
Fern thought. On her way up, she met Andli, who was already climbing
down. Fern wasn't surprised. These people knew one another's thoughts.

Andli hugged Fern. "Don't worry," she said in Human Talk. "Go up
with the others." She wiped a tear off Fern's cheek and made her way
downhill.

Fern retrieved Simbi's backpack and finished the climb. "How is she?"
Tira asked in English.

Fern turned away so Tira wouldn't see her cry. "I don't know."

Simbi's parents made it to the top and sat down. Behind them came
Andli and Taran. Simbi was asleep in her grandfather's arms. He laid
the child down beside her mother. Andli crushed a handful of herbs and
smeared the pulp on Simbi's arms and legs.

"Is she okay?" Fern asked.

Taran nodded. "Just a few scratches."

Fern sighed with relief. To Simbi's parents, she said, "Estut miryit.
I'm so sorry."

Taran translated Belan's reply. "This is hard for everyone. You did your
best. We appreciate all you do for us. Tekuyate."

Fern's legs quivered so badly she could barely walk over to join the rest
of her family. Was she really that tired? More likely it was the fright
of Simbi's accident. She collapsed on the ground and rubbed her calves.
She was relieved when Taran told her they would eat and rest before
continuing their journey.

Lunch was a biscuit and a handful of greens. Then everyone lay down
for naps. Fern rested her head on her backpack but, tired though she

was, she had trouble falling asleep. Her heart wept for the weka, the very elderly ones, who had stayed behind when they fled from the village.

Geltan, Taran's great-grandfather, was among them. Something he'd said when she was new to this world came to mind. Taran had translated his words for her. "He said you are troubled and unhappy. He thinks your road to healing will be long and difficult."

Her feet attested to the long and difficult road they were taking, but that's not what Geltan meant. After losing her home and family on Earth, Fern had barely healed emotionally before she was once again torn from her new home, from everything familiar, and set out on another path to uncertainty.

A sudden roar disturbed her thoughts. She grabbed her backpack, ready to run from another volcano, but when she looked around, no one else seemed alarmed. The sound came from the river. She dashed to the edge of the cliff and stared down. A torrent raged through the gorge. The path was flooded! Fern shivered. Another close call.

Rain began to fall in the forest around them, but Fern didn't feel a drop. The elders sat in deep meditation, putting up a force field to shelter everyone.

Fern returned to her family circle. Her sisters and brothers were napping. Her sister-in-law, Sela, nursed her baby. Taran and Rina sat in deep meditation. Doran and Andli appeared to be resting, but alert. Although their plural marriage had been a shock to Fern at first, by now she felt secure having two mothers and two fathers. All four were kind and patient. She lay back down and dozed off.

When people around her began to stir, Fern woke and slipped off into the woods to relieve herself. When she returned, everyone was ready to resume walking. Doran, whose knowledge of the wilderness made him the leader on the journey, was conferring with a couple of elders. Fern wished she could ask him how he knew which way to go, but he didn't speak English. So she asked Taran. "Has Doran been here before? Does he know this part of the country?"

"No. This territory is unfamiliar to him. He's been to the sea, but not by this route. We couldn't take our usual path because of the eruption."

"Then how does he know where to go?"

"Noba advises him. She has the gift of ethenos and scouts out a path for him. Besides, almost all rivers eventually lead to the sea."

Fern looked at Noba, Andli's mother, with new respect. Fern also had the gift of ethenos, astral or etheric projection. She used it to visit the family she'd left on Earth, but she didn't know it could be used to explore this planet. She wished she could talk with Noba, but Noba didn't speak English. Only Taran and Tira.

Once the company had assembled, Doran headed downhill. Fern put on her hat, hoisted her backpack, and Simbi joined her. Fern's brother Forsil began to play a tune on his flute, and others took up the song. Fern stepped in time with the rhythm. She understood some of the words but could pronounce only a few, so she hummed along. They rejoined the river where walking was easier.

Because they were traveling with small children, they stopped frequently to rest. At one break, Simbi said, "I want skri," and pointed at Fern's backpack. One reason they were friends was that Fern's grasp of the language was on the toddler's level. Fern tried to tell Simbi they were not allowed to snack and would eat later, but she couldn't find the right words. Simbi ran to her parents. They explained that she'd have to wait and sent her back to Fern.

Fern's stomach, too, felt empty. Their light breakfast and meager lunch hadn't been enough. At the village, there'd always been plenty of food and she could eat whenever she wanted to. Fern picked a handful of lenitrus, edible wild leaves, for her and Simbi to munch on until supper.

Late in the afternoon, Fern heard the distant sound of falling water. It reminded her of the cascade downriver from their abandoned village. As they proceeded, the noise grew louder and the river's current flowed more swiftly. Someone began a new song and others joined in. It was a cheerful tune about a waterfall. Fern didn't know all the words, but the burden on her heart lifted.

Before they reached the falls, the villagers laid down their backpacks. Fern did the same, more than ready for a rest stop, but curiosity drew her to the waterfall. The river tumbled over a series of cataracts into a wide jungle below. After a few minutes of admiration, Fern scanned the cliff, looking for a way down.

Tira came up beside her. "We're going to camp here tonight."

"Really? It's too early to stop."

"Yes, but when we get down there, it'll be hotter and more humid. We'll take advantage of the cooler mountain air one more night. When you get done sight-seeing, gather some lenitrus."

Fern resented Tira telling her what to do. She knew she was supposed to collect lenitrus for supper. Tira was her age, not old enough to boss her around. She looked at the vegetation below and spotted several likely plants. To reach them, she almost slid down the rocky slope. Doran would need to find a better path than this.

She was delighted to find wispis and a few others she recognized. Before picking leaves off each plant, she bowed her head and asked its permission. This was the way of her new people. She was careful not to harvest more leaves than the plant could spare. Afterward, she thanked it.

When she returned to the encampment, the villagers had formed a loose circle of families similar to the arrangement of their houses in their lost village. In the center, they'd set a ring of stones where Alta was building a fire. On one side of the fire circle, someone had laid a large flat stone supported by smaller rocks. After the fire burned down, Alta would shove hot coals under the stone and bake pancakes the size of large pizzas. The elders were already mixing meal with water.

Fern added her armful of lenitrus to the pile on a nearby cloth. Without being told, she gathered her share of firewood. Then she returned to where she'd left her backpack. It was gone. She joined her family and found that someone had moved it for her.

Rina looked in the backpack of each family member to count the number of skri—biscuits made of nut meal—that were left. She then talked

7

with the adults of other households. All looked concerned. Fern wondered how long their supplies would last.

"Are we running out of food?" she asked Taran.

"We'll need to ration it for a few days, but don't worry, we won't starve before we reach the sea."

"Why don't we stop and collect nuts?"

"Have you seen any nut trees?"

No, she hadn't. "I thought they grew all over the world."

"Think about it. How many plants on Earth grow all over that world?"

He was right. "What kind of food will we find at the sea?"

"There are nut trees and other plants you're used to, plus some that don't grow in the mountains."

"Are there any fish?"

Taran shook his head. "No animal life. Not even in the sea."

At first, this had been one of the strangest things to Fern. Her new people had come to this world the same way she had, by wrashiru, and had been here only a little over a century. No one could explain what twist of evolution was responsible for the absence of animal life on this planet. Otherwise, the place was very Earth-like, and its ecosystems worked perfectly. Part of her education had been Doran's teachings, with Tira translating. He had described some of the fascinating ways plants were pollinated and seeds dispersed without the help of animals.

Waiting for supper gave everyone time to bathe. Parents took the younger children upstream to a pool where the current wasn't too swift. The more adventurous went down to take showers in the falls. Fern removed the cord she wore around her neck and tucked it into her basket. It held a little pouch which contained three precious things: a medallion made from a lock of her mother's hair, a dried flower from the miaven tree on her mother's grave, and a small egg-shaped stone.

She climbed down to the falls, loosened her hair, and braced herself for the cold water. She missed the warm stream near the village where she used to bathe. Nearly everyone else shed their tunics, but Fern hadn't been able to overcome the modesty instilled in her as a child.

She plunged under the torrent fully clothed and gave her hair, body, and tunic a thorough rinsing.

When she was done, she climbed back to camp, averting her gaze from the naked bathers, especially the males, mainly the boys who'd shown an interest in her as a potential mate. She slipped behind a bush to change into her other tunic and hung the wet one to dry. Then she replaced the cord around her neck, letting the pouch hang against her heart. Finally, she combed her hair and braided it. On this journey, there was no time to fix hair every morning like they had back in the village.

When the family assembled for supper, Rina set down only one pancake topped with lenitrus and dressing. Previous nights, each family had been given several, and everyone had eaten their fill. Tonight, the adults, except Sela who was nursing and couldn't be denied food, stood aside while the children ate. This meant there wasn't enough to go around. Fern glanced at nearby families and saw that they, too, were feeding their children first.

Fern tore off an edge of pancake and wrapped it around as much lenitrus as it would hold. She'd fill up on vegetables and let the adults have the rest of her bread. Tira and Forsil were doing the same.

"Eat," Andli encouraged them. "There's more coming." Rina brought over another pancake, a small one.

After supper, Simbi came to get her doll from Fern. Even the toddlers carried something, if no more than their clothes and blanket, but Simbi had no room in her backpack for a doll. Her parents had intended to leave it, because it was replaceable, but that would have broken Simbi's heart. Fern, who had few possessions, carried it for her.

Everyone had left belongings behind. Fern had abandoned the precious rocking chair which had been made for her mother. It had given Mama comfort when she was dying. The sentiment had made it irreplaceable, but of course, it was too much to carry.

As it grew dark, the family laid out blankets and the younger ones went to sleep. Fern missed nights on the sameg, the common area of their village, when everyone gathered to sing, dance, and tell stories. No one had the energy to dance after walking all day, but a few sat around the fire to sing. Forsil played his flute and someone, perhaps Rina, drummed in accompaniment.

Fern stretched out on her blanket and looked at the stars that peeped through the tree branches. The small moon was high in the sky, but she didn't see the large moon. It was past full and hadn't risen yet.

CHAPTER 2
PATH TO THE SEA

In the morning, despite a scanty breakfast, Fern's mood was lighter. Doran led them away from the river to find a more gradual descent from the mountain heights. They rejoined the river downstream from the falls. Fern paused to listen. She could hear the falling water in the distance.

Tira had been right—the air was hotter and more humid in the lowlands. Despite the deep shade of the jungle, it was oppressive, worse than August in Florida. Here, Fern didn't need her hat. She tucked it into her backpack and felt slightly cooler without it. Before long, her tunic was soaked with sweat. No one sang while they walked. When they stopped for lunch, everyone went swimming, clothes and all.

Fern stepped out of the cool water, refreshed for the moment, but before her tunic dried, she began to sweat again. She rinsed off during each rest stop.

That afternoon, Simbi became petulant and collapsed on the ground. When Fern tried to take her hand, she pulled away. "No. Simbi want go namai."

Fern wasn't sure what she meant. She tried to pick her up, but Simbi only wriggled out of her arms and cried. "Simbi want go namai!"

Tira, who had been walking ahead with their little sister Ara, came back to help.

"I don't understand," Fern said. "I know she's tired."

Simbi let Tira hold her. "What's wrong?"

The child buried her face in Tira's chest and said, "Want go namai."

Tira looked up at Fern and said in English, "She wants to go home." Tira tried to explain to Simbi that she couldn't go home, but the child began to cry.

Fern felt helpless. Once again, she'd failed in her care of Simbi. When Simbi's parents caught up with them, the child rushed to her mother. Taran, who had taken up the rear, said. "If you can go a little further, we're looking for a good place to rest."

Farsa said something Fern couldn't understand. Tira translated. "She suggests you and Simbi walk with them for a while."

Simbi was content to hold Fern's hand as long as her mother was near. From time to time Farsa or her mate would give words of encouragement to both their daughter and Fern.

Finally, they stopped for the night. Fern bathed and changed into her dry tunic. After she hung up her wet one, she planned to gather lenitrus, but Tira pulled her aside.

"Doran has found another edible plant," she said.

Doran stood beside a bush, lecturing a group of young people and children. The shrub's branches were tipped with fleshy green fan-shaped structures. Fern had seen these bushes in the jungle but hadn't thought about them being edible. Doran picked a fan and, while talking, pointed to its several parts before he stripped away a few outer layers and handed out the pieces. The inner part that clasped the stem was white.

Fern tried to follow what he said. When Doran nibbled the white part of his leaf, she did the same. It had a sweet, delicate flavor, but the green part was tough. The others talked among themselves and dispersed into the forest. Fern started to follow, but Doran beckoned to her. He repeated what he'd told everyone else while Tira translated. "It's actually a flower, and these are petals."

With no insects to attract, flowers on this world were inconspicuous, with no color or scent. On Earth, Fern had seen brightly colored tropical flowers that were shaped like this, but to her knowledge, none were edible. She wished she knew their name, even though they wouldn't be related to these plants.

Tira continued. "The whole plant is safe to eat, but it's too tough, except for the tender white part." Doran half-peeled off another petal and pointed to where it attached to the stem. Nestled between petal and stem was a seed the size of a pea. "These are edible, too, but they need to be cooked. The sea people grind them up and add them to skri. Doran says to scatter them around away from the plants so they can grow. Also, harvest only mature flowers. The seeds in the younger ones aren't ripe enough to sprout."

Fern nodded. "What are they called?"

Tira answered with an unpronounceable word. Even when she spoke it slowly, Fern shook her head. "I'll call them fan-flowers for now."

Fern found an area where no one else had picked fan-flowers. She found a similar bush that had tall spikes of tight, unopened blossoms. That might be a male plant, she thought. They must be pollinated by wind.

As she gathered the edible flowers, she thought about how Doran had persuaded the miaven tree on her mother's grave to bloom with purplish blossoms. She thought how beautiful these fan-flowers would be if they were a different color, perhaps red or yellow. Maybe when they had time, she'd talk to Doran about this.

Having a new item on the menu made their insufficient supper slightly more satisfying. After pancakes had been baked, a boy a little younger than Fern tried toasting the tough part of a fan-flower on the stone. Fern watched him bite into it. It must have been tough still, because he shook his head and tossed it into the fire.

Fern's wet tunic hardly dried in the muggy night. By mid-morning, the other was saturated. At the next rest stop, several of the smaller children took off their clothes. Their parents tried to keep them dressed.

"Why can't they just go naked?" Fern asked Tira. "They'd be cooler."

"Their tunics wick moisture away from the skin. When it evaporates, it cools them."

"I don't see much evaporation in this humidity."

Tira ignored her.

Simbi took off her tunic. Fern looked at her parents inquiringly. Farsa appeared too tired to care. Belan shrugged his shoulders, so Fern let Simbi go naked. She didn't mind unclothed children, but she was glad the adults stayed dressed. They walked through the day with their spare tunics hanging from their backpacks, trying to get them dry.

As if the discomfort of the jungle wasn't enough, they were almost out of food. When they stopped for lunch, Rina took the remaining skri out of Fern's backpack, broke them in half, and distributed the halves to the children. At least fan-flowers were available. They were more satisfying than lenitrus. When Fern realized the adults went without skri, she felt guilty for not sharing hers with them.

After her nap, Fern stood on the riverbank and peered downstream through the undergrowth. Her eyes followed the current as it twisted around snags and over rocks. She wondered how many miles they'd come.

Did these people have a measurement for distance? She should ask Taran, but she expected an answer similar to her inquiry about time. Their days were not segmented by hours or minutes. There were no weeks or months or even years, only the cycle of the Full Moons. Otherwise, they just let time flow.

She looked back the way they'd come. There was hardly any evidence of a path, as though only a few, not a hundred, people had passed through. Weary though they were, they made little impact on the wilderness. She looked ahead where there was no path, yet Doran would find one.

Many of the trees and other plants looked the same as those she'd grown used to in the mountains. Although this was a different river, it reminded her of the one that had flowed by their village. She was homesick for a place that no longer existed. No wonder Simbi was having a hard time. Well, she had survived homesickness for Earth. She'd survive this, too.

As they walked through the afternoon, Fern paid more attention to the vegetation, wondering what else was edible. Surely, Doran would know.

At supper, their family got one pancake half the size of the usual ones. Instead of joining them, the parents wandered into the woods to forage. Sela divided the pancake among herself and the six children. Fern ate half of hers without thinking. Sela finished hers and began nursing the baby.

Fern looked at Tira and Forsil who also held half-eaten pieces. The three made eye contact with one another, then without speaking, handed Sela the rest of their food and left before she could object.

Fern found Doran in the forest. She pointed to a plant that looked tender enough to chew and said the word for eat. He smiled and plucked two leaves, handing one to her. He bit his leaf and made a face. Fern hesitated, then nibbled on hers. It was so bitter she spat it out, and they both laughed. Doran said something, but the only word she caught was, "Kirrib." Maybe he meant it was good in soup.

At night, nearly everyone else slept naked, but Fern usually wore her clothes to bed. That night, neither of her tunics were dry, so she hung them up and trusted the darkness to hide her nudity. At least there were no mosquitoes.

Other than lenitrus, there was no breakfast. Little Simbi was more miserable than ever and refused to eat more vegetables. Every time she said she was hungry, Fern encouraged her to drink water. Thank goodness we're by a river, she thought.

That afternoon, they passed an ancient tree with a huge growth on its side. No one paid much attention to it until one of the children began to laugh. Rina, who had been trudging along, threw up her head, dropped her backpack, and ran to the tree. Almost reverently, she caressed the swelling as if she were touching a pregnant belly. In fact, it was as round as a ripe belly and stuck out from the tree in the same way.

Doran followed her, and he, too, ran his hands over the large ball, careful not to disturb its grey bark. He spoke to Rina, but she threw up her hands in resignation and returned to her backpack. She slung it over her shoulders and resumed walking. Doran stood before the tree for a few minutes before he returned to his place at the head of the group. What was that all about? Fern was almost too tired to be curious.

The next morning, it was as hot and humid as ever, but a slight breeze carried a hint of salt air. At midday, Fern heard a shout in the distance. Soon they met a new group of people, all carrying baskets. They set them down, opened them, and took out food. The parents of small children wasted no time distributing skri.

Fern grabbed a biscuit and withdrew to where she could watch the villagers and newcomers greet one another. She hadn't been so shy when she lived on Earth. Perhaps the language barrier made her wary of strangers.

One young man rushed to Tira, hugged and kissed her, and attached himself to their household. He reminded Fern of Tira's brother Tiril, the young man she had fallen in love with before he left for Earth, but this youth's skin was more golden. His eyes had flecks of gold among the green, and even his hair had gold highlights where it had been bleached by the sun.

Tira brought him over. "Fern, this is Ansil, Tiril's brother. He's the one who made the rocking chair for your mother."

Ansil's smile resembled Tiril's.

Fern's heart brightened. She said, "Tekuyate." Then she asked Tira, "Is he is your brother, too?"

"No. He and Tiril have the same mother, Lila. His father is Rogan, the one in the green tunic. We're not closely related by blood."

Rogan was talking with Taran. Fern saw his resemblance to Ansil. Rogan's skin was lighter than most and his hair had those same golden highlights. However, his eyes were more the color of ripe olives.

Fern nibbled on her second skri and sorted out the men's relationship. Both had been Lila's mates, Taran before he'd mated with Andli and

Rina, and now Rogan. She saw no conflict between the men. They acted like best friends, not rivals for the same woman.

Fern shook her head. Would she ever get used to the ways of these people? She hoped that, providing she wasn't able to return to Earth, she wouldn't be expected to enter into one of these plural marriages.

After a good lunch and rest, they resumed walking. Simbi was happier with a full belly. So was Fern. By mid-afternoon, a pleasant breeze wafted toward them and the air cooled. Soon they reached a cliff where the river cascaded over rocks and the blue sea winked through the trees. Fern filled her lungs with salt air and stepped off the path to where she could get a better view.

It had been too long since she'd gone to a beach. An expanse of beautiful white sand stretched below. Large boulders stood in the water, which was so clear she could see patches of water plants on the bottom. She let the wind evaporate the sweat from her face.

Simbi tugged at her. Everyone else was moving on. The path twisted its way down among rocks. Evening was approaching and they had to get to the bottom of this cliff before dark.

By now, Simbi's mother was barely able to walk. How could she climb down? One of the sea people had brought a rope. Farsa's mate make a sling so he could lower her from one ledge to the next. Farsa set her mouth in a tight line as though she were in pain, but she didn't complain.

Simbi was eager to follow her mother. At a particularly steep part of the path, her tired feet slipped from under her and she fell.

"Not again!" Helplessly, Fern watched the child tumble down until one of the sea people caught her. Fern descended as fast as she dared. Simbi cried for her mother but her parents were below them on the cliff. Fern checked Simbi for injuries. A few scrapes and bruises, but she couldn't put her weight on one leg. Fern felt for broken bones. Simbi howled. The man who had caught her ran his hands lightly over her leg and frowned. He gathered Simbi in his arms and carried her down the path.

On a wide ledge below, Andli waited for them. The man set Simbi down and Andli gently massaged the child's body, head to toe, lastly the injured leg. Simbi stopped crying and eventually stood up and limped along, holding Fern's hand. They climbed down the rest of the way with no further mishap.

At the beach, a small group of sea people welcomed them with campfires and fresh pancakes. Simbi ran to her parents. One of her grandmothers took charge and led Simbi to the water to bathe.

Fern joined her family. For supper, they had several pancakes piled with lenitrus, some of which was unfamiliar. "I guess they have plants here that don't grow in the mountains," she said.

Tira answered, "That's right. And they also have plants in the water. Some of this lenitrus is seaweed."

After they ate, the travelers stripped off their clothes and went swimming. The sea people set up racks near the fires where freshly washed tunics could be draped to dry. Under cover of darkness, Fern bathed in the river and washed both tunics. She put one on and hung the other by the fire. Then she walked along the shore until her tunic was dry enough to sleep in.

She tasted the seawater and was surprised to find it not as salty as the Atlantic Ocean. The light of the small moon, almost full, glowed on the crests of waves which tickled the sand. She peered at the horizon and wondered how far the sea stretched.

Most of the travelers went to bed, but some joined the sea people at the campfires to sing and tell stories. Lying on her blanket on the sand with her sisters, listening to the waves and the music, smelling the campfires and salt air, Fern recalled camping trips to the beach with her family on Earth. She and her sisters used to pick up shells and chase crabs which disappeared into little holes in the sand. No crabs or shellfish here, but her family, like these people, would sit by a fire at night and tell stories.

Fern remembered her little sisters begging to hear, for the hundredth time, the story of how their parents met.

Daddy had been a senior in college and Mama was in nursing school. Both had gone to St. Augustine on spring break and were visiting the Castillo de San Marcos. Mama had become separated from her friends.

Daddy always started the story with, "Here I was, on the battlements of this ancient castle, and I spied a damsel in distress."

"Nonsense. I was in no distress."

"Here was this beautiful maiden with golden hair that shone in the sun, and she had been abandoned by her retinue."

"So this crazy Irishman comes up and wants to talk to me."

"She must have thought I was a pirate, come to carry her off."

"Well, that's about what you did." Everyone always laughed.

Like her sisters, Fern never tired of the story. The Old Fort was such a romantic setting in which to meet the man of one's dreams. On these thoughts, she drifted into a restful sleep.

CHAPTER 3
THE SEA PEOPLE

Fern slept so soundly she didn't wake until she heard the melody of the morning song. By habit, her mind filled in the English words Tiril had taught her:

> Light from the stars begins to fade
> And gathers in the sleeping east.
> We bade goodnight to cool, dark hours
> And welcome in the bright, warm day.
> Our hearts are filled with gratitude
> For this green world, blue sky, and sea,
> And for the sun and moons and stars,
> And for the miracles of life.

She scrambled to her feet and faced east with everyone else. The rising sun painted both sky and sea purple and red. She drank in the salt air and spread her limbs to let the soft breeze wash over her skin.

Tira called Fern over to a tidal pool near the mouth of the river. Ansil burst to the surface with his hands under water, holding something that looked like a flower. Fern tried to look at the flower, not his naked body. When he lifted it above the surface, it closed into a tight brown nut.

"What is it?" Fern asked.

"An oyster," Tira said. "Well, not really an oyster, it's a plant, but we call it 'ostrica.'"

Ansil flicked his wrist and it opened. Fleshy leaves radiated from the center like a lotus blossom. "Eat it," he said in English.

The petals had a delicate, slightly sweet flavor, similar to the fan-flowers.

Ansil dove for another and gave it to Fern. She flicked her wrist as he had done, but nothing happened. Ansil laughed.

"You have to open it with your mind," Tira said.

"Oh."

Ansil smiled into her eyes. His gaze coursed through every nerve in her body. She sucked in her breath. He touched the ostrica. She felt a tingle, and it opened.

"Tekuyate." She stepped back, away from him, and sat down to eat it.

Tira and Ansil gathered more ostrica and distributed them among the children. When Fern's equanimity returned, she helped them. She noticed the children had little trouble opening theirs. When no one was looking, she tried again, but the tight nut refused to open. She had to ask a child to help her.

After breakfast and a swim, the company walked southward along the beach. As before, Simbi walked with Fern, but she wanted to stay close to her mother, whose pace was painfully slow. Farsa's mate, Belan, and both sets of grandparents hovered around her. It must be awful having to walk all this distance when she's pregnant, Fern thought.

The soft sand massaged her feet. She felt at home with the sea on one side and palm-like trees on the other. The breeze threatened to take her hat. She stopped, took two pieces of yarn out of her backpack, attached them to the hat, and tied them under her chin. "Wind, do your best," she said.

The cool sea air improved everyone's mood and they sang as they walked. Simbi and Fern sang the ditties they had taught each other, in English and Human Talk.

Before the first rest stop, Farsa sat down in the shade. Belan knelt beside her and rubbed her back. He called Taran and Fern over and spoke to them. The only words Fern understood were "tekuyate" and "Simbi."

Taran said, "He thanks you for helping with Simbi, but you no longer need to be responsible for her, so you can go on."

Fern looked to where the other adolescents, including Tira and Ansil, were walking ahead. None of them appeared to be in charge of small children anymore.

"The hard part of the journey is over," Taran said. "You can relax now."

Much as Fern loved Simbi, she was glad to be relieved of her care. She joined the other young people. When she looked back, Simbi's family lagged far behind.

She caught herself looking for shells on the beach, even though they couldn't exist on this world. She waded in the shallows and wished she had time to explore the rocks that skirted the shore. When the sun climbed higher and grew hotter, she and her companions moved into the shade of the trees along the beach.

Late that afternoon, they came to a large river with a strong current. Fern wondered how they could cross it. "Boats," Ansil responded to her unspoken question. A picture flashed through her mind—a sailboat gliding across the mouth of the river.

Fern looked around but saw no boats.

Ansil continued to talk to Fern. She caught the word "barca" but didn't know what it meant.

Tira said, "They stored the boats behind the dunes where the tide can't carry them off. We'll get them out tomorrow when we're ready to cross the river. 'Barca' means boat. It's Italian. We don't know if the thortles had a word for boat, because they never told us. One of our cousins who visited Italy brought 'barca' into our language. Also 'ostrica.'"

Fern realized Tira had read her thoughts. She'd let her guard down when she tried to understand what Ansil said. She was surprised to hear Tira mention the thortles so casually. Tira was usually reluctant to talk about that alien race that enslaved her ancestors. Whenever Fern asked about them, Tira's answers were tinged with dread. Taran's reactions were more extreme. If the subject came up, he would struggle to control a deep-seated anger.

Most of what Fern knew about the thortles she had learned from Tiril. He'd told her they were a space-faring race. They collected specimens from many planets, including Earth, and exhibited them in zoos. When they discovered that certain humans had useful mental powers, they captured and bred psychics to work for them. Communication over vast distances was limited to the speed of light, but telepathy was instantaneous. The human slaves' ability to send and receive messages enabled the thortles to manage their interstellar empire.

The ancestors of the people Fern now lived among had escaped from the thortles, but imbedded in their psyche was a fear that if they were discovered, the thortles might capture and enslave them again. Only Tiril had been willing to talk about them. Now he was far away, visiting Earth, and she could no longer ask him questions.

Fern noticed a change in her sister's demeanor after Ansil joined them. Tira acted more spirited and, at the same time, more relaxed. Fern couldn't blame Tira for liking Ansil. He was a nice-looking young man. Since Tira and Ansil weren't closely related by blood, he was a potential mate.

She followed Tira and Ansil to a tidal pool and heard them say something about ostrica. While others built fires, gathered lenitrus, and prepared supper, the young people dove for ostrica and collected enough for everyone. Fern sheepishly asked for help opening hers.

Not until after dark did Simbi's family reach camp. Simbi took her doll from Fern and fell asleep over supper. Farsa was too exhausted to eat, but Belan coaxed her to nibble on an ostrica. Singing around the campfire that evening was quiet and restrained. It reminded Fern of the evening before Rufan and Sela's baby was born.

In the morning, Ansil and the men dragged several catamarans from behind the dunes to the mouth of the river. From what Ansil had pictured in her mind, Fern expected sails, but none were evident. They loaded the backpacks on the barcas and tied them in place. The sailors then launched their boats into the river and steered them into the swift current, which carried them in an arc beyond the mouth of the river.

They used this momentum to paddle the barcas to the opposite bank. Once unloaded, the boats returned for passengers.

Strong swimmers crossed the river by themselves. Fern knew she couldn't beat the current and went a little way upriver to enter the water. She let the flow carry her downstream while she swam across, and she ended up where everybody else did.

Once everyone had reached the other side, the sailors retrieved masts and sails from behind the trees where they'd stored them. Simbi and her parents were settled on a barca. Backpacks were secured on the others, and most of the villagers set out walking.

Ansil had room for one passenger and invited Fern to accompany him. It had been so long since she'd gone sailing! As they skimmed along, she examined his craft. The twin hulls were made of wooden frames covered by smooth bark. Struts supported the mast and hammock, which was woven of tightly-spun cord. The sailcloth was a finer weave, with brightly colored designs worked in. Fern scrutinized the fabrics. They were made of a material unknown to her. They must have fibers here that don't grow in the mountains, she thought. Everything was sealed with a waxy substance.

Ansil handled the boat almost effortlessly. When he needed to tack, he let Fern hold the tiller. Apparently satisfied with her skill, he allowed her to sail.

At midday, they went ashore and waited for the walkers. After lunch, Fern took a nap. When she woke, to her disappointment, Ansil had already left, and Tira had gone with him.

As the company set out, Fern noticed Farsa was still sitting in the shade, Simbi by her side.

"It's time for the baby to be born," Taran said. "We can go on. Farsa's family will stay here with her."

Farsa's parents and Belan's emerged from the woods with poles and "palm" fronds. "Are they building her a house?" Fern asked.

"Only a temporary shelter so she'll be comfortable. The baby has chosen an inconvenient time, but at least he waited until we reached the sea."

Andli, who was a skilled midwife, showed no signs of staying with Farsa. "Won't she need Andli's help?"

Taran shook his head. "They're not expecting any complications, and there are two sets of grandparents to assist."

They reached the village of the sea people that evening. It looked similar to the mountain village, a semi-circle of thatched houses around a common area. This one was a built on a shelf of land well above the beach, with wide steps leading up to it. The fire pit, similar to that in the mountain village, was situated on the landward side of the sameg, where the sea winds would blow the smoke away from the houses. Behind it, hills rose into the mountains.

A throng of people descended upon them, including some of the elders and weka they'd left in the mountain village, but not all. Fern's heart ached for Taran and Rina's great-grandparents who were not able to wrashiru to safety. They'd given up their lives to stay behind and put up a force field against the volcanic ash and gasses, to shield the rest of the villagers, allowing them to escape from danger.

A woman approached Fern and said in English, "I'm so glad to see you again." It was Lila, who had gone to Earth with Taran and Tira. Fern had met her when she woke after arriving by wrashiru. Lila hugged her. "Come, I'll show you where you'll stay." She escorted Fern to a house. "You and your sisters may sleep in our room. Rogan and I will sleep on the sameg."

Four pallets were arranged around the room. Fern recognized her own blanket on one. Above it, someone had hung her backpack. "Tekuyate," Fern said and hugged Lila.

Supper was cooked on the sameg but the food was carried to the beach. On an area of hard-packed sand, there was room for everyone to gather around campfires to eat and socialize.

Fern was lost in the sea of faces. Lila and Taran chatted with friends they'd not seen in some time. Tira was glued to Ansil. Fern ate with her sisters, Tala and Ara, who also seemed overwhelmed by the hundred or so cousins they didn't know well. After supper, the crowd cleared the area and sat around what was now a dance floor. When the music began, Fern was too tired to dance, but she listened to half-understood songs and stories.

During a break in the music, Fern was surprised to hear her name. She looked up to find every eye on her, every face smiling.

Taran placed a hand on her shoulder. "We've been telling our cousins about how you alerted us to the lava flow near the village. Everyone is grateful to you."

Fern managed a bashful smile.

A hundred voices said, "Tekuyate."

"I didn't do anything special," Fern said. "The water in the creek was hot, so I told Tira."

"It's a good thing you did," Lila said.

Not long after, the younger girls went to bed, and Fern followed. On the beach, talking, singing, and dancing went on most of the night. Tira didn't come to bed until all was quiet.

The next morning, Fern noticed that people were staring at her. She had forgotten how different she was from the people on this planet. When she'd first arrived in the mountain village, her blonde hair and blue eyes made her stand out among the dark haired, green eyed descendants of all the races of Earth.

After breakfast and tidying up, the family resumed their practice of fixing one another's hair in intricate patterns of braided strands, pinned up off the neck to keep them cool. By now Fern's hair had grown to her waist. It was straight and fine and, when she danced in the evenings, the hairdo would often come apart. She'd learned to comb and braid it at night before going to bed so it wouldn't be tangled in the morning, but last night she'd been too tired. Andli and Rina had to untangle it before they could plait it. Their efforts drew an audience of children. Her younger siblings, Tala, Ara, and Donal, became instantly popular when they introduced their golden-haired sister to new-found friends.

The older boys of the sea village watched from a respectful distance, but she knew what was on their mind. In the mountain village, she'd been courted by every adolescent boy, even though she was too young to mate. It was more than her appearance that attracted them. Interbreeding was a concern in such a small population and only distant cousins were allowed to have children together. Fern was not related to anyone, which made her a potential mate for any man on the planet.

But she wanted to go home to Earth, not get tied to a husband. Or children. The mountain boys had lost interest when Fern failed to encourage them. The only one she had allowed herself to have feelings for was Tiril. But he hadn't been interested in a relationship. He was going to Earth and would be gone for years. And now he was on Earth, where she wanted to be, but she couldn't get there.

After her mothers finished Fern's hair and released her, a boy approached and said, "Buenos días, señorita Fern. Mi nombre es Arlon."

After a moment of surprise, she replied, "Buenos días." They exchanged a few pleasantries, but Fern's middle school Spanish was inadequate for much conversation. She rushed to find Lila.

"There's a boy here who speaks Spanish."

"Yes," Lila said, "Arlon and his parents visited Earth and lived in Mexico."

"Why Mexico?"

"When we go to Earth, we try to fit in. We can easily pass as Americans, since you are a society of mixed races, and we are believable as Hispanics." She laughed. "But we'd stand out in some countries on Earth, where you'd fit right in."

Early that morning, a few sailors had launched their boats, but at the time Fern couldn't find anyone who could tell her why. She knew they hadn't gone fishing, because there were no fish. About midday, a cheer rose from the beach. The barcas returned with Farsa and her family. Belan hopped from a boat and helped beach it. Farsa handed him a little bundle which he held against his chest while Farsa's father lifted her off the boat. Belan passed the bundle back to Farsa and they waded ashore.

The crowd parted to let them pass. When Simbi spotted Fern, she ran up and hugged her. Once they were in the shade, Farsa sat down and took the blanket off the baby. Fern craned her neck for a peek. Simbi took her hand and pulled her over to Farsa. Beaming, Simbi fondled the newborn's head and said, in Human Talk, "This my baby. He name Melir."

Farsa smiled at Fern and spoke to her mate. Belan took little Melir from Farsa's arms and, to Fern's surprise, handed him to her. She clutched him tightly, afraid to drop him. As Belan helped Farsa to her feet, Taran came to Fern's side. "They want you to carry the baby to the house where they'll be staying."

Fern was amazed that they'd trust her with this helpless infant after Simbi had been hurt twice in her care. She carefully carried little Melir up the steps and across the sameg, then gently placed him in Farsa's arms.

Later, when the excitement settled down, Fern asked Taran, "Are we going to stay here?"

"For the time being, but not forever. We'll look for a place to build a new village, then we'll move on."

"Will we build our new village near here?"

"No. In the mountains."

"How long until we do that?"

"I don't know. We have to choose a place. In the meantime, we have family and friends we haven't seen in a long time, and we want to enjoy their company."

"It's nice to have someone else who speaks English. I mean Lila. I won't have to bother you so much."

"Fern, you are not a bother, but Lila will enjoy your company. So will the ones that don't understand English. You'll make new friends here."

He was right. That night she joined the festivities. Since she was a good dancer she was much sought after as a partner for couples' dances. Now there were twice as many young men to compete for her.

After dancing nonstop several times, Fern decided to sit out the next one. Then the musicians struck up an Irish jig. She forgot her fatigue and jumped to her feet. Midway through the dance, she noticed more people were watching than dancing, and she was the center of attention. She froze in embarrassment. In the mountain village, Fern had taught everyone the Irish dances her father had taught her.

Tira said, "They'd like you to teach them the jig."

"Okay. Ask the musicians to slow down."

Tira spoke to the musicians and announced Fern's intentions. Then she and a few of the mountain people who already knew the steps stood by Fern, facing a line of new students. Fern drew a deep breath and hoped not to mess up. The musicians resumed playing. Her feet found the music and took over. As her pupils caught on, the music increased in tempo. Before long, the dance floor was filled with Irish dancers.

Later, as she lay in bed, Fern couldn't help thinking about her father and how she missed him. The last time she'd seen him flashed into her mind. The night after the ice storm. They had no electricity and were using the fireplace for heat. She woke and went downstairs where Daddy was adding wood to the fire. She'd stayed a few minutes, warming herself, then went back to bed.

She would never forget the uneasiness she felt, but hadn't acted on, when she looked back at him, lounging in his chair by the hearth. She allowed herself a few tears. The house had caught fire that night. She got her sisters out through a window, then tried to rescue her parents. She couldn't find Daddy, and Mama was overcome by smoke. Fern had been unable to help her, except—that's when she and her mother wrashirued to this world. Her father died in the fire, and everyone thought she and her mother had, too.

She missed her sisters. She sat up and tried to meditate, to use ethenos to visit them, but she couldn't concentrate. The breathing of the other children in the room interrupted her focus. Other members of Lila's and Rogan's family occupied the adjacent bedrooms. Anticipating when they, and Tira, would retire for the night kept her on edge.

Back in the mountain village, she had a private place to meditate, the little hut the people had built for her and her mother. No one bothered her there. Sitting in her mother's rocking chair had enabled her to find the part of her mind from which she could project her etheric body.

Whenever she was successful, Fern could watch her sisters and grandparents go about their daily lives, but she couldn't interact with them, and they weren't aware of her presence. If she found them asleep, she'd talk to them. Many nights Fern had told her sisters she was still alive, on another world. She would describe that world to them and relate stories about her new life.

This night, unable concentrate enough to use ethenos, Fern soothed herself by revisiting the dream she'd had the first night after their escape from the volcano eruption. If at any time she'd needed solace, it was then.

That night, she'd dreamed of her sisters in their grandmother's kitchen. The girls were drawing pictures of her wearing the tunics Andli had made her and the landscape she'd described to them while they slept. It was no ordinary dream. It had the characteristics of ethenos—it was real. To know they were able to hear her when she talked to them in their sleep was a balm to her soul. In order to visit them again, she needed to find a sanctuary, someplace where she could be alone and meditate undisturbed.

CHAPTER 4
NEW FRIENDS

Being guests didn't excuse the mountain people from chores. They were expected to fetch their share of water, lenitrus, and firewood, just as they had in their old village. Rogan took Fern and her siblings to a nearby spring for water and showed them places where they could collect food and firewood. Together, Rogan and Doran took them into the sea at low tide to show them which seaweeds were edible.

Fern's heart lifted at the possibility of new territory to explore, which she did at every opportunity, walking along the beach or climbing into the hills above the village. A throng of children, Simbi among them, always followed her. Simbi had adopted Fern as a big sister and, when her parents were busy with the new baby, she clung to Fern.

At times, Fern wanted to be alone, and the children were a distraction, but she didn't know how to tell them that. She thought of asking Tira or Lila to explain it to them but didn't want to hurt their feelings.

When she strolled along the beach, however, she enjoyed their company. She had trouble talking with them but found other ways to communicate, mostly through pantomime. Although there were no seashells, Fern found rocks of many colors in the sand and couldn't help collecting them. The pouch she attached to her belt when she gathered lenitrus was handy for carrying rocks, too.

When the children learned how much she liked pretty stones, they helped. They found so many, it was hard to decide which ones to keep. In the mountain village, she kept her rock collections at her mother's hut. Here she had no place to call her own, so she arranged them beside the doorway of Lila's house.

At low tide, the children took her among the offshore boulders and showed her caves carved out by the waves. Together they explored them. Fern's parents had instilled in her a responsibility for her little sisters. She'd learned to keep a close watch on them in places that might be dangerous, like the beach. However, Fern didn't know the names of most of these children and felt uncomfortable having to supervise them. She wondered if their parents knew they were with her.

One day, she found a girl hunting for children who had hidden in caves. Fern helped her find them and didn't rest until all were accounted for. When she returned to the sameg, she told Lila about this.

Lila smiled. "They were playing Hide and Seek. Someone who visited Earth brought the game back. They probably want you to play with them. Their parents know where the children are and what they're doing. They stay in touch with them mentally. Besides, they know they're safe with you."

The next time the children followed her to the beach, she played Hide and Seek with them, but no matter how cleverly she tried to hide, Fern was the first to be found.

Arlon often accompanied Fern on food-gathering excursions. She welcomed the opportunity to talk with someone besides toddlers and English-speakers. As they struggled to understand each other, her fluency in Spanish improved faster than her command of Human Talk. One day, Arlon sent his sister to Fern with a bracelet. She knew what that meant. He was attracted to her as a potential mate. She wasn't interested in his courtship, but it would be unkind not to accept his gift.

Arlon wasn't her only admirer. Other young men sent their sisters with little presents and, at the evening campfires, their competition to dance with her became obvious. She expected Tira to be jealous of the attention she got, but Tira spent most of her time with Ansil, the only young man who hadn't send her a gift.

Despite this popularity, Fern felt lonely. The English-speaking people, and even Andli, were so busy catching up on news they had little time for her. She'd grown comfortable with the people of the mountain village, but now she was surrounded by so many strangers it was hard to relax. She missed her mother more than ever. She missed sitting in the rocking chair in her mother's hut, now reduced to ashes. So much of her past life had been reduced to ashes.

She desperately needed privacy. On Earth, she had her own room. In the mountain village, her mother's hut. Now there seemed to be nowhere she could be alone. Even the latrine was a place for socializing. She refused to open her mind to others, so no one picked up on her needs.

One day, she managed to slip off by herself into the hills south of the village. No one pursued her. Perhaps her would-be followers sensed her need. She came to a creek she hadn't encountered before and waded upstream to a little pool that reminded her of her old bathing place in the mountains. On the bank grew a profusion of ahnti plants, and at the foot of a great erguvon tree was a space just large enough to sit or lie on the ground. She felt almost at home.

She'd always thought of erguvons, with their heart-shaped leaves, as friendly trees. Careful not to disturb the ahnti plants, she climbed the bank, sat against the tree, and relaxed. This clump of ahnti was the largest she'd ever seen. Their fern-like leaves were shriveled and turning brown, but she knew they'd revive when it rained. They were highly valued for their medicinal properties, and as Fern sat quietly among them, she could almost feel healing energy emanate from them.

Preparing for meditation, Fern did her breathing exercises. But instead of slipping into meditation, she began to cry. She wept for her parents, her home, her life on Earth. She cried for the mountain village which had been home for so long. Her little sisters stood forth in her mind. How she missed them, but she was in no state to contact them by ethenos.

Instead, she fell asleep. While she slept, she dreamed of them. They were walking with their grandparents along the parapets of the Old Fort in St. Augustine. While the adults gazed out to sea, the girls climbed on a cannon. Grandma turned and, laughing, snapped their picture.

In her dream, Fern was part of a tour group, listening to a man dressed as a sixteenth century Spanish soldier. "This fortress has never fallen to siege," he declared, then moved on. Fern was swept along with the group, but her grandparents and sisters were not part of the tour. She wanted to join them but she lacked freedom of movement.

As her family went their way, her desire to follow them seemed to tear the fabric of the dream. Before it faded, a young man, lagging behind the tour group, turned to face her. She found herself looking into green eyes, and Tiril's smile. The vision dissolved.

She woke knowing this was no ordinary dream. She had seen her family through Tiril's eyes, but how did he get into her mind? Had he sensed her loneliness from across the universe? How did he know where to find her family? Why would he interrupt his busy life to help her see them? At least she was reassured that her sisters were safe and well.

Whenever she could, Fern returned to this place. No one bothered her here. Every time, she meditated and tried to visit her sisters. She wasn't always successful, but when she was, she caught vignettes of their daily life. Tiril did not appear in her dreams again for some time.

When the large moon became full, Fern remembered her intentions to keep track of time. In the old village, on a post in her mother's hut, she'd left twenty three marks for the number of times the small moon had been full since her arrival on this world. Of course, she'd been unable to bring the post with her and it had suffered the same fate as everything else. She needed another way to keep track of the months, something she could take with her when she moved on.

Under the erguvon tree, she found a straight stick about a foot long and an inch in diameter. She thanked the tree for it and peeled off the bark. The wood was smooth and almost golden. She borrowed a knife from Rina and etched lines on one side—twenty three for the full moons when she lived in the mountains and one for the time it was full after they reached the sea. These marks nearly covered one side, but the stick had more sides. She hoped she wouldn't be here long enough to use the whole thing. She tucked it in her basket.

The next day she had a visitor at her secret place. Ansil quietly arrived while she was deep in meditation. When she became aware of his presence, she came out of her trance. Although he spoke in Human Talk, she understood him fully when he said, "So, you have found this place. This is where I go when I want to be alone."

"Estut miryit." She continued in English, "I'm sorry. I didn't know. Sometimes I just need to be by myself, and this seems to be the only place no one follows me."

He nodded. "I know." Although he spoke in Human Talk, she understood him. "We have this whole world to ourselves. You'd expect we could have privacy. You're welcome to use this place whenever you like."

He sat across from her and they talked for a long time, he in his language and she in English, yet they were able to comprehend what each other said. This hadn't happened with anyone else. She thanked him again for constructing her mother's chair. He offered to make another, but she shook her head. "It wouldn't be the same. My mother wouldn't have sat in it."

"I was happy to be able to provide her comfort. I like your mother very much. I was grieved when she left us."

Taran was on the sameg when Fern returned. She told him about her conversation with Ansil, but he didn't act surprised. "True communication is not words, but understanding. Ansil has strong psychic ability, as you do. In that, you've found a common language."

Despite Ansil's permission to use his retreat, she was careful not to go to it unless she knew he was otherwise occupied, and he never returned when she was there. She found healing in solitude. Her spirits lifted and she began to enjoy herself. She became more involved with the young people, learning their games if not their language. She was glad of Arlon's company, especially as her command of Spanish improved, but with Ansil, she felt she could talk about almost anything.

* * *

The young people in the mountain village had grown used to Fern's bouts of self-imposed isolation and knew when to leave her alone. Not so here. The children of the sea people insisted she participate in their activities, including their games.

Fern recalled the time she'd joined a footrace in the mountain village. An older girl had run past her and shouted something that Fern took to be a taunt. The memory still stung. She hadn't believed Tira's explanation that the point of the race was to excel, not win, and the girl was only encouraging her to run faster.

Now Fern discovered she'd misunderstood the intent of such competitions. Ansil assured her, "We inspire excellence in one another, and we give each other tips on how to streamline our movements."

Arlon introduced her to a game similar to soccer. "The objective is to score points, not for a team but for the entire group. I played soccer in Mexico and didn't understand about competition at first." He laughed. "They thought I was weird. I was trying to play for cooperation. Before long, though, I caught on."

Fern stopped worrying about getting the rules wrong and started to enjoy herself. She joined another game, the goal of which was to keep the ball in the air, being thrown to as many participants as possible, including the less skilled. A small child clumsily threw a ball in Fern's direction. She reached for it, but stumbled and collapsed on the ground, laughing. Everyone laughed with her.

One day, Ansil took Fern sailing. The barca almost flew across the crests of waves. She so enjoyed the wind in her hair, droplets of salt spray on her face, and Ansil's company. They sailed to an offshore island where Ansil gathered seafood and Fern collected stones. "On Earth, we'd find shells on the beach," she said.

"Yes, Tiril has shown me the wonders of your sea shores."

"How?"

"He lets me enter his mind."

She remembered the vision she'd had through Tiril's eyes of her sisters and grandparents at the Castillo. Is that what happened? Hungry though she was for visions of Earth, she wasn't sure she wanted to enter Tiril's mind again, and she certainly didn't want anyone in hers.

There were sailboat races. Ansil often won. He explained that the races were not just a contest but an effort to learn more efficient sailing techniques. Besides, they were fun. In some races the sailors took riders, and he always took Tira. "She rides as one with the boat," he said. Fern couldn't help a twinge of jealousy, even though he took her sailing often enough.

One day, they sailed beyond the sight of land. Fern felt uneasy. "Have you been out this far before?"

"Are you worried we'll get lost? Yes. I've gone further than this, but not so far I couldn't get back the same day. I've also sailed along the shore for many days. It's so beautiful."

"Do you know how big this sea is?"

"No. Someday I want to find out. Who knows? I may go all the way around the world and end up back here."

Fern thought about stories she'd heard of the weka who leave home to explore the world on foot. Why not explore by boat, too? "Has anyone sailed that far?"

"No. Maybe I'll be the first."

"Will you take anyone with you?"

He smiled into her eyes. "Maybe."

Something quivered inside Fern. She'd love to accompany him on such a voyage, if she couldn't go home. A cloud passed over. Would Ansil want a plural marriage? He and Tira were so close.

CHAPTER 5
LIFE WITH THE SEA PEOPLE

Fern found Lila to be open to questions and willing to give answers. One day she asked Lila, "Someone told me that on the thortle world, people were able to alter their genetic code. Can you all still do that?"

"Yes, it can be done, if needed."

"Then why not do it when two close cousins fall in love? Then they could have children together."

Lila shook her head. "There are risks. It can open what you call a 'Pandora's box.' We saw that on the thortle world. Changing an undesirable trait can interfere with desirable ones. There's more to be gained by letting Nature take her course."

Fern nodded.

Lila continued, "We don't inquire into your genetic background. You may have undesirable traits in your family history, but we wouldn't alter your genes. We'll take the bad with the good."

Fern hadn't thought about that. No, she wouldn't want her genes altered. That would be a violation of her deeper self. "My grandfather was bald, and my father was starting to be, so if I had sons, they might carry those genes. I haven't seen any bald men here."

Lila frowned. "No, that was a trait the thortles tried to breed out of us. They thought it was an imperfection and they culled out men who went bald. So men who started to go bald altered their genes to grow hair. But you don't need to worry about your sons. If they don't want to be bald, they can do the same."

Fern grumbled, "Sometimes I think I'm only wanted for my fresh genes."

"Oh, Fern," Lila hugged her. "I won't deny that we need to freshen our gene pool, but you are valued for yourself, not just your genes."

Fern thought about these people's control over their bodies. They could not only heal themselves and alter their genes, they could alter their very body chemistry. Life on Earth is composed of left-handed molecules. It was the same on the thortle world, but on this world, molecules were right-handed. To transition between here and Earth, one's body chemistry had to change. When Fern arrived on the planet, she was unconscious. Andli and other healers were able to alter her body chemistry. Her mother was not so lucky. Unable to change, Mama was unable to take nutrition, and so she died. Fern suspected this other-handedness could be some protection from the thortles taking over this planet.

Another day, Fern asked Lila, "I've noticed you have only one mate."

Lila smiled. "As you know, Taran and I were mates, but he loves the mountains and I feel most alive by the sea. Wherever we lived, one of us was unhappy, so we decided to part. I still consider Taran, and his other mates, and you children, too, as my family. Rogan and I were happy until I went to Earth. Then he was lonely, so he took another mate, Risa."

She laughed. "Although he has no desire to visit Earth himself, he seems to like women who do. Risa is in Italy now and my birth daughter is with her. Rogan and I are taking care of the children she birthed."

"So two of your children are on Earth now? Her and Tiril? Are they together?"

"They see each other occasionally, but Tiril is going to college."

"How can you bear to be separated from them?" Her unvoiced question was, how can the children bear to be separated from you?

"We're not entirely cut off. We stay in contact. Remember, our people are used to living this way. Families were constantly being separated on the thortle world."

Fern was silent a moment. "Tira told me 'thortle' means 'captor.' Do they have a name for themselves?"

"Yes, but we don't use it. Naming something gives it reality, makes a stronger bond with it. We don't want to be bonded to them."

"Taran said something like that once. You know, the only times I've seen Taran get mad was when he talked about the thortles."

"Yes." Lila sighed. "That is a demon he wrestles with. All of us lived on the thortle world in the past, but we don't all remember those lives. Taran does. He remembers a life as a man called ElSoDan. He took a mate who'd been recently captured and helped her recover from the horrors she experienced. Then they had several children. One was born with a deformity, so all the children were destroyed."

Fern gasped.

"His mate was allowed to live, only because she had strong psychic powers, but her womb was removed. ElSoDan wasn't sterilized because he was from an old bloodline that had proven itself. They wanted to breed him with other women, but he refused."

"I had no idea! No wonder he hates them so."

"Yes, that's something he tries to overcome. Hate is counterproductive."

"What do you mean?" Fern asked.

"Hate binds you to another the same as love does. Taran doesn't want to be bound to the thortles, so he works on dispelling the hate. He's trying to forgive the thortles, to learn acceptance. It's not an easy task."

"Acceptance? After what they did to him?" Fern forgot that the incident occurred perhaps centuries ago, to another person, not the Taran she knew.

"The thortles don't act out of malice. They are purely practical—they have no emotions. They would destroy a bloodline among themselves if it had an undesirable genetic mutation. When one of them becomes old, or sick, or injured and unable to perform its function, it's put to death. Evil, as we understand it, doesn't describe them. It's just the way they are. This is something Taran, and most of the rest of us, struggles with."

Fern now viewed Taran in a new light. She wished she could ask him more, but she didn't want to stir up bad memories. Then she noticed she hadn't seen him for a few days and Doran was also absent. When she asked Lila where they were, her answer was vague, that they were away on some business.

The next day the men returned. Taran carried a large bundle of firewood, but Doran's sling was filled with what looked like a large wooden ball. Taran unloaded his firewood without comment, then Doran put his burden on the woodpile with a grin. Fern heard a shriek behind her, and Rina tore past. She threw herself on the great ball and began talking rapidly in a high-pitched voice. Now Taran was grinning, too. Rina took the ball off the woodpile and threw her arms around Doran, then Taran.

Fern crept forward to see what the fuss was about. The wooden ball was the large growth they'd seen on the side of a tree on their journey. She wondered how Doran had managed to carry such a heavy thing, until she discovered it was hollow.

Taran was happy to enlighten her. "In English, this is called a burl. Sometimes when a tree suffers an injury, such as losing a limb, it'll grow one over the wound. We seldom find one so big, or so hollow. Rina really wanted this one, and the tree was willing to give it to her, but at the time, we couldn't carry it, so we decided to surprise her."

Fern had always marveled how these people knew each other's thoughts. When she'd become aware that they could read hers as well, she had rebelled and learned to shield her mind from them. At times this resulted in her needs not being met, but she stubbornly guarded her privacy. She thought about how Doran and Taran had surprised Rina. They wouldn't have been able to had she picked up on their thoughts. Apparently, when appropriate, they could shield their minds like she did.

When Rina had time, she smoothed the rim of the burl and leveled the bottom so it would sit well, like a large bowl. Then she carefully removed the bark, exposing the grain of the wood which contained patterns of beautiful colors. Slowly, patiently, using the grain for inspiration, she carved the wood, and a piece of art began to emerge. This happily occupied her spare time for the remainder of their stay.

* * *

Fern felt like a guest at an extended family reunion. People she was unacquainted with acted like they knew her. She tried to learn their names, but there were so many of them. It was emotionally burdensome. To cope, she slept more and spent as much time as she could in Ansil's sanctuary.

On the positive side, new foods helped diminish her craving for meat. As in the mountains, the basic fare was skri, kirrib, and lenitrus, but here they had a wider choice of flavorings. They even grilled vegetables wrapped in seaweed. Cooks engaged in friendly competition to make the tastiest dishes.

One day Fern woke from a nap to a silent house. Instead of enjoying the solitude, she felt the emptiness. Her sisters were off somewhere with cousins. It dawned on her that she missed the family togetherness she'd experienced in their old village. With no house of their own, the family no longer ate or slept together. About the only thing they did was fix one another's hair every morning.

That afternoon she found Jorsil in the company of a young woman, Tana, the same one he danced with every night almost to the exclusion of others. She asked Tira if they were courting.

"Yes," Tira said. "They're getting to know each other better. I don't know if they'll mate, but they're not closely related, so they can."

"If they mate, where will they live?"

"I don't know. They'll have to decide."

Fern hoped they'd choose the mountains. Otherwise, even though she couldn't converse with Jorsil, she'd miss him.

* * *

Fern always swam in her clothes. Sometimes the children would touch her tunic and look at her inquiringly. One day when she and Lila were shelling nuts, Fern said, "Do people wonder why I always keep my clothes on?"

Lila smiled. "The adults understand that things were different where you came from. The explanation we give to children who are too young to understand is that your fair skin is more sensitive to the sun."

Fern nodded. "Did people wear clothes on the thortle world?"

"Oh, yes. It was cool there, in the hives anyway." She paused to think. "There's a very old story about when our people lived in zoos, before the thortles discovered our psychic abilities. We were treated like animals and went naked. I don't know why they didn't understand humans' need for clothing. Maybe they captured people from the tropics where they didn't wear clothes. In warm places that was no problem, but in colder climates, when they turned us outside so they could clean the cages, we suffered."

She grimaced. "At least the thortles were good zookeepers and tried to keep their exhibits healthy, so when they figured out that humans needed warmth, they clothed them. Once they discovered our psychic abilities, everything changed."

"If you don't know your history for certain, that is, where you originally came from, how do you know about the zoos?"

"The thortles keep good records for breeding purposes, and some of us had access to those records."

"You don't seem to mind talking about the thortle world like Tira and Taran do."

Lila nodded.

"Do you remember living there?"

"Yes, but not the really bad experiences like they do. I don't recall being captured. I know I was born there, and remember ordinary things about life, like growing up and learning to read, working, mates and children. But I don't remember lives on Earth or any other world. I'm not sure why. Perhaps I don't need such memories."

They finished shelling their nuts. Lila rose to take the nutmeats to the fire pit and Fern followed with the hulls.

Fern said, "I've heard stories about the First Parents, Moses and Rila, and their children, but almost nothing about the thortle world. I'd think you'd have lots of stories about life there."

"We have some, not many. There wasn't much to tell. Life was boring at best. We had no challenges, other than keeping ourselves and our loved ones alive. Our 'world' was too small. We languished. Most of the stories we had were told to us by new captives from Earth. We weren't allowed writing materials, so stories had to be passed down orally. If stories had no lasting significance, they'd be lost. When we came here, our people wanted to forget that world. That may have been unwise, but you can understand why."

Lila began to grind the nutmeats. Fern looked for something to do so she could stay with her. She began to stack bowls that had been washed and left to dry. She said, "What little I know about that place, I think it would make interesting stories. I mean, it was so different from here. And from Earth."

"You're right. I remember being taken on spaceships, but we weren't allowed to see outside. Most of us had no contact with other peoples. I suspect the thortles kept our existence a secret. While I was on the ship, one thortle was assigned to me and my fellow workers, but I couldn't say we got to know it well. We didn't even know its name, if it had one. They gave us numbers, so they probably went by numbers, too. There was no friendship between our races."

She frowned. "Humans on Earth at least love their animals." Lila poured the flour into a large bowl and added water.

Fern watched her add other ingredients. "Why do you say 'it?' Don't they have males and females? Or something like that?"

"We don't know. There were individual differences, like patterns on their carapaces, but if there were gender differences, we didn't know. They may be all male, or all female like worker ants and bees on Earth, or both. Or neither. We don't know if they have families, or if one 'queen' populates a hive. They kept such information from us."

"What kind of work did you do?"

"That incarnation of me did what many of our people did. We acted like radios, sending and receiving messages. As you know, radio waves are limited to the speed of light, but thought is not. Being able to communicate vast distances, without having to wait for messages, gave the thortles an advantage over peoples who didn't use psychic powers."

"Do you know what their world looks like outside the hives?"

"Not really. Some people explored it by etheric projection, but they said very little about it. If they displeased the thortles, they'd suffer retribution. Moses explored it and said their natural world looks much like Earth, and this world. He wrashirued outside and found that the air was different, thinner. The thortles piped enriched air into our living space. And probably into the zoo cages when they kept us there."

"What, exactly, do the thortles look like?"

Lila sighed. "Like big insects. Only, they wear clothes."

* * *

One day Fern saw Lila help a couple beach their boat and turn it over to inspect the hull. "Does it need to be repaired?" Fern asked.

Lila said, "Yes. We're going to go gather materials. Would you like to come along?" Fern jumped at the opportunity to do something different. Lila handed her a basket and donned an apron with several pockets.

The four of them went into the forest to a place where vines grew up into the trees. "What are those?" Fern asked. "I never saw any like them in the mountains."

"They don't grow there. We've tried to transplant them, but they don't like high altitudes. They have strong fibers we use for ropes and sails."

"Do you make clothes out of them, too?"

"No, they're too coarse for clothing and not as abundant as the reeds we use."

After the usual silent communication with the plants, the woman climbed a tree and cut a few branches from a vine, carefully loosened the tendrils, and dropped them to the ground. The man climbed a neighboring tree and did the same. Lila began to separate and coil the vines.

Fern helped her. "They are two different kinds."

"Yes and no. They're male and female of the same species. They grow together like this to ensure pollination. This one," she pointed to the thicker stalk, "is the male. He grows up into the tree. When he's mature, he releases a compound that signals the female seed to sprout. She entwines him as she grows. When she reaches his pollen-bearing buds, she blooms, and that triggers him to open his flower and pollinate her." She pointed to slender vines that stretched from tree to tree. "She then grows laterally and drops her ripe seeds some distance from their host tree."

"Wow! What do you call them?"

Lila told her, but even after several tries, Fern couldn't work her mouth around the word. She shook her head. "I'll just call them Romeo and Juliet."

The couple descended from the trees and picked up the coiled vines. "Tekuyate," they said and headed back toward the village. Lila beckoned Fern to follow her. "I'm going to look for ingredients for resin."

They gathered seeds from a shrub Fern was unfamiliar with. Lila put them in a pocket of her apron. She collected sticky sap that oozed from another tree, wrapped it in leaves, and pocketed it. In a stream bed, she groped through the mud until she found a few handfuls of clay Then they filled Fern's basket with leaves, thanked the plants and stream, and returned to the village.

The man and woman let the vines soak in a large crock, much as Andli soaked reeds for cloth, until the soft parts fell away from the fibers. Fern helped Lila process her ingredients to make resin. She explained everything to Fern, primarily in English, but many of the words were unfamiliar and the process was so technical Fern couldn't commit it to memory. "You must be a chemist," Fern said.

"Yes. And when I was on Earth, I studied chemistry."

"Is that where you learned all this?"

"By no means not all of it. I had a great deal of knowledge to begin with, but what I learned on Earth enhanced it."

"How did you learn what you already knew?"

"From other chemists, like Andli. And I look into the plants and minerals, and examine the elements, how they combine and separate, and how they can be recombined to make what I need."

"Like Doran looks into plants."

Lila nodded.

"Andli's a chemist, too?"

"Of course. How else could she make her dyes?"

"Did your people learn chemistry on the thortle world?"

"No, the thortles didn't educate us in anything they couldn't use us for. A few of us have been able to access some of their writings and learn from them, but we have to be careful."

Chapter 6
Tempest

Once again, Taran was away, this time for days. Rina and several others were absent as well. Fern recalled hearing conversations she hadn't understood and knew she'd missed out on something, but she didn't want to admit her ignorance by asking Tira, or even Lila. She waited until Taran returned to ask him where they'd been.

"We've been scouting a site for our new village."

"Oh. Have you found one?"

"Not yet."

She looked inland beyond the foothills. "Why not these mountains? That would be close enough for everybody to visit more often."

He shook his head. "We're still looking for the best place."

"I don't understand why it's so hard. You have a whole planet to choose from, don't you?"

"Yes, but it's a democratic process. We have to choose a location that will make everyone happy. The site of our old village was so perfect, it's hard to match. Another consideration is safety. We don't want to fall victim to another catastrophe."

Fern's eyes widened. "Right!"

She wished they could stay here forever, but this village was too crowded. Nearly two hundred people were squeezed into a space designed for half that number, and the sameg was not large enough to add many more houses. Well, while they were still here, she intended to enjoy the beach as much as possible.

During their stay, the weather, for the most part, was beautiful. The usual afternoon thunderstorms left more than enough time for beach-combing and foraging and didn't interfere with social activities. But one day the sky stayed cloudy. Fern sensed an anxious watchfulness among the adults. It reminded her of the days preceding the volcanic eruption. "Do you have any volcanoes around here?" she asked Lila.

"No, not for at least a hundred miles."

The next morning a light rain fell and the wind came in little puffs that made the trees dance. The weka sat in meditation and put an "umbrella" over the sameg. By midday, the weather cleared and the sky was blue again. Later it rained harder and the wind thrashed the trees. The sea angrily pounded the rocks, shooting columns of spray into the air.

Sailors dragged their boats out of the water and carried them inland. Fern and Tira helped Ansil move his. At high tide, waves crashed against the bank the village was built on, sending droplets of spray as high as the sameg.

Fern recalled similar weather from her childhood on Earth. "Are we having a hurricane?"

"Yes," Tira said. "One is on the way."

Cooks baked a large supply of skri. Lila asked Fern to help carry food, bedding, and belongings to caves in the hills. She showed Fern which cave their family would occupy. Everything that could be blown away was secured. As the weather worsened, the children were sent to the caves. Simbi came by to hug Fern when her family took refuge. Fern and Andli took their younger children and Lila's to their cave. Andli's brother and his family; their mother, Noba; and a few of Lila's close relatives joined them. It was getting crowded.

Between squalls, Jorsil and Rogan arrived. The caves were high above the storm surge and deep enough to offer shelter from driving rain, but they weren't very comfortable and the stone floor was cold. The bedding had been piled in the back of the cave and the children were urged to lie down. The parents showed no desire to rest, and neither did Fern.

As the storm's violence increased, she walked to the cave's mouth and watched the wind batter the trees. She looked for Taran, Rina, Doran, and Tira, but they didn't come. Nor did Lila and Ansil. She retreated when cold rain blew into the cave.

Finally, she asked Andli where the others were. Andli said they had stayed behind to gentle the storm. Fern thought she'd misunderstood, but Andli explained that those with the strongest ability had remained in the village, in meditation, to protect everyone from danger. She assured Fern that she was in contact with them and they were safe.

Fern couldn't help a twinge of jealousy. Tira had been included and, as usual, she was left out. She found a quiet nook where she could isolate herself with her discontent. She knew she wasn't as skilled in psychic matters as Tira, but it still stung.

She thought back to a hurricane that had hit St. Augustine when she lived there. Her parents stayed up all night listening to a battery powered radio, tracking the storm. Fern wanted to experience the eye of the hurricane, but she fell asleep, and by morning the winds had subsided. Her parents assured her she hadn't missed anything. They hadn't been in the direct path, and the eye hadn't passed over them.

This time, Fern hoped the worst of the storm would bypass them. St. Augustine was a coastal city but her family had lived inland, miles from the beach, where they'd been reasonably safe in their sturdy house. Here, they were exposed to raw Nature, hunkered in caves and thatched houses. She listened to the wind hiss and moan. She didn't remember the Florida storm being this fierce.

Many of the children slept and required no tending. In soft voices, the adults told stories to those who were awake. Occasionally someone sang soothingly. Night came. Fern wrapped her blanket around her and entered meditation. She tried to cast a safety net around her loved ones.

She found herself in a large, dark bubble, aware of the presence of Lila, Taran, Ansil, and others. She reached out and found Tira, Rina, and Doran. She attempted no contact, saw and heard nothing, but experienced a sense of perfect safety. She tried to add to that atmosphere and not detract from it.

As her awareness sharpened, Fern sensed this was unlike the force field the weka put over the sameg to shelter it from rain. This "gentling" absorbed the power of the storm and used it for protection. Fern didn't try to become involved with what she didn't understand, but she projected a mantle of safety around those gentling the storm.

As the tempest eased, the gentling relaxed, and Fern fell asleep. She woke to gray light filtering into the cave. The storm had abated. Those who'd remained in the village came for food and dry clothes. All were safe.

Suddenly, a cry came from a nearby cave, and moments later a hysterical child, little Tandil's sister, rushed in. Fern understood her to say that her brother was missing. The younger children were told to remain with Tala. Fern followed the parents to the cave where Tandil's family had sheltered.

His parents and grandparents stood outside, concern on their faces, but not the alarm Fern felt. When Ansil and other sailors ran toward the beach, her stomach knotted.

"Fern," said Taran, "we need to search for Tandil. His family senses he's safe, but he's frightened and they can't locate him. There's a lot of storm damage, so be careful."

Tandil's grandparents were directing people to fan out and cover every area. Fern headed in the direction she was given, calling, "Tandil!" She listened for an answer. Silence. No one else was yelling. She halted. She'd never find him if she let anxiety drive her. She drew a deep, calming breath. Everyone else was probably searching with their minds as well as their eyes and ears.

Fern closed her eyes and tried to open her mind, but she sensed nothing. She thought, why would he leave the cave during a hurricane? Because his mother had been among those gentling the storm. Tandil, an independent, mischievous little boy, was very close to his mother.

Fern retraced her steps back to Tandil's family's cave. Which way did the wind blow last night? She closed her eyes and drifted downhill, towards the village but slanting left, as the wind would have pushed a small boy. She peeked through her eyelids to watch where she was going, but she could drift better with them shut.

Suddenly, her feet gave way beneath her and she slid down a muddy bank into a gully. Collecting herself, she checked for injury. No harm, only dirt. Nearby, a voice said, "Ferni?" A small hand touched her shoulder.

"Tandil! You're safe." She looked into his red-rimmed eyes and hugged him. "Everyone's looking for you." They struggled up the mud-covered bank together. Fern couldn't think of what to say in Human Talk, so she yelled, "Aqui!"

In a few moments, a woman from the sea village arrived. She shouted in Human Talk and led Fern and Tandil to the sameg. Tandil's parents hurried over and embraced him. Then they questioned him. Fern caught enough of his reply to know he'd left the cave to look for his mother, fell into the ravine and, not knowing where he was, sheltered under an overhanging rock until he heard Fern.

Now that it was all over, her legs felt like jelly. She wanted to sit, but the sameg was a sea of mud, fallen branches, and leaf litter. A nearby tree had toppled, narrowly missing the houses. Fern made her way over and sat on the trunk, breathing deeply to calm her pounding heart. She tried to brush the mud off her tunic.

Tandil's mother rushed to Fern and took her hands. "Tekuyate," she said. Everyone crowded on the sameg, wet and dirty, but smiling with relief and gratitude.

Taran took Fern's hand. "While everyone else was trying to locate Tandil mentally, you used simple logic, and it worked."

Fern burst into tears. "I'm just glad he's safe."

"Yes," Taran said. "Everyone is safe, and you played your part." He smiled at her with pride.

Had he been aware of her feeble efforts to keep him and the others safe?

Taran said, "You also showed good judgement during the storm. You didn't interfere with what was beyond your capacity, but you gave us what help you could."

The sun shone as though nothing had happened. The houses were miraculously intact, due to the gentling, but the thatch needed mending and everything was soaked. Alta and the sea people's fire maker kindled fires to dry belongings. Fern was amazed at their ability to make fire when all the fuel was wet.

It took two days for the sameg to dry and longer for the interiors of the houses. Everyone worked overtime to clear the sameg and beach of debris. They slept in shifts in the caves.

Although there were twice as many hands to do the work, there was also twice the need for food. The stores ran low. So many plants had been damaged, they had to walk a long way to forage for lenitrus. The raging sea had taken a toll on the water plants, too.

The storm had blown a profusion of nuts off the trees. These were easy to collect, but as days went by, many sprouted on the ground. It was the practice, going back to the people's first arrival on the planet, not to eat nuts that sprouted on their own. They had to be collected and planted some distance from other nut trees where they would have room to grow.

At night, everyone gathered on the sameg and beach, but no one had the energy to dance.

Finally, repairs and clean-up from the hurricane were completed. Fern was relieved to hear they would be moving soon. Taran said, "We've chosen the site for our new village. It's a safe place, and plenty of food grows there. It's farther from here than our old village, but within a half day's walk is a view of the sea. Several of us will wrashiru there and start building. The rest of you will join us on foot."

Rina went with him, leaving her burl with Lila. Ansil and a few other sea people also left, as well as some of the weka, but Andli, Doran, and Tira remained. "Why didn't you wrashiru with the others?" Fern asked Tira.

"I have no special skills for building houses," Tira said. "So I'll walk with you."

The children of the sea village wanted to know why the mountain people couldn't always live with them. Fern overheard Lila's explanation but didn't quite understand her. "What did you tell them?"

"That it's not wise for us to all live in one place. If a disaster wiped out all of us, it would be very difficult to start over. That's one reason we have more than one village, in different places."

"What do you mean start over? If everyone died, there'd be no starting over."

"We'd be forced to be reborn and live on Earth until we could wrashiru here and begin again. It would be a long, difficult process. It would take many generations."

"But if you were reborn on Earth, why wouldn't you stay there?"

"Because this is our home."

* * *

After Ansil and Taran left, Fern spent more time with Arlon. He liked to talk about his experiences on Earth. Fern enjoyed these conversations, but they made her homesick. Once Arlon told about his family's trip to Disney World. His account dredged up an unsettling memory.

On her thirteenth birthday, Fern's family had gone to Disney. The first part of the day was delightful. Then, in line for Small World, she had encountered Tira.

She didn't know who Tira was at the time, of course, nor Taran or Lila, who were with her. They were just three of thousands of nameless tourists, dressed like everyone else, blending in with the crowd. But Tira made eye contact, and the way she looked at Fern, absorbing her with her eyes, was unnerving. A few seconds later, Fern lost sight of Tira, but an ominous feeling dogged her the rest of the day. After that, she was terrified of the stars.

Fern tried to relate this to Arlon. Perhaps talking about it would ease her distress. But despite her improvement in Spanish, she lacked the vocabulary to express herself. At such times, she usually looked to one of the English speakers for help, but neither Lila nor Tira were around. After struggling unsuccessfully to make herself understood, both she and Arlon gave up in frustration. This put Fern in a bad mood and she snapped at Ara, which caused the child to cry.

By this time Lila returned, Fern had apologized and Ara's feelings had been soothed, but Fern remained sullen. She no longer wanted to talk about her Disney experience. While she helped Lila rinse the vegetables, she asked, "How is it that everyone here is so good?" Her unvoiced question was, "Except me?" "It can't be because all the bad ones were left on the thortle world."

Lila compressed her lips. "One thing that happened to us as a people is that many negative traits were bred out of us. The thortles wouldn't allow a rebellious captive to breed. They wanted slaves who were compliant and easy to manage." She shook the water out of the greens and sorted them. "That had an effect on us. In some ways, it was a good thing, but it diminished us, took away our gumption." She handed Fern a handful of lenitrus and a large bowl.

"But what about Moses? He wasn't exactly compliant."

"Moses was cunning. While he lived on Earth, as a slave before the Civil War, he learned how to appear compliant, even when his heart was raging, and he did the same thing on the thortle world. The thortles couldn't read his thoughts and feelings, only his behavior. That's how he survived on both worlds."

That made sense. Fern broke the greens into bite-size pieces. "How did the thortles know who to kidnap? How did they know who had psychic powers?"

Lila began to combine ingredients for salad dressing. "At first, they only took specimens for their zoos. When they found out that some of them had useful talents, they'd take a few of the psychic captives back to Earth to search for others like themselves. When they discovered some of us could wrashiru, they made their slaves locate others with that ability and trick them to come to the thortle world."

"So, the psychics sold each other into slavery?"

Lila frowned. "Yes, and that trait was not bred out of us. That's why we're cautious about contacting our cousins on the thortle world. But many who sold out their kind did it only because their families were held hostage. They did it only to protect their loved ones."

Yes, Fern thought, I would have done much to protect my family.

CHAPTER 7
RETURN TO THE MOUNTAINS

Fern helped Andli weave new moccasins and hats for the journey. A few men and women of the sea village were to accompany them. Lila explained, "They're going with you to help carry things and build houses. Then they'll come home. When you pack your basket, take only what's necessary so you have room for food. The rest of your things will be sent later."

Fern left the spindle and yarn she'd carried from the mountain village with Lila. They wouldn't be making new clothes before they built houses. She looped the cord with the little pouch around her neck. It contained things precious to her: the medallion Andli made of a lock of her mother's hair, the dried flower Fern had picked from the miaven tree on her mother's grave, and the egg-shaped pebble she'd found when she'd gone to the volcano fields with Tiril. She also secreted her erguvon-stick calendar in her backpack. To her, it was more essential than food. She left her rock collection by Lila's house. She could always find more.

Most of the elders and parents with small children, including Simbi's family, showed no signs of preparation. "They'll join you when the new village is ready," Lila said. "Ara will stay with me for now." Fern wondered how Andli could bear to leave her child, but Ara seemed happy with Lila. The sea people accompanying them carried Taran's and Rina's baskets and those of others who had wrashirued.

Sailors took them up the coastline to where they would turn inland, a different route from the way they came. They camped on the beach overnight and set out early. Here, the cliffs skirting the sea were as steep as those on their previous journey, but at least there was a path with switchbacks. It still took much of the day to climb to their next campsite. Fern's moccasins held out, but she wished she had good tough jeans to protect her legs from the rocky climb. Andli found herbs to treat their scrapes and bruises.

The path ended where the jungle began. When Doran marched into the forest, Fern asked, "How does he know which way to go?"

Tira said, "Noba advises him. She uses ethenos to scout out a path."

Fern had wondered why Noba accompanied them instead of staying at the sea village with the other great-grandparents. She hadn't thought about there being no trail yet from the sea village to their new one. Once again, she wished she could talk with Noba to compare experiences with ethenos. She could, through a translator, but it would be cumbersome.

Fan-flowers grew in this forest. When they stopped to rest, Fern asked Tira to help her talk to Doran. She told him about similar flowers that grew on Earth and asked if he could convince these to turn colors. Doran held a fan-flower in his hands and closed his eyes. An image of a bright red fan-flower flashed into Fern's mind. No—it wasn't a fan-flower! It was the tropical flower Fern remembered but had no name for. Doran had accessed her mind. She immediately threw up her guard. Doran looked at her, cocked his head, and said, "Hmmm."

They spent only one day in the jungle heat before they reached cooler uplands. Now travel became more leisurely. They carried plenty of food and had no reason to hurry. When it rained, they walked on unless there was lightning. At night, they huddled under makeshift shelters because no one in the group had the ability to put up an "umbrella."

The family ate and slept together, which comforted Fern. To her surprise, Jorsil also slept with them. He had a faraway look in his eyes. She suspected he missed Tana.

One night when the moons rose, Fern noticed that both seemed to be growing full together. The large moon was only a few nights from full and the small one was waxing. She hadn't kept track of the large moon and wondered if this was one of those times both would be full within days of one another, or if the Full Moons approached. She asked Tira.

"Yes, but we won't have a feast this time."

"Oh. I guess we won't reach the new village in time." She thought about the sea village, still recovering from the devastation of the hurricane. "I wonder what the sea people are doing."

"They'll have a small celebration."

"Why didn't we just stay there a few more days? We could have celebrated together."

Tira shook her head. "It's not wise. When the moons are in conjunction, the pull of the tides is stronger than usual, and things can happen."

"What kind of things?"

"Earthquakes, and such."

"What? Are they in danger? At the sea village?"

"No more than usual. It's just a precaution. We shouldn't have stayed there as long as we did, but everyone was having such a good time. Until the hurricane, that is."

Walking gave Fern plenty of time to think. Thinking brought up questions. Fern missed Lila and Taran, whom she could ask almost anything. If she could find the right words, she asked Andli. If not, Tira was always willing to talk. Once Fern said, "Lila said everybody who lives on this world has chosen to live here. What about other planets? Do people always get reborn on the same one or do they change worlds?"

"Usually people stay with their loved ones, or whoever they're connected to. That means they generally come back to the same planet. Sometimes people from Earth or the thortle world come here, but none of us wants to go back to the thortle world, neither do people from Earth."

Fern mulled over this. People who were captured by the thortles left loved ones behind on Earth. Of course, most of captives formed new families on the thortle world, but what happened when they were reborn? Perhaps they went back to Earth in the next life, but not everybody did, because babies were born on the thortle world, too. Either way, would they be separated forever from those they loved?

"Tira, do you remember any past lives?"

Tira nodded. "I have some awareness, but not many details. Our task in life is to focus on the present, not the past." She sounded like Taran.

"Were all your lives here, or do you remember the thortle world?"

Tira frowned. "I remember more about that world than I care to, and I don't want to talk about it." Then her face softened. "I do remember another place, though. I had these memories even before I visited Earth. I remember snow and mountains. It was beautiful, but very cold. I remember a house with a set of horns above the door. There was a fireplace, but it was smoky inside, and if you didn't stay near the fire, it was cold. I was having trouble breathing. I think I was dying."

Despite the heat of the day, Fern shivered.

A new question popped into Fern's mind. She asked Tira, "If people from the thortle world get reincarnated here, how do they know where to come if this place is such a secret?"

"After the body dies, the person is open to a lot of things they weren't aware of in life. And there are special souls that guide you after death. If someone is receptive to it, they'll be guided here to be reborn."

That night at supper, Tira said, "Fern, when I saw you at Disney World, I knew I'd see you again. That's why I was staring at you. I wondered when and where we'd meet again. My mind told me it would be here, but I thought that was impossible."

"Yeah. It really freaked me out. And I didn't understand why. It wasn't just because you were staring at me, it was something else."

"You picked up on that, too? I'm sorry I ruined your birthday."

"It wasn't your fault. I guess it was the latent psychic ability my mother said I have." Then she remembered she'd never talked to Tira about the incident or told her it had been her birthday. Tira had been reading her again. Fern closed her mind, got up, and walked away. She didn't return until her vexation dissolved.

That night, the nearly full moons outshone all but the brightest stars. Fern thought about her former fear of the stars. "Tira, are you still awake?"

"Um hm."

"After I saw you at Disney, I was afraid of the stars. It was a full-blown phobia. It's a real disorder—siderophobia—I looked it up. I wasn't like that before. I used to love the stars. But afterwards, I was okay on cloudy nights, but if I could see the stars, I'd get really spooked, like someone was watching me. I haven't been that way since I came here. Not at all."

Tira sat up abruptly. "Did you tell Taran about this?"

"No. I never thought to."

"I wish you had. He'd have cautioned you about contact with the thortles."

"He did, but he said I didn't have much to worry about because I had no connection to them. I thought I was afraid because somehow I knew I'd be coming here. After I came here, I wasn't afraid of the stars anymore."

"Maybe," said Tira. "Or maybe it's because you're safe here. Maybe the thortles were after you!"

A sense of doom fell to the pit of Fern's being. "Do you really think so?" What would she have done if they had taken her? "Can they track me here?"

"I don't think so. They don't know about 'here.' We'll have to talk to Taran."

"Why would it start when I saw you at Disney?"

"Maybe our meeting alerted you that they were watching. Or maybe, I don't think so, and I sure hope not, but maybe I alerted them to you."

Fern thought about her complicated feelings toward Tira. Maybe this accounted for them. "Do they know about you all when you visit Earth?"

"We have to be on guard. And we are very, very careful when we wrashiru between here and there."

"So coming here may have saved me from the thortles? What about my sisters? Are they safe? What about Tiril?"

"He's safe. And he thinks your sisters are, too. We'll talk to Taran when we get there."

Fern lay back and looked at the stars. The same old dread no longer haunted her, but somehow she felt she must remain on guard.

The next night, both moons rose, one after another, and climbed into the heavens. The group sang to the rising moons and prepared a hasty supper, but instead of making camp, they resumed their trek. Jorsil played his flute and they walked and sang under the bright sky. At midnight, when the small moon crept across the face of the large one, they stopped. Andli dug into her basket and handed out skri. Fern tasted hers. It was sweet! "Tekuyate," she said between bites.

Andli smiled. Other adults had also horded sweet cakes in their backpacks, so everybody got one. Fern took out her erguvon stick and scratched a wider than usual mark, to signify the full of both moons. Then she lay back and watched the eclipse, not as perfect as her first one, but still marvelous. After the small moon hurried on its way, the throng resumed walking, singing as they went. When the moons began to settle behind the trees, they stopped to sleep for the rest of the night.

A few days later, they reached the site of their new village, approaching from the east as the sun westered among banks of pink and purple clouds. Doran led them to a rocky ledge that afforded a view of the valley and mountains beyond. Not as massive as the mountains around their old village, these looked older. Rounded tops descended gracefully to a lazy river. Beneath forested slopes nestled a green valley where the river widened into a small lake. On a shoulder of a hill above the lake was a level area, the site for their new village. From the distance, Fern could see people setting posts for houses.

They descended to the valley, forded the river, and climbed the hill. The builders were grateful for the skri and clothing they brought.

"This is good," Ansil said, munching on skri. "We've had only pancakes and lenitrus. I hope someone brought a stew pot."

"No," Tira said. "That'd be too heavy to carry. We'll have to make one."

Fern looked around at what they'd accomplished. In addition to preparing the ground and laying out plans for the village, they'd made hats to shade their faces, lit a fire, and fashioned tools from wood and stone.

"We don't have hot springs here," Taran said, "but also no volcanoes. The lake is shallow, though, and the river moves slowly enough for the sun to warm the water."

At supper, Ansil sat between Fern and Tira and the three chatted about their recent adventures. After they'd eaten, everyone went to the lake. Instead of joining the others on the shore, Fern was drawn to a little spit of land where a grove of miaven trees grew. To the left was a small cove, just large enough for one or two to bathe. Although she'd lost much of her modesty by now, she was happy to find a place with relative privacy. As Taran promised, the water was comfortably warm.

After bathing, everyone gathered on the sameg around the fire. No one had the energy to dance, but Jorsil played a few tunes on his flute to accompany songs. They slept on the new sameg, which the weka sheltered from rain.

CHAPTER 8
BUILDING ANEW

Breakfast was pancakes and lenitrus. The builders resumed work and others took up tasks they were most suited for. Fern wondered why they went to so much trouble to build houses. "Why not just keep an 'umbrella' up?"

Taran answered, "It takes a lot of someone's energy to do that. Besides, a cozy house is shelter for the heart and mind as well as the body."

She felt that way, too.

Doran took a group to gather food. Fern was surprised by the size of the nuts. "They're so small."

"This is their natural size," Doran said and Tira translated. "It will take time to coax the trees to grow them larger." They scouted the best places to find lenitrus and Doran taught them to identify new edible plants that grew here. Fern was disappointed there were no fan-flowers.

Late in the morning, they ceased work and took their lunches to shady places near the sameg. Tira and Fern told Taran about her fear of the stars.

He was silent for a while, then spoke in a low voice, "I had a sense that you might be at risk. I didn't want to alarm you, but that's why I gave you a warning. I believe you're safe here, but you may not have been safe on Earth. Maybe that's why you haven't been able to wrashiru back."

For her and Tira, a pair of teenagers, to speculate about thortles stalking her had been one thing. For Taran to take it seriously brought home its unwelcome reality. Fern swallowed. "What about my sisters? Are they safe?"

"Tiril's monitoring their safety. He's seen no indication they're at risk."

Her relief was quickly replaced by dread. "If—if the thortles were after me, do you think they'd look for me here? Am I putting this world in danger?"

Taran shook his head. "No. When they lost track of you on Earth, they would have targeted someone else."

"Oh, dear."

Taran said, "Fern, single handedly you cannot save the world. And you cannot save two worlds. You saved your sisters from the fire, you saved our people from the volcano, and you found Tandil when he was lost, but it's not your role to save everyone from every possible disaster. Others must do their part. And some tragedies are unavoidable."

* * *

Their old village, built on the bank of a river, required a short climb to haul water to the sameg. Here, the closest water came from a spring-fed creek which ran just below the sameg. It provided enough for drinking and cooking, but water for washing had to be carried from the lake. Fern asked Taran, "Why didn't we build closer to the river?"

"This valley occasionally floods, and we don't want the houses washed away."

The geologists, Darsan and Tirna, laid the stone foundation for the new fire pit and ovens. Fern wondered, since they were building everything new, couldn't they make some improvements? She asked, "Why build the fire pit so far from the houses? Wouldn't it be more convenient if it was closer, like in the middle of the sameg?"

Taran replied, "Yes, it would be convenient, but the risk of catching our houses on fire would be greater. You've seen how sparks fly."

Yes, she had. She shuddered to think about it.

"We positioned it so the prevailing winds will blow the smoke away from the houses. Much thought was put into our planning."

They built two cisterns, one for drinking water and one for washing, out of stone lined with hardened clay. One morning, as she hauled water,

Fern thought about the water problem. Although Taran was busy, she interrupted him, "Why don't we build the village around the creek so the water would be right here and we wouldn't have to carry it?"

"Because after heavy rains, this creek floods. If we built around it, our sameg would turn to mud." He took her down to the creek and showed her the evidence, traces of debris almost at the foot of the new fire pit.

She accepted this but kept thinking. Would there be some way to divert a controlled amount of water from the spring to the cistern? Like a water pipe? She wished she knew more about such things.

The next day while out collecting firewood, Fern came across a stand of bamboo. Some stalks were as big around as her leg. And they were hollow. Maybe she had the answer to the water problem, but she didn't tell anyone because there was so much else to do and no time for extra projects. But whenever she was in the vicinity, she would search the bamboo stand for dead stalks. She trimmed them with a knife to manageable lengths and stacked them. If she didn't have too much to carry back to the village site, she'd bring one pipe at a time and stockpile them nearby.

Taran gave her a quizzical look. She explained her idea. He raised his eyebrows but didn't object.

* * *

The masons quarried rock for the fire pit from an old landside some distance away. They cut the stones to fit together perfectly without mortar. Fern was foraging for food while much of this was done and later wondered how they cut the stones.

Tira said, "Darsan asks the rocks to split for him."

She remembered their expedition to the volcano fields so long ago and how Darsan had asked the mountain to give him shards of obsidian. So, he could also split stones for building. The next day she watched a couple of strong men lift the pieces into place. How had they managed to carry them so far? She couldn't find the right words and the men didn't understand her question. No one else was around to ask, and afterwards she got busy and forgot.

Fern helped dig clay out of the riverbank to fashion earthen pots and bowls which were hardened in the fire. Now they could make kirrib. The first pot of soup was cause for celebration. Andli had brought some savory herbs from the sea village which made the kirrib especially tasty. Everyone gathered on the sameg to eat supper together. Fern sat near Andli and Doran. After his first sip of soup, Doran complimented Andli, and Fern understood some of what he said, "I am finding new plants here. Some of them have interesting flavors."

Andli was pleased. "You must show them to me."

Fern said, "Me, too."

Doran smiled at her and spoke slowly. "When I am sure they are edible, I will teach you all about them."

Once the ovens were built, they were able to bake skri. Fern was tired of pancakes. She helped gather seed pods that resembled pine cones and extract the seeds, which were sweet. They made sweet cakes to celebrate completion of the ovens and held a dance. When Fern nibbled on her cake, it almost felt like a Feast of the Full Moons, although the moons were in different phases and in separate parts of the sky. She danced nearly every dance.

When she took a break, Ansil was dancing with Tira. Her heart sank. She felt a special bond with Ansil, but Tira had monopolized his attentions. Then for the next dance, Ansil asked Fern, lifting her spirits. Her heart danced with him.

* * *

Rina, Ansil, and other woodworkers oversaw building new houses. In their old village, Fern had helped build Rufan and Sela's house. These were constructed the same way. Those who had wrashirued here had collected building materials and set supporting posts before Fern arrived. As the frames took shape, she marveled at their graceful forms which, however humble, could compete with Earth's best architecture for beauty. It almost seemed a shame to cover them with thatch.

Most of the wood was from dead trees but once the framing was complete, they needed supple wood for wattles. Fern remembered how strange the idea of weaving wood had seemed when they built Rufan and Sela's house.

Doran chose the trees to cut. Fern followed him to a young grove in the river valley. He sat before a sapling which was half a hand width in diameter, and went into meditation. Fern sat at a respectful distance and tried to imagine his conversation with the tree. After a while, he rose and tied a string around its trunk. Fern watched him wend his way through the grove, stop by a tree, bow his head for a moment, then mark it with string. Bregan came after him, respectfully cut the saplings down, and trimmed the branches. Fern helped carry them to the sameg where Bregan split them into slats.

Anyone could weave wattles through the upright posts, but Fern especially enjoyed it. She knew that once the exterior of the first house was finished, she would be busy weaving mats for the interior. And they had many houses to build.

In the old village, and at the sea village when they made repairs after the hurricane, they used large palm-like fronds for thatch. Here, a new material was available. Tall grasses with wide leaves grew in swampy areas. When Tira brought the first armload to the building site, Fern asked, "What's this for?"

Tira took a leaf and folded it over a wattle. "We didn't have these at our old village. On Earth, we visited an Indian village reenactment. They used cattails to thatch their houses. Andli thought these would be easier to work with and do just as good a job. She said we'll use conventional thatch for the roofs."

Fern was skeptical at first, but she found these grass blades were more supple and easier to bend than the materials they used for mats. She tried different methods until she found one she liked. Starting at the bottom, she layered each row over the one below it so it would shed water. Not that it rains on the sameg, she thought. Unless for some reason the weka can't keep the umbrella up. She looked across the river in the direction of the sea. *Could we get a hurricane this far inland?*

After completing part of a wall, she asked Taran to look at it.

He studied her work and nodded. "Yes, this looks like the method the Native Americans used."

Fern taught her technique to others. This freed her to help Andli and other thatchers with the roof. As usual, the builders left a space for air circulation between the wall and roof. They bundled "palm" fronds and, starting at the eaves, lashed them to the rafters, each row overlapping the one below, so the roof would shed water. Lastly, they built a large awning in front of the door where people could sit in the shade.

One morning, when Fern picked up a sling and headed out to gather firewood, Taran stopped her. "Let Tira do your chores. Andli needs your expertise." He smiled and reached for her sling. "And I'm going to fetch firewood."

After the exteriors were finished, they worked on the interiors. Anyone could weave simple mats for floors, which had to be replaced regularly, but those for the walls were artistic endeavors. The members of each household discussed what patterns they wanted, and Fern and Andli wove them. When they attached the panels to the walls with twine, the pieces fit together almost seamlessly. Fern was pleased with the result.

Rina and Ansil put the finishing touches on houses by carving designs on the lintels and door posts. When Ansil's job framing houses was finished, unless he was carving, he helped with other work. Fern watched him accompany Tira into the woods to collect firewood and food, and her heart sank. She wanted to be with him. One consolation was that her talent for weaving was valued and Tira showed no special proficiency in anything.

The first house was given to the weka. The day it was finished, they moved their bedding and belongings in. Fern was puzzled that, instead of sitting under their awning like they'd done at the old village, they stayed on the sameg, or wherever their inclinations took them, for the rest of the day. That evening, when they were ready to retire for the night, everyone else rose to their feet and followed the weka to their house, singing as they went. Fern was reminded of how the village sang Rufan and Sela to their new home in the old village. She had always thought of the ritual as a marriage rite. Apparently it was a housewarming.

After that, homes for grandparents were completed, then families, and lastly for those who'd remained at the sea village. In Fern's new house, the girls' room was larger, to accommodate four girls, and the boys' room was smaller, since Jorsil now slept on the sameg and only Donal remained in the home.

One day, Fern found Rina carving on the lintel of the front doorway of their house. She remembered the carvings in their old home. These were different. It didn't surprise her that Rina made new designs, but when Fern saw carvings above the girls' bedroom doorway framed with ahnti leaves, she asked Tira, "What is this?"

"They're writings in our language, embellished to make them decorative." Tira ran her finger across the lintel and read, "May love eternally surround and guide our daughters Tira, Fern, Tala, and Ara."

Fern peered at the symbols bordered by ahnti leaves. "So this is my name in Human Talk? I never knew this was your writing. I always thought they were only decorations."

Tira's face reddened. "Estut miryit. I should have told you."

Fern stayed in front of the doorway after Tira left. To see her name included with the other daughters warmed her heart. She had always felt loved, and the parents never treated her differently from the others, but to see her name written with theirs was another matter. She rushed to Rina and hugged her. "Tekuyate."

Now Fern took an interest in written Human Talk. She asked to see words printed, if only scratched in the dirt. When Rina noticed her interest, she asked Bregan to split a thin board from a short log. Rina sanded it smooth and applied a resin. Once it was dry, she handed the board to Fern and asked Taran to translate for her. "This is a slate so you can practice writing."

"Tekuyate," Fern said. "I wonder where can I find chalk?"

"It doesn't exist here," Taran said. "Use charcoal."

Seeing and writing words was a key to the language Fern had lacked. Now learning new words and phrases became easier. When she wanted to say something in Human Talk, she asked Tira or Taran to write it on her slate. She wrote down the pronunciation and translation and studied it until she'd mastered the phrase.

With the houses nearly finished, Fern began to work on her proposed water pipe. Uphill, she had located a more robust spring whose creek flowed in a different direction, but it was close enough to supply water. She cleaned out the core of each length of bamboo. With only vague ideas about how to fit the pieces together, she enlisted Ansil's help. She told him how her father had replaced plumbing in their house with PVC pipe and glue. Ansil listened to her and said, "I will read about this."

Fern asked, "How?"

"I'll ask Tiril to help me find the information."

The next day, he said, "If we had stalks large enough to fit on the outside of the pipes, we could make collars to join the ends together, like your father did." Unfortunately, she had chosen the largest diameter stalks she could find and there were few larger. So they found smaller pieces which fit inside the larger ones and joined them that way.

Fern set one end of her pipe by the spring and, over many days, she ran it down to the sameg, burrowing through underbrush carefully, so she wouldn't harm anything. In low places she propped it up with rocks. When Ansil saw that, he made wooden stanchions to support the pipe.

Finally, it was all together. Fern set one end over the cistern for drinking water and made her way uphill to lay the other end in the pool. She put her hand over the end and felt a current, which told her that water was flowing into the pipe. She nearly flew down to the village, but only a small trickle fell into the cistern. She looked along the pipe and at the first joint, she saw why. It was leaking. She followed the pipeline uphill. Every joint leaked. She sat down in the mud and cried.

Rina came to her. Using words and gestures, she helped Fern understand that the problem was that the joints were not watertight. Rina reminded her they used resin to make the bamboo bottles watertight, but the length of the line would require a lot of resin.

Before the day was out, the flow increased a little. Rina explained that the water made the wood swell, closing some of the gaps. However, the leaking didn't stop. That night, a pair of enthusiastic dancers, forgetting about the pipe, bumped into it, and water spewed across the sameg. The contrite couple helped Fern move the end of the pipe off the sameg to where it would drain into the creek.

The next day, while they were shelling nuts, Fern asked Andli if she knew how to make resin. Andli deferred to Motan, a grandfather who had been hoping to find an apprentice to bequeath his knowledge and skills to. He was overjoyed to be given a pupil, until he learned that Fern was not interested in chemistry, only how to make resin. He agreed to teach her anyway, hoping she would change her mind.

Either Tira or Ansil would accompany her as translator. Fern had no trouble learning to identify and collect the various ingredients. She easily learned how to process and purify them in readiness for combining them, but when it came to getting the measurements right, it just didn't work.

Like Lila had done, Motan measured ingredients with his fingertips or the palms of his hands. Even when Fern was sure she had measured correctly, her results were a failure. Ansil carved her a set of measuring cups and spoons. With them, she measured the ingredients after Motan did and wrote the recipe on her slate. It still didn't turn out right.

"You need to feel the amounts, not measure them," Tira informed her. So she let Tira measure, and Tira's batch was successful. Fern was abashed, but there was nothing to do but accept Tira's partnership in this endeavor.

The first successful batch of resin was too hard and brittle. It sealed the bamboo joints perfectly, but then it cracked and leaked. "It needs to give some," Tira decided. "It's impossible to keep this long pipe rigid enough."

Motan and Tira concocted a gummier resin which sealed successfully and was fluid enough to move with the inevitable sway of the pipe. This delivered water to the cistern as intended, but the water tasted like resin. It was undrinkable.

Tira seemed genuinely disappointed. "You put so much work into it."

Yes. So much work—for nothing! Fern threw up her hands and screamed, "You people will never get anywhere! You do nothing to better yourselves!" She grabbed the end of the pipe and jerked it away from the cistern. She was angry enough to tear the whole thing apart, but Andli gently restrained her.

Taran took the end of the pipe and moved it off the sameg. Andli held Fern until she stopped crying. Then Taran came to her and said, "We need to empty the cistern and clean it out."

Fern hung her head and began to bail out the cistern.

Taran said, "All is not lost. Even though we can't drink the water from the pipe, we can still wash with it." He set the pipe to run into the cistern for lake water. "Now we won't have to haul water from the lake."

Fern had the satisfaction that, after all, her water pipe made life easier for her people.

CHAPTER 9
THE LIBRARY

The helpers from the sea village went home. Jorsil left to rejoin Tana, but Ansil stayed. Everyone had more time for leisure and for projects they'd put on hold. Musicians made new instruments. Although not a musician, Ansil helped them with the woodwork. Fern helped Andli collect and process plants for fabrics.

Ara arrived with a group of families from the sea village, who also brought Rina's bowl and Fern's spindle. Rina resumed carving the sides of the bowl and asked Fern to spin very fine, strong thread and weave it into cloth for a drum head. The next group brought rope for a new tetherball and swings. When Bregan split a board for a swing, Fern said to Tira, "I have an idea. Why don't we make a teeter-totter for the children?"

She and Tira debated on how long the board should be. Neither had measured a see-saw when they were on Earth. Finally, Ansil said, "Two arm spans."

"How do you know?" Fern asked.

He shrugged his shoulders. "I asked Tiril to measure one."

Once completed, before anyone else would ride the see-saw, Fern and Tira each mounted an end and showed them how it worked. The children enjoyed it, and even the adults waited their turns to ride.

* * *

Fern had been too busy to meditate or visit her sisters. She faithfully recorded each full of the small moon on her erguvon stick but hadn't kept up with the passage of time on Earth. She tried to remember when she'd last seen her family—after summer vacation, when the girls were back in school.

One morning she asked Taran, "What date is it on Earth?"

He closed his eyes and concentrated. "It's about mid December."

"That means I missed Thanksgiving!" She stomped off to do her chores. She relied on Taran to tell her when it was on Earth. It was hard for her to keep track, since the days here were nearly twenty seven Earth-hours long. Somehow, Taran was able to calculate the time difference, but he didn't always remember to tell her when milestones approached.

After she finished, Fern went to her miaven grove. She'd never told anyone she'd chosen this as her special place, yet everyone seemed to understand and no one bothered her here. She tried to meditate but anger and frustration broke her concentration. Desperately, she tried ethenos, but instead of projecting herself into her grandparents' home, her mind bounced among the miaven trees. She looked up at the branches. A breeze stirred their leaves. Could Doran coax them to bloom like he did the one on her mother's grave? But even if he did, it wouldn't be the same.

She missed the solitude of her mother's hut and the comfort of the rocking chair. If only she could share the holidays with her sisters, or at least see what they were doing! No one celebrated Christmas here. Although Taran said the Feast of the Full Moons was special to them, like Christmas was for her, it wasn't the same. And it didn't come every year. Soon it would be January. Thoughts of ice storm and house fire raged through her.

She threw herself on the ground and cried. The sound of children playing on the sameg cut through her. What she wouldn't give to listen to her own sisters play! It was her own fault. Lately, her life had been so full, she'd hardly thought about them. She sat up and wiped her eyes. Then she stared at her hands, smudged with dirt and tears, and went to the lake's edge to wash.

Fern missed the pool by her mother's hut, but this water was pleasant, as warm as a Florida lake in summer. Her new bathing place, screened by the miaven trees, gave her privacy. She stripped off her tunic, went into the water, and let it ease her taut muscles and nerves.

After she bathed, she let herself drip dry, shook debris out of her tunic, and dressed. When she emerged from her grove, Taran was returning from gathering lenitrus. She remembered her rudeness that morning. He had kindly given her an approximate date, and she'd complained about missing Thanksgiving. She went to him. "Estut miryit."

"I'm sorry, too, Fern. I'm not sensitive to your need for holidays."

"So, I've been here almost two years."

He nodded.

"I haven't been able to see my sisters in a long time."

"You've been distracted. A lot has been going on. You need to take time for yourself, meditate more. I'm willing to help guide your mind, whenever you're ready."

"I know." She accompanied him back to the sameg.

Fern took his advice. Every day after chores, she rinsed off in the lake and sat in her miaven grove to meditate. Sorrow and disappointment subsided. Her mind became better focused. She was able to ethenos again.

To her delight, she was present for Christmas. She watched her sisters open their gifts of new clothes, games, and toys. She'd forgotten how lavish their life was. When the youngest carried her new CD player into her bedroom, Fern followed. The closet and drawers burst with clothing, and books and toys spilled off the shelves. Did she have so much stuff when she was ten? What would Tala and Ara think of all this? Upon reflection, Fern decided she and her foster sisters were just as happy with what little they had. They never went hungry and were kept warm and safe. Most important, they were loved.

She was unable to visit her family again until January. She found her grandparents and sisters, dressed for winter, walking through a cemetery. Grandma carried a potted poinsettia and Grandpa a shovel.

"You know this plant probably won't survive the next frost," he said.

"I know, but this is what the girls wanted, and who knows?"

Fern followed them to a black marble headstone. On it were her parents' names and her own. She wept with the family while they planted the poinsettia on the grave.

"Fern's not really here," the youngest said.

"No," said Grandma. "She's really in Heaven. But I'm sure she can see the flowers."

"Yes," her other sister said. "She likes flowers."

With tears in her eyes, she embraced each of her sisters, even though she knew they couldn't feel her presence.

* * *

Across the lake rose the high ridge from which, Taran said, one could glimpse the sea. Fern occasionally spotted Ansil standing on the rocky peak, a miniscule figure against the wide sky. One day after finishing her chores, she climbed the ridge. By now there should have been a path, made by Ansil or other climbers, but she couldn't find it. It was a hard climb, but she was anxious to view the sea.

By the time she reached the top, she was disappointed. She imagined a faint salt smell on the landward breeze but all she could see were trees. She followed the ridge to the west and climbed a pinnacle where, at last, she spotted a silver glimmer in the distance. So much for a view of the sea.

She didn't go back there again because of the lengthy climb. Besides, if it was Ansil's private place, she didn't want to impose. One day, she asked him about it.

"Yes, I go there to be alone," he said. "And also to look at the sea. I miss the sea. You are welcome anytime. I'll know you're coming. Sometimes I only go there to read."

To read! How she missed reading. The long days and longer nights would be so much more pleasant if she could curl up with a book. "Just how do you read? I know it's a mental thing, but how do you do it?"

Ansil frowned. "Taran hasn't taught you to read?"

"He offered to, but I didn't want to let him into my mind."

"I understand. You can't be expected to adopt all our ways at once. It's good to proceed slowly and do only what's comfortable. When I read, I go into my library."

"Where is it?" In her explorations with ethenos, the only library she'd found was the one at her old school on Earth. She'd been unable to remove a book from the shelves, let alone read it.

Ansil grinned and pointed to his head.

She didn't want him in her mind. How would it feel to be in his? She drew a deep breath and said, "Can you teach me to read?"

He smiled. "First, I'll help you find your library."

They went to her miaven grove and sat on the ground facing each other. Something stirred in Fern and she yearned for him to kiss her. Immediately, she hid that impulse and concentrated on their purpose. Ansil gave no indication that he'd been aware of her errant thought.

In a soothing voice, he led her into a hypnotic state, much as Taran used to. Her focus turned from the sounds and sensations of the world —the wind in the trees, distant murmuring voices, the cool leaves on which she sat. She became aware of a long, dim hallway. Soft carpet caressed her bare feet. Ansil took her hand and led her to a room lined with bookshelves and furnished with easy chairs and antique lamps. Fern felt at home.

She scanned the shelves. When her life on Earth had been interrupted, she was halfway through a Nancy Drew mystery. The book appeared on the shelf in front of her. She removed it, opened it, and was delighted to be able to read the words.

She looked across the room. Ansil sat in a chair, reading. Instead of his tunic, he wore jeans and a tee shirt with a picture of a sailboat. She looked down at herself. She was wearing shorts and what had once been her favorite blouse. How odd, she thought. She chose a chair, curled her legs under her, propped the book on the chair's arm, and read several chapters.

Finally, she marked her place, closed the book, and looked across the room at Ansil.

He asked, "Are you ready to go?"

She nodded. He set his book aside and stood up. Fern went to him and hugged him. "Tekuyate."

He led her back through the polished wooden door of the library, down the carpeted hall, and through a garden gate to the miaven grove.

Fern became aware of sitting on the ground. The sounds of the lake returned. She opened her eyes. She and Ansil were wearing their tunics again, and she was happily tired from hours of reading. A few cleansing breaths dissipated the fatigue. Fern knew she had let Ansil into her mind, but she felt safe with him. "Was that a real library?"

"Not an actual material one. What you saw is a framework constructed in your mind."

"How did you do it?'

"I didn't. You did. I only took you to the door."

"Why were you wearing Earth clothes?"

"Was I?"

"Yes. I was, too." She described the room and everything in it, including his clothes.

"That's curious. I saw it quite differently."

"What were you reading?"

"Some poetry written by Hartha, the granddaughter of Moses and Rila."

She shook her head sadly. "No one's told me about the books your people have written."

"Estut miryit. It seems we have neglected many things."

"It's partly my fault. I've resisted learning things. I've wasted my time only trying to learn to wrashiru."

"The songs and stories we share on the sameg at night are mostly our creations."

"I know, but I thought they were only oral traditions. Why are there books in Human Talk in my library?"

"It was from *my* library. In my mind, that's where I was. You can access anything in the universe in your library. You only have to be able to read the words. Some of us can read languages besides Human Talk. It's a rare gift. One has to be able to follow the thinking processes of a very alien people."

"It seemed so easy to get there. I wish I'd let Taran teach me before."

The following afternoon, Fern tried, unsuccessfully, to find her library and had to ask Ansil for help. Again, he guided her into a hypnotic state and down the corridor. He sat across the room from her and read, as before. This time, she asked to see his book. The cover looked like any book on Earth except that it was blank. Inside, it looked like a computer screen, with strange symbols in neat rows and columns. As she looked more closely, a few symbols looked familiar. They were similar to designs Rina had carved and lettering she'd written on her slate, but none of the words were familiar.

"This is written in the language of the thortles," he confirmed. "But it's Shakespeare's *Midsummer Night's Dream*."

"I didn't think the thortles would be interested in Shakespeare."

"They're not. They have no respect for humans or our accomplishments. Besides, they don't bother with poetry or fiction. Lila's father translated this into our language. It wasn't easy. Human Talk didn't have a lot of the words he needed. The thortles never taught us the names for things found in nature because we didn't need them for our work. When we came here, Moses gave us some words and we devised others, but we still had no words for animals or fairies. Lila's father borrowed the English words and figured out how to write them in the thortle characters."

After this, Fern paid even more attention to the written language. Ansil helped her recognize more words and, in her library, they found children's books from Earth that had been translated into Human Talk. By comparing those writings with the ones in English, Fern began to decipher the new language, and her command of it slowly increased.

Fern required a few more lessons before she was able to find the library on her own. Another time she asked to see Ansil's book. Inside the cover, a three dimensional shape with strange symbols floated in and out of focus. The stationary corners were embellished with pictures that resembled flowers and vines. She didn't recognize those symbols. They looked different from thortle characters.

"What language is this?"

"It's the writings of the…." She failed to catch the sounds or meaning of the word he said.

"Who?"

"A gentle people on a planet you have no name for."

"How can you read their language?"

"I once visited their world."

"Really? Tell me about them."

"It was a brief visit, because they don't encourage tourists. I also lived with them during one of my lifetimes."

"What do they look like?"

"They are small people. Like us, they have two eyes, two ears, a mouth, nose, arms and legs, but you would not mistake them for one of us. If you saw one, you might think it was an elf, or a doll. And they have strong psychic powers."

"You had a past life among them?"

"Yes. I remember very little about that life, but I think they accepted me as a visitor because I had once lived with them. They seemed to know more about it than I did."

"Tell me more."

He described a world that looked much like this planet and Earth, with oceans, mountains, forests, and deserts. When he told her about their animals, they sounded similar to those on Earth, in appearance. He described their cities and their space ships, their psychic abilities, their culture, and their arts. She could almost see their world through his eyes.

"Do the thortles kidnap them?"

"No, they don't bother them. They are a space faring people with strong allies. The thortles fear them."

"Do they have books I can read?"

"No, none have been translated into English or any other Earth language. However, when you learn our language, you'll be able to read some of their writings." He smiled proudly. "I myself have translated a few of their children's stories. They are quite delightful."

The next time she asked for his help, Ansil had her lead the way to the library. She realized her dependence on him was not because she needed his assistance but because she enjoyed his company. It was so home-like to sit across the room from him while they both read.

One day, reading alone in her library, Fern fell asleep and dreamed of her sisters. They were at a softball game, and the older one was at bat. She swung—a loud crack—and the ball flew into the backfield. "Run!" Fern found herself screaming, "Run to second! Keep running! No, stop! Stay there." The player at third base streaked home. In the audience, Fern's youngest sister jumped with excitement and her grandparents applauded wildly. A young man with "Coach" on his shirt yelled, "Good job!" Then he turned to Fern and smiled. It was Tiril! The shock woke her.

She had mixed feelings about what Tiril was doing. She'd asked him to check on her sisters, not to become involved with them. What's more, she wasn't sure she wanted him to enter her mind like that, or rather, have her enter his. At the same time, she was grateful to him for further assurance that her sisters were leading a normal life.

CHAPTER 10
COURTSHIP

If Tira was jealous of the attention Ansil gave Fern, she didn't show it, but Fern couldn't help being envious of the time he spent with Tira. They would go on long walks together, or sit and talk while shelling nuts, sometimes leaving Fern out of the conversation. One night when she couldn't sleep, Fern tried to go to her library, but she was too agitated. She looked for Ansil on the sameg, but he wasn't there. When she returned to her bedroom, Tira was gone. The girls were free to come and go as they wished, day or night, but Fern harbored an uncomfortable suspicion which she didn't mention to anyone. She only let it smolder into envious resentment.

The next day, still in a bad mood, Fern sat in front of the house, spinning. Ansil joined her, carving tiny pieces of wood. If he picked up on her anger, he didn't show it. He spoke kindly to her, as always. Eventually, her mood softened. When Ansil asked her to spin him some fine, tough cord, she was happy to do so.

A few days later, he presented her with a necklace of wooden beads of many colors, etched with intricate designs.

That's what he'd been carving. "It's beautiful," she said, and almost forgave him, until she saw Tira wearing a similar necklace. Without saying a thing, she ran to her miaven grove. She tried to snatch the necklace from her neck but the cord was too strong to break. She pulled it off over her head. The etchings on the beads skinned her ear. "Ouch!" She threw the necklace into the lake. Then she cried. She hated Tira. And she hated Ansil.

Once she had run the gamut of emotions, she tried to reason with herself. Other than giving her a necklace, Ansil made no romantic overtures, as other young men had. Like Tiril, he treated her like a sister. Why was she attracted to such boys when others were interested in her? Ansil was one of the few males on the planet with whom Tira could mate. They had known each other a long time and it was obvious they liked each other. Ansil was kind to Fern. She had let him into her mind more than any other person, even Andli. He'd been a thoughtful teacher.

She couldn't help the feelings she had for him, but she remembered she'd felt the same way about Tiril, and she got over him. It was unfair to deny Tira her chance at happiness. But it still hurt.

She couldn't reason herself out of the way she felt, but she resolved to not let it spoil her relationship with Ansil. Maybe things would work out. She wasn't old enough for marriage, anyway. Besides, she hadn't entirely lost hope of returning to Earth. The thought fleetingly crossed her mind that Ansil was courting both of them, but she dismissed it.

The necklace! How far had she thrown it? She waded into the water. She had to find it. She picked up a pebble to toss, to estimate how far she'd the flung necklace, but she didn't remember which direction she'd thrown it.

Andli was swimming nearby. She must have sensed Fern's anguish. She came over and touched Fern's ear, which was bleeding. Fern had forgotten all about it. Andli rinsed off the blood, examined the scratch, and said, "It will soon heal." Then she hugged her, and Fern let loose another flow of tears. No words were exchanged, but Fern felt Andli knew what was troubling her. Soon she felt better.

Andli touched Fern's neck and said something. Fern pointed at the lake. Andli dived under the water and Fern followed. But how could they find such a small thing among the rocks, sand, and leaf litter covering the lake bottom? Fern closed her eyes and let her mind reach out. Suddenly her hand found the necklace. With relief, she surfaced and showed it to Andli, and they returned to the village together.

* * *

Fern's library became a refuge even more comforting than her miaven grove, but she hadn't been able to visit or even dream about her sisters in a while. She considered asking for assistance but hesitated to let anyone into her mind, even Ansil. One day she had an idea. On her way down the corridor to the library, she envisioned a television set, and when she entered the room, there was a TV on a stand across from her chair. Her heart beat with anticipation. She ran across the room and pressed the power button.

The picture showed the playground at her grandparents' church, surrounded by picnic tables and Easter baskets. Fern's sisters sat with other children, eating fried chicken. Fern's mouth watered. She'd almost forgotten the taste of meat. The image panned to another table where her grandparents dined with other adults. One of them was Tiril! He turned in her direction, lifted a chicken leg, made eye contact, and grinned. She was so shocked, the screen went dark. With shaky fingers, she pushed the button several times but couldn't get it to turn back on.

Later, she told Ansil about it.

"Didn't you ask him to check on them?"

"Yes, but not to get—it's creepy."

"He won't harm your family. He joined your grandparents' church and got to know them that way."

"But do they know who he is? Do they know anything about him?"

"They know he's a college student and will be moving on once he graduates. And that's true. He's going to college, and he'll come home when he's done. He's learning many curious things about your people. He'll tell you all about it when he comes back."

"How do you know all this?"

He gave her a funny look. "Why, I'm in contact with him, of course."

* * *

After Fern finished her Nancy Drew book, she read another, then a third. By then, she was tired of them. They were appropriate for a middle-schooler, but she had outgrown them. Besides, her library seemed limitless. Anything she desired appeared on a shelf. She read *Jane Eyre* and her emotions ached with the heroine through torment and love.

Inspired by Ansil's reading *A Midsummer Night's Dream*, she read *Romeo and Juliet*. She chose a paperback aimed at students, with footnotes to help her understand the archaic language and sixteenth century references. She enjoyed the story but thought the couple was stupid to end their short lives the way they did. Why, Juliet was younger than she was, too young to get so serious about a boy.

Fern thought about her friends back home. They'd be in tenth grade. Some of them might be dating. Her parents had told her she couldn't date until she was sixteen.

She smiled when she thought about her first week of middle school. She'd gone home one day sporting a bracelet a boy in class had given her, one he'd crafted at summer camp. "Guess what!" She'd flashed her wrist. "I'm going with Peter."

Instead of congratulating her, her parents had glanced sideways at each other and Daddy growled, "You can have all the boyfriends you want at school but you can't go out on dates until you're sixteen."

His lack of enthusiasm had dampened her spirits, but now she could laugh at her naïveté. Later, she'd overheard her mother say, "Don't be so hard on her. She's growing up, you know. I started dating when I was fifteen."

Her father had sighed and said, "I know, but I see too many freshman girls at school, some of them only fourteen, going with senior boys, and they're seventeen and eighteen. I'll not have that. I don't want to be a grandfather before I'm forty."

When would she be sixteen? She faithfully kept track of time and had added ten marks on her erguvon stick since the Full Moons. She still used the television set in her library to check on her sisters but discovered that by meditating in the library, she could easily project herself to Earth.

Each time, she looked at a calendar to see what month it was, but she didn't always know what day. She remembered her family observing her fifteenth birthday almost a year ago. A lot had happened since then.

When she became sixteen, she'd have her parents' permission to date. But what was dating here? Young men and women danced with each other, but everyone danced with one another. Couples went into the woods and were gone for hours. What did they do there? She let her imagination run. Couples who spent much time together eventually set up a household. There seemed to be no marriage ceremony. The villagers helped the pair build a house and sang them home on the night they moved in. And sometimes another adult or two joined the family with little fanfare.

In the past, young men of their village had sent their sisters to Fern with gifts. At the village by the sea, Arlon and other boys had done the same. Ansil had given her a necklace, but he also made one for Tira. Some mornings Ansil plaited Tira's hair, which Fern suspected was an act of courtship.

One day, she spied two people on Ansil's ridge and Tira was nowhere to be found. More and more, the pair was absent from the village at the same time, day or night. Fern's parents had been protective of her, but here she was allowed to go anywhere, anytime, with anyone. And so was Tira. Fern's parents had given her strict guidelines to prevent them from "becoming grandparents before they were forty." To Fern's knowledge, none of Tira's parents had so cautioned her. Of course, with everyone's minds so open to everyone else's, they probably knew what she was up to.

Here, people were more open about sex than where she'd grown up, and no one had given Fern a frank talk about boys like her parents had. She would have been uncomfortable to discuss this with Taran and wouldn't have listened to Tira. With Andli and Rina, there was the language barrier. She and Lila had talked about many things, but not this, only that she was free to mate with any man on the planet.

Although she, too, spent hours alone with Ansil, no one said anything. Did they trust them that much? Why didn't parents on Earth trust their children? This was another unfathomable difference between the cultures.

What about pregnancy? She recalled the first time she'd had a period after she came here. She'd asked Tira for supplies. To her surprise, Tira didn't know what to do. She said they used mind control to manage reproduction, and that she wouldn't start her menses until she was ready to bear children. They went to Andli for instructions.

Fern had no intention of deviating from her parents' teachings. She would wait until sixteen to "date," and until she was married.... Well, she hoped to be back on Earth by then.

At night, sweaty dancers rinsed off in the lake. Fern usually bathed in the lee of her little grove for privacy, but when it was dark enough, she joined the others at the beach. One such night, after she shed her tunic and rinsed it out, Fern swam out into the lake, just far enough to touch bottom with her feet and let the water caress her skin. Ansil swam to her. She was aware of his nakedness and her own. Her hair had come undone when she danced, only one braid remaining intact. Ansil reached over and started undoing it. Fern giggled. When he finished, he handed her the hair fasteners and, chuckling, ran his fingers through her locks. She laughed and splashed him. He laughed in turn and swam across the lake. Later, by the light of the moons, she saw someone on the ridge.

The next morning, Ansil approached Fern. "Would you like me to plait your hair?"

She hesitated. He always did a good job with Tira's, but... "Uh, no. That's okay."

"Any time, I'll be happy to."

"Sure. Thanks." Shortly after, when she saw him fixing Tira's hair, it was hard not to feel jealous. She hoped they didn't pick up on her feelings.

Later that day, Ansil met her as she carried her firewood to the sameg. "I'm going up the mountain to look at the sea. Would you like to come?"

"Sure." She deposited her wood on the pile and grabbed a few skri and two bags for lenitrus.

He led her up a trail which bent more to the east. "I didn't know about this path," she said. The walking was easier and faster than the route she'd taken before. At the top, she smelled the sea breeze and glimpsed deep blue shining in the distance. She turned landward and saw a miniscule cluster of huts, tiny people, and a cooking fire. "I brought some skri, if you get hungry."

"Tekuyate." He touched her arm. "This way." Another path took them to a rocky outcropping where, far below, beyond the treetops, an expanse of sparkling water met the sky at a dark blue line.

"I guess I went the wrong way before. Is this your special place?"

He nodded.

She wondered if he had brought Tira here, or only to the top of the ridge, but she didn't ask.

They sat on a rock and watched the sun play on the water. "I'm thinking of going back for a while," he said. "I miss the sea. And I miss my mother."

"I bet you do." She thought about going with him, but she didn't want to leave Andli.

"I won't be gone forever. I'll come back."

Fern watched a few puffy clouds race across the sea and realized she was looking for birds. With a sigh, she remembered there were none.

"What's wrong?"

"I was thinking about birds. A place like this on Earth, you'd see seagulls, maybe pelicans. And other birds, too. Songbirds. It's so quiet here."

"Yes, Tiril is quite taken with your birds, especially the songbirds."

The wind in the trees reminded her this world was not entirely silent. "Where's your village from here? Is it below us?"

"No." He pointed east. "It would be a good day's sailing in that direction."

She thought about him sailing to this part of the sea, but a boat would be too small to see from this distance. As she gazed down the green precipice to the silver sea, then to the sky growing pink with the evening sun, she almost wished he would kiss her. But if he read her thoughts he didn't act on them, and nothing but deep friendship passed between them.

The next morning, Fern learned that Tira was to accompany Ansil to the sea village. She hid her tears and went to her grove to cry. She half hoped Ansil would come to her, to comfort her, but she also put up a mental barrier to keep him away. That day, she avoided everyone, performing her domestic chores quickly, and walked as far away as she could to collect firewood.

On her way back, Andli met her. "Fern, you are upset."

Fern dropped her wood and allowed Andli to embrace her. "I'm in love with Ansil," she confessed.

"I know. He loves you, too."

"But he's taking Tira to the sea village with him. Are they going to be married?"

"Probably, someday, but they're still very young. Fern, there's nothing to stop you from marrying them also."

Fern shook her head, "No. I don't want that. I wasn't brought up that way." She spoke in English but Andli seemed to understand.

"You're still very young. Someday you may feel differently. Or you may find a man who'll be content with your wishes."

Where would she find such a man? On Earth, maybe, not here. But she wasn't on Earth and despaired of ever going back. She nodded anyway.

Andli picked up Fern's firewood and carried it to where she'd left her own. Fern picked up Andli's and they returned to the village.

Rather than going to the sameg that night, Fern hid in her grove and tried to think. Back in middle school, her infatuation with Peter had been short lived, as had been her passion for a series of other boys, including Tiril. At least Tira couldn't marry Tiril. He was her brother. But could she ever get over Ansil? With him, she'd achieved a degree of intimacy lacking in prior relationships. She'd let him into her mind.

To her surprise, Tira came and stood outside the grove, "Fern? May I join you?"

Fern rose to her feet and went out to meet her.

Tira said, "Fern, I am sorry to have distressed you. Esmilu tefi. I love you. You are my sister." She threw her arms around Fern.

Fern reluctantly hugged her back. "Estut miryit," she said, "I should feel happy for you. It's just that, I'm confused. I'm still not used to your ways."

Tira took off the necklace Ansil had made her and put it around Fern's neck. "I want you to take this for safekeeping, until I return."

Fern fingered it. It was no nicer than her own. "Why don't you take it with you?"

"I can't. We're not walking."

Of course. Why should they? Both could wrashiru. Fern couldn't go with them if she wanted. At least they wouldn't be spending many days alone together in the wilderness.

After Tira left, Ansil came. He took Fern in his arms and said, "I will say goodbye for now, but I'll return." This time he did kiss her—long and sweet. She let herself melt into his embrace. "Esmilu tefi," he said. He kissed her again. Then he left.

The sensation lingered on Fern's lips a few minutes. But it was wrong, all wrong. "No!" she screamed into the night. "Wait! Come back!" But no one came. Laughter and music echoed from the sameg. She put a hand over her thundering heart and found Tira's necklace. Despair spiraled into rage. She snatched at the necklace and the string snapped. Beads flew about the grove. Fern crumpled to the ground and bawled. Why did nothing work out for her?

When she'd exhausted herself, she conceded Tira couldn't help loving Ansil any more than she could. But why did he kiss her and tell her he loved her? It was so cruel! But no, Ansil was trying to be kind. To give her a promise of hope. He knew how she felt about him. Why didn't he understand she couldn't share him with another woman? Yet Tira was willing to share. In a way, she wished she could, too. But it was impossible.

She had destroyed the necklace Ansil had painstakingly made for Tira, which Tira had entrusted into her care. Chastened, Fern searched the grove in the dark until she had gathered as many beads as she could find. When she returned to the village, Ansil and Tira were gone.

The next day, Fern spun the strongest, finest cord she could, hunted through the grove until she found each and every bead, and restrung the necklace. Then she put it away among her own belongings where it would be safe.

CHAPTER 11
EDUCATION

In their old village, Taran had taught an English class. Now, with Fern's help, he resumed it. Not all of the English students from their old village joined them. A few had remained at the sea and others were too busy with new stages of their lives. Most of the current students were hardly fluent enough to carry on a conversation, so with Tira gone, Fern still had only Taran to talk to. Her comprehension of Human Talk improved day by day, but she was still self-conscious about speaking it with anyone but Andli and the toddlers.

This brought Fern to an awakening. The toddlers with whom she first conversed in baby talk had become children with language skills that outpaced hers. Fern now babbled with toddlers who were born after she'd come here. Even Simbi corrected her speech. No wonder Ansil didn't seriously court her. Who would want a wife who couldn't talk to her own children?

She tried harder to master the language. Seeing and copying the written words helped, but her greatest impediment came from failure to think in Human Talk. How did these folk manage to think in the language of the thortles? Were skills like wrashiru facilitated by the structure of their thinking?

She asked Taran.

"Certainly, mental skills are influenced by thinking in a language, but we don't think as the thortles do. Actually, we don't speak as they do, either. Human Talk changed greatly after we came here. Moses gave us words that the thortle language, or what we knew of it, didn't have. We also borrowed words from other Earth languages, and even devised some words of our own."

Just knowing she didn't have to think in the language of the dreaded thortles eased Fern's mind.

* * *

Fern never thought she'd miss Tira. She hadn't been aware how much she depended on her sister, and now she was lonely. She considered walking to the village by the sea, but it was so far. If she could wrashiru …but if she could wrashiru to the sea, she could go back to Earth. She consented to allow Taran to train her mind.

They sat in meditation and he guided her. Ethenos became easier and she checked on her sisters on Earth regularly. One day she found her family in the cafeteria at the elementary school where the elder sister was graduating. Fern was days from turning sixteen! She tried to visit them on her birthday, to see if they celebrated, but she was too late for the party. Her disappointment was offset by finding a half-eaten birthday cake in the kitchen.

With ethenos becoming routine, the next step could be wrashiru. Fern renewed hopes of returning to Earth. The implications of this possibility crowded her thoughts. If she returned, how could she explain her disappearance? Explain where she'd been? Who would believe her?

After her next session with Taran, she asked, "If I can learn wrashiru, and I go back to Earth, then what? I've been gone almost three years. What do I tell people?"

Taran stroked his beard. "I've wondered about that myself. It's not a problem for us, because we're only visitors. We have cover stories about where we moved from, so we don't have to explain how we popped into existence. When we're ready to come home, we just tell people we're moving elsewhere. If you told the truth, no one would believe you, and they'd treat you like you were crazy. If the government believed you, they might use you for research, and you wouldn't lead a normal life. Your immediate family might accept you, but old friends are likely to distance you. It's a quandary."

Fern looked down at the matt she sat on. "I could say I bumped my head trying to get out of the house and had amnesia. Or I was kidnapped and just got free." She looked at Taran. He wore a patronizing half-smile. "I know. It sounds like a plot from a bad movie."

"It does. There is half a plan. You would go to our friends, the Devoirs, and they would get in touch with your grandparents. Most likely, they'd believe you. From there, a cover story could be concocted. Possibly amnesia or kidnapping could be part of it."

Fern shrugged. "I guess it's too soon to worry about it now. I have to learn to wrashiru first."

"That's right."

After this, she thought about all the people here she had come to love, and the idea of returning to Earth became bittersweet. She would miss this family, especially Andli, and the friends she'd made. But if she could master wrashiru, perhaps she could come back to visit. The important thing was to get home.

Another consideration was that she had missed two and a half years of school and was seriously behind. She had to catch up with her classmates on Earth. Education here was so different. She didn't think about the practical skills she'd gained, the information gleaned from various teachers, or all she'd learned about the history and culture of these people. This was not education as she knew it on Earth. These people were highly intelligent, but primitive. They focused on the nebulous world of the mind and spirit and did little to advance themselves otherwise.

With a library full of books, education was at her fingertips. She thought about her eighth grade textbooks and imagined them into her library. She began with science, picking up mid-year where she'd left. Despite her best intentions, she found the book boring and had trouble staying focused. She thumbed through it and decided that manatees were an interesting topic, so she found a book about them.

Back in her grove, Fern thought about the rivers that flowed into the sea and wondered if manatees would like living here. Why not? They were vegetarians. Wouldn't it be nice to swim with those gentle beasts? But this world had no manatees and probably never would. The book said they were in danger of going extinct. Fern hugged her knees and buried her face. She wished she could bring all the manatees here where they'd have a chance to survive, but that was impossible. She raised her head but the scenery failed to lift her spirits. There were no fish in the lake, no birds or butterflies, no deer in the forests. Not even mosquitoes to bite her, or cockroaches to infest the thatched roofs or mat floors of their house.

* * *

After struggling to finish eighth grade studies, Fern visited the high school where her father once taught, looked at the ninth grade textbooks, and imagined them into her library. Among other subjects, college bound students took a foreign language. Well, she was learning a foreign language, but how could she explain this one back on Earth? Ninth graders also took physical education and a choice of art. She had these covered. With all the physical activity, she was in excellent condition, and she'd been immersed in the arts—weaving, music, performances on the sameg.

Although she'd always been good at math, learning algebra from a textbook was daunting. She asked Taran for advice.

"What are you having difficulty with?" he asked.

"Well, I know most of the terms, and there's a glossary in the back of the book, but it requires a whole different kind of thinking. It's hard to wrap my mind around it."

"That's understandable. It would help if I could see the book."

"I know. But it's in my library."

"Take me to your library."

"Is that possible?"

"Didn't Ansil accompany you there?"

They sat in meditation and Fern led Taran to her library. It felt so weird for him to be there. She set the book on the table. When Taran sat down to study it, Fern noticed he was wearing his tunic. She looked at herself. She was dressed in jeans and a sweater. Ansil always wore Earth clothes in her library, but Taran's appearance was unchanged.

"Pull up another chair," he said. "Show me what you're having trouble with."

They sat together and went over her questions. She was surprised he knew so much about math. "How did you learn algebra?"

"Mathematics is part of the structure of the universe. And I studied your math when I visited Earth."

A few days later, she was stumped by an equation.

When she asked for help, Taran said, "Do I need to go to your library?"

To tell the truth, she didn't want anyone there, except perhaps Ansil. "If I could remember it, I could write it on my slate and you wouldn't have to."

He smiled. "Your mind is better trained than that. Stop and think. Let your mind stretch out."

She closed her eyes and "stretched out" her mind. The equation flashed in front of her. "I've got it." With eyes still shut, she wrote it on her slate. When she looked at her writing, she said, "Wow, that's sloppy."

"It's okay. I can make it out."

Fern tried not to bother Taran with every problem, unless she couldn't solve it on her own. In some of their mental training lessons, she let him enter her mind and show her the relationships among numbers. As he helped her mentally explore the worlds of math, Fern began to appreciate how beautiful the structure of the universe was.

These people used a base-twelve numbering system, not ten like Fern was used to. When counting on their fingers, they started and ended with the thumbs, which gave them six numbers on each hand. Taran told her the thortles used the dozenal system, as he called it. "Moses tried to teach us base-ten, but we were set in our ways, and he didn't live long enough to change us." Taran taught her the dozenal system, but she always used the one she knew.

One day Fern helped Andli set up a loom. Andli counted on her fingers, as Fern had seen her and others do before. Fern didn't interrupt, only watched Andli's fingers fold and unfold, over and over. She never saw people write numbers down, not even scratched in the dirt. She suspected they kept the figures in their heads. She knew Andli was trying to determine how much thread she needed for the loom's warp.

Finally, Andli paused and said, "El jin," and began to attach the threads.

Fern had to figure it on her slate, but was able to convert the number. El jin was one hundred twenty in base-ten.

Later, she asked Taran what Andli was doing with her fingers.

"You know what an abacus is, don't you?"

"Yes, I had one once, but it was only a toy."

"It's more than a toy. People in some cultures on Earth do complicated calculations on them. We use our fingers for the abacus. And, yes, we can keep a lot of figures in our minds."

Once again, he had answered a question she hadn't asked.

Fern had an easier time with Science. The same natural laws applied here as on Earth, with the addition of the "paranormal" factor. Photosynthesis intrigued her. One day she wanted to know more about how it worked. She asked Taran, "What is your word for photosynthesis?"

"You just said it."

"Okay. I guess the thortles never educated humans about plants."

"That's right."

To the best of her ability, Fern asked Doran in Human Talk, "I know what photosynthesis is, but how does it work?"

"Ah," said Doran and gave her an explanation she could only half follow.

"I'm afraid I don't understand."

Doran nodded. "Let's try again." This time he spoke more slowly, while his hands performed a complex ballet.

Suddenly, a ray of light flashed into Fern's mind and she saw electrons move, molecules separate and recombine, and she tasted the sweetness of sugar. It was almost overwhelming. All she could say was, "Tekuyate."

"What else do you want to know?"

"Uh, nothing I can think of right now." Once again, she had let him enter her mind. As with Andli, she knew she could trust Doran, yet this made her uncomfortable.

At the same time, she admired his expertise. Without the advantage of a microscope or laboratory, Doran could see into a plant and understand its inner workings, just as Andli could a human body. By letting them into her mind, she could experience what they knew. Andli could heal a person and Doran could influence plants. She had seen him make the miaven tree on her mother's grave blossom. Their old village had been surrounded by nut trees with fruits the size of her fist. Here, the nuts were as small as pecans, but they were already growing larger.

One day after collecting nuts, Fern asked Doran, "How big can the nuts get?"

"No larger than they were at our old village. The trees couldn't hold them if they got too big."

"Why not make the branches stronger?"

Doran cocked his head. "I don't *make* things grow bigger. I ask the plants to do it for us. It would be unreasonable to ask too much of them."

* * *

Whenever she felt melancholy, Fern took refuge in her little grove to be alone with her thoughts, to weep for her losses. She'd think about her mother's hut, the rocking chair, and her mother's grave with its miaven tree covered with purple-red flowers. Fern didn't ask Doran to make the miavens in her grove bloom. The tree on her mother's grave had been special, the only one with flowers. She missed flowers, but even with no blossoms, she loved miaven trees.

One day, she let her mind wander, gazing at her surroundings, the soft shade of the trees, the sparkling of the sun on the lake, the mountains in the background. Then she looked at a miaven tree and was surprised to see a tiny red leaf. She stood up and examined it. The bracts around the miniscule blossom were turning color. Glancing around, she found more.

Within a few days, the grove was covered with purple-red flowers. She ran to Doran and thanked him. He looked puzzled. Believing he hadn't understood her, she asked Taran to translate. Doran's reply was, "No, Fern, I didn't make the flowers. You did."

But how? She had only admired the trees and thought about flowers. Had Doran's teachings, guiding her mind inside plants, taken root and given her an ability she'd never dreamed possible?

One evening, Fern lay on the side of the hill watching the stars come out. She recalled nights back home when her father had taken out the telescope and expounded on the wonders of the universe. She'd enjoyed stargazing until she saw Tira at Disney World and developed sidero-phobia. Grateful that the stars no longer terrified her, she regretted the missed opportunities to learn more from her father. Perhaps he'd be proud of her if she studied astronomy.

She hurried to her grove, entered meditation, and went to her library. After devouring articles about galaxies, black holes, and the Big Bang, she realized how little the people of Earth knew about the greater uni-verse. Information in a recent writing contradicted that in an older one. Scientists had found planets around other stars by clues such as the suns wobbling or blinking, but they didn't know about worlds where other peoples might, and do, live. Most serious scientists didn't seem to be-lieve in UFOs. Of course, there were no books in English, or probably in any other language, about this planet. She wanted to know more.

She went to Taran.

"What would you like to know?" he asked.

"Tell me about this world, its solar system."

"This world is much like Earth, a water planet. It's about the same size, judging by the feel of gravity, but it's much younger, still in the process of evolving. Our people will have the pleasure of watching life here unfold. We will, of course, influence its development, as we already do."

He glanced at the sky. "Our sun is much like Earth's, about the same size and color, but younger. As you know, our days are longer, about twenty seven hours as you count time on Earth. Because we originated on Earth, we find the rhythm of days uncomfortably long, like you do. Having two moons causes more pull than Earth's one moon does. This influences the tides and ground movement more."

"Does this sun have other planets, like Earth's sun does?"

"Yes."

"What can you tell me about them?"

"I'll show them to you tonight."

"What's the rest of this world like? I only know what I've seen."

"Very similar to Earth. We live in the tropical area because life is easier. Here in the mountains, it's cooler because of the altitude. By the sea, the breezes make it cool. Just like Earth, there is ice at the poles. Someday, you can explore it for yourself. Just remember, we want to stay hidden from other peoples of the universe. We don't want the thortles to find us, and we don't want anyone else to see our world as a nice place to colonize."

"But they wouldn't be able to live here, unless they changed their body chemistry."

"That's right, the thortles couldn't, but there may be other planets where the molecules of life are right handed, like here. We don't know, but it makes sense that there would be."

Later, as the stars came out, Fern pointed to a bright one close to the horizon. "Is that a planet?"

He nodded and showed her two more, one which was very faint and hard to see.

She had noticed one planet in the west just after sunset on many occasions. It wasn't visible tonight, but she described it to him. "Is that one closer to the sun?"

"That's right. And others aren't visible right now. They're on the other side of the world."

She pointed. "I've wondered about that one. It's the brightest thing in the sky other than the sun and moons."

"You'd call that a Jovian planet. It is a big ball of gas, like Jupiter."

"Do any of them have moons?"

"I'm sure they do. That seems to be the order of things. Every inhabited world we know of has other planets around their sun, and many of those planets have moons. None of our sister planets are inhabited."

This solar system seemed so much like the one she was born in, she felt homesick again. "I wish I could see Earth's sun from here."

He was quiet a moment, as though he understood her yearning. "I purposely don't inquire about the placement of stars to make it harder for the thortles to find us. In all probability, Earth's sun is not visible from here anyway. We don't experience space the way you do. To us, time and space are all one, which is why we can move through space instantaneously. I know about our sister planets because I've observed them, and I studied a little astronomy on Earth."

Fern thought a while. "If time and space are one, can you also move through time?"

Taran smiled. "It would make sense, but we don't. Psychologically, there are more complications involved in time travel than in space travel."

She pondered the truth of this. "Do any of the peoples of the universe travel in time?"

"We don't know about all the people in the universe, but it is said the"—he uttered a word more foreign than Human Talk—"bend time, which is how they traverse through space, but the truth is a well-kept secret. Even Ansil, who had a lifetime with them, hadn't been able to find the answer."

The villagers were gathering on the sameg and she could hear the musicians tuning their instruments, but Taran seemed to be in no hurry to join them, so she continued with her questions.

"I wonder where the thortle world is in relation to Earth."

"I don't know, but I suspect it's rather close, in astronomical terms, since they travel by spaceships and have time to carry their victims back before they die of old age. It's possible, of course, that they use wormholes, or techniques like stasis."

To Fern's quizzical expression, he added, "That's basically putting people in a suspended state, like frozen sleep, for the duration of the voyage. They didn't share such information with us, and they may have transportation methods we can't even imagine."

After this, Fern paid more attention to the stars. She learned to track their paths across the sky. She had favorites, like the two blue giants that she once thought were Orion's belt, except that there was no third star, and the pair of small pink ones that reminded her of her little sisters. She told Taran, "When I look at the night sky, I imagine pictures in the stars, like constellations, only mine make more sense than the ones I knew on Earth." She pointed out some.

"That's curious. Our people had no experience with constellations. We see patterns in the stars, but we haven't named them like people on Earth do."

Other nights, he pointed out distant galaxies he was able to see.

One evening, while the family shared a late supper in front of their house, Fern watched the colors of the sky fade from blue to pink and purple, then to the dark blue that allowed the stars to shine. The first to come out was the bright one that hung low over the horizon and reminded her of Venus. "Taran, do you ever visit the other planets in this solar system by wrashiru?"

He grinned. "What do you think would happen to someone who materialized on a place with no breathable air?"

"Oh. What about ethenos?"

"I haven't, but some of the weka have."

This put a seed into Fern's mind. If she could travel on Earth by ethenos, why not here? But instead of visiting the sister planets, she projected herself to the village by the sea. Everyone was asleep. Tira and Ansil slept on the sameg separately, to her relief, she with the young women, he with the young men. Fern was old enough to sleep on the sameg herself, but she wasn't emotionally ready to leave the sanctuary of the room she shared with her foster sisters.

Encouraged by this experience, she projected herself to the site of their old village, but found no trace of it, only a sheet of lava. Not even the lake or the waterfall remained. The river valley was half filled, the forests around it burned. She hovered over where the meadow had been and imagined the location of the graveyard. If by ethenos she could plant a new miaven tree on her mother's grave, she would. But her mother was not there, only the mantle she'd worn in life. Perhaps she would encounter her mother someday in another form. She returned to her grove of miaven trees for another good cry.

CHAPTER 12
EXPLORING

Fern had etched two more marks on her erguvon stick calendar. She moved on to study geology. After reading the books she had available, she decided to talk to their geologist, Darsan. Taran helped translate her questions. Darsan was happy to answer them, and he was curious about what scientists on Earth knew. When Fern told him what she learned from her textbook, Darsan frowned.

"What's wrong?" Fern asked.

Taran stifled a laugh. "Darsan thinks the scientists on Earth are backward, they have primitive ideas about how things work."

Fern couldn't conceive of her home planet being backward. "But, I'm sure they know more. That's just what they put in my schoolbook. Maybe they don't think kids could understand more."

Taran shook his head. "If that's what they think about their students, they're wasting a lot of potential."

History was interesting, as long as she avoided the textbook. How did her father manage to teach such a boring subject? She remembered watching documentaries on television with him. Afterward, he would elaborate on the topic, and sometimes he'd bring Fern and her sisters library books on the subject.

Fern emulated her father and looked for reading material on history in her library. Some were novels. Even though they were fiction, she assumed there was enough truth in them to be worthwhile.

One day while studying geography, Fern had an idea. If she could use ethenos to visit her sisters, why couldn't she visit other places on Earth? The year her life had been interrupted, she was supposed to go on a class trip to Washington, D.C. Now she projected herself into the middle of the Mall and gazed in wonder at the buildings and museums she'd only read about. Like a ghost, she could follow a tour group or explore on her own. She had no fear. No one could harm her, because she wasn't really there.

She made several trips to D.C., then New York City. Afterwards, she went abroad to places she'd dreamed of—Stonehenge, the pyramids of Egypt, the Great Wall of China. Fern had a great time until, at the Parthenon in Greece, she had an unnerving experience. Tour groups covered the Acropolis but were not allowed in the ancient temples. After eavesdropping on a tour guide who gave an extensive history of the Parthenon to a group of American tourists, Fern went exploring on her own. No barrier stopped her etheric body from climbing the marble steps and walking among the columns. Despite her physical body being light years away, she felt the ancient magic imbued in the Temple of Athena.

Then she sensed a presence. Looking around, she saw a woman on the perimeter of a tour group staring at her. No, she wasn't looking at the building. She made eye contact with Fern, smiled at her, and beckoned, as though she wanted to talk with her. Fern was so alarmed she withdrew, back to her library. Who was that woman? How could she see her? What did she think Fern was? In her travels, this was the only time she had such an experience.

She told Taran about it.

He nodded. "Apparently, you met someone with clear vision. She was probably as surprised as you were. That's why she wanted to talk to you."

"Was she one of us?"

"You mean someone from here? There are a handful of us on Earth right now, but no, I don't think she's one of them."

"I wish I had talked to her. I didn't get a bad feeling from her, but she did frighten me."

"It's wise to be cautious."

Fern thought for a moment. "Do you suppose she was a slave of the thortles? Looking for psychic people to kidnap?"

"That's not their usual modus operandi, as far as I know. She was probably just an Earthling with strong psychic abilities."

"When I'm in ethenos, can the thortles find me?"

He shook his head. "Even if one of their scouts noticed you, I don't think they could track you."

"So they couldn't follow me here."

"No. But whenever in doubt, do what you did in Athens and come straight home."

When Fern thought it over, she recalled how Tiril was able to see her when she was in ethenos. Could he hear her if she talked to him? Mulling over her conservation with Taran, she realized she'd asked if the woman was "one of us." What did she mean by that?

On other trips, Fern wandered away from the attractions to go among the people of the countries she visited. She was interested in seeing how they lived. In the great cities of the world, she witnessed poverty and violence in the shadows of historical splendor, conditions a tour group wouldn't experience. This disturbed her enough to want to avoid Earth's troubles. She discussed it with Taran.

"Yes," he said. "The universe is full of tragedy. You were sheltered as a child, and here we are quite sheltered as well."

"Do you think things like that could happen here? I don't mean right now, but in the future? When there are more people?"

"I don't know. Right now, everyone here is peaceful. As our population increases, we may become subject to the same ills as humans on Earth, but we don't know. One reason some of us study Earth is to learn from its mistakes so we can avoid them here."

In middle school, teachers had encouraged students to read about "current events" but it was so boring. Now Fern took an interest in her old home and its people and began to read newspapers. What she learned disturbed her. In one paper, she read about a suicide bombing in Israel, a flood in Bangladesh, and ethnic "cleansing" in Africa. She was able to travel in safety and witness some of these events first hand. Her heart bled for the people. But adults and nature misbehaving in distant parts of the Earth was difficult enough, then she read an account of a boy her own age in Missouri who killed his entire family.

Taran was helping Andli with a loom when Fern related that story to him. Apparently, Andli understood everything she said. Although Andli kept her attention on her work, Fern felt comfort wrap around her shoulders, easing her tension and sorrow.

Taran said, "We are fortunate. This place is a paradise, compared to the rest of the universe. Our biggest worry here is Nature."

Fern decided not to further explore the troubles of Earth, especially since there was nothing she could do about them.

But she itched to travel. Where should she go next? When she went somewhere on Earth, she only had to think about her destination to project herself there. Here, most destinations were a mystery. She looked at the large moon and toyed with the idea of visiting it, but the thought of going to that cold, lifeless place, even by ethenos, was scary. Better to enjoy it from the relative safety of this warm planet.

By ethenos, she wandered about the immediate vicinity of the village, going as far as the ridge across the lake, but traveling at ground level was too limiting. She projected herself into the air and found herself flying. The exhilaration gave way to terror—of falling, even though she consciously knew she couldn't get hurt when not in material form.

At her next session with Taran, Fern asked, "Can you help me with this fear of flying?"

After a few lessons, she found the freedom she imagined birds to have.

At first, she explored familiar areas. She floated over the ridge and down to the sea. How she missed the beach! She yearned to wade into the waves, feel them crashing into her, and taste the salt. This was a drawback of ethenos, being unable to fully experience something. She followed the coastline to the sea village but steered clear of the inhabitants, not sure how to interact with any who could sense her presence. From there she retraced the path they had taken to their new village.

These travels emboldened her to explore new places. While she knew, rationally, that she couldn't get lost—all she had to do was wake up—Fern went only cautiously into unfamiliar territory. When she did, she found other people. The first was a very old couple camping by a warm spring. She reported this to Taran.

"That would be Doran's grandparents. They've been gone since before you came to us."

"Why did they go?"

"They wanted to explore the world, and their children and grandchildren were grown."

Fern had noticed more comings and goings among the elders than by younger people, but she always assumed they were visiting the village by the sea. "Do many of the weka go off like that?"

"Yes. They're free to go their own ways once they've fulfilled their obligations to the young."

At her next opportunity, Fern checked on the couple again and found them walking away from the spring. She followed their movements and eventually they joined two women. She began to feel uncomfortable watching them unseen and asked Taran if she was violating their privacy.

"They know you've been watching them. If they didn't want you to, they'd put up a barrier and you wouldn't be able to."

"How do they feed themselves?"

"Their needs are few and their resources many."

Although she suspected there was more to be said, Taran didn't elaborate.

"Why do they walk and not wrashiru? Or use ethenos?"

"There is a pleasure in exploring that you can get only from walking. Also, there's a different focus. Haven't you noticed it?"

She had. Ethenos had a surreal quality to it, like a dream, but she could cover more territory that way.

* * *

Fern continued her studies, now moving into tenth grade schoolwork. Sometimes she thought about Tiril, who was attending college on Earth. After being educated here, did he have trouble adapting? As if in answer to her thoughts, Fern encountered him on her next visit.

She projected herself into her grandparents' house. It was Saturday, and Grandma was teaching her sisters to follow a recipe for chocolate cake. How she missed chocolate!

She moved outside to look for Grandpa and found him in the carport, leaning under the hood of a car. He wasn't alone. The other man straightened up, turned, and smiled at her. It was Tiril! What on Earth was he doing here? Her grandfather also stood up and looked around. "What are you starin' at?" he asked.

"That humming bird," Tiril replied.

A humming bird feeder hung in the yard. A dominant male was chasing away the other birds. When Fern looked back at Tiril, he winked at her. She smiled and turned back to watch the hummers. It was so nice to see birds again. To her surprise, Tiril walked past her to the feeder where he held up his index finger. The male alighted on his finger and remained perched there long enough for the other birds to steal a quick drink. When the bird saw this, he jerked his head at Tiril and, in a tiny voice, scolded him before flying back to his post.

Grandpa watched with gaping jaws. "How in hang did you do that?"

Tiril shrugged his shoulders and said, "I don't know. I never tried it before."

CHAPTER 13
METIA

The large moon was full, the smaller one waxing, and the nights were filled with light. Life for Fern had settled into a gentle routine. She was making progress in Human Talk and socialized more with the villagers. She now could better understand and enjoy the stories that were told every evening on the sameg. She continued to study schoolwork from Earth and made improvement in her studies with Taran.

One day Fern sat with Andli under the awning in front of their house when cries of joyous greeting rose from the river. They set down their work and hurried over. A very old woman, surrounded by a throng of villagers, made her way up the hill toward the sameg.

"Metia!" Andli rushed down to meet her. Fern followed. The crowd led the weka to the fire pit where someone laid down a mat for her to sit on. Others brought her kirrib and skri. Metia seemed overwhelmed by their attentions, but she took it in stride. Although she must have been hungry, she only sipped the soup and nibbled on the skri while answering a barrage of questions.

Taran appeared. With a catch in his voice, he told Fern, "Metia is the daughter of Hannah and granddaughter of Moses and Rila. She has been walking about the planet since before you joined us."

To Fern, Hannah and her parents were the subjects of myth. She had no idea any of Hannah's offspring could still be alive. "How old is she?"

Taran said, "Old enough to have great-great-great-grandchildren. In Earth years, she's well over a hundred." He paused to calculate. "Probably around one hundred and ten. You have just met a living legend."

Fern stared at her. That old, and she was walking through the wilderness by herself! The weka's long white hair hung in one braid down her back. She was quite thin and her tunic had been mended in more places than it was whole. She wore no hat and her only adornment was a necklace with one large blue gemstone. Yet other than being thin, she didn't seem frail and appeared to be in good health.

While Metia ate, Andli rushed home and returned with the new tunic she'd just finished for Tala, who was the same size as the old woman. Andli handed the tunic to Tala who, instead of looking disappointed, beamed with pride as she presented it to Metia.

"Tekuyate," Metia said. "The love that imbues this garment will comfort me to the end of my days."

Fern had no trouble understanding her.

Narvil and his brother went to Metia. "We've moved out of our room and will sleep on the sameg. We'll be honored if you take our room."

Metia smiled. "Ah, I feel honored."

At the fireside that night, Metia told of her travels. Taran sat beside Fern to translate, which was unusual. He normally let her listen by herself and only later would he answer any questions she had. She realized he wanted her to hear every word of Metia's story. Fern was so enthralled, she understood much of what Metia said even before he translated.

Metia had been walking with her mate for more than four Full Moons, and she decided to return home after he died. She'd left his remains sitting on a mountain top.

"You live in one of the best places on this world," Metia said. "I have traveled to where it rains every day and the heat is oppressive. These places have much food but one cannot travel far without needing to rest, and there are marshes one cannot walk through without great difficulty. The best way to travel there, for the ungifted, would be 'barca without sails.'" Metia looked directly at Fern when she said this, and into Fern's mind flashed an image of a canoe.

"To the far south," Metia continued, "the air grows colder and the mountains are covered with 'water that does not move.' It falls from the sky in crystals." Metia looked at Fern again.

Fern felt compelled to speak. "Snow. The crystals falling from the sky are snow."

The audience looked at her. One after another, they repeated the word "snow."

Fern hesitated, then added, "And the water that doesn't move is called 'ice.'"

Metia smiled and repeated the word "ice" as did her listeners. At that moment, Fern understood there were still things on this world that the thortle language, at least what these people knew of it, had no words for. Moreover, she could make contributions to Human Talk, and others were willing to learn from her.

When Metia said goodnight and went to bed, Fern, too, felt sleepy. Once snuggled on her pallet, she thought about how Metia had prompted her to utter the English words she needed. The barrier she had erected around her mind had not kept Metia out, but this breach didn't bother her. For some reason, she felt a bond with this ancient woman.

As a weka, Metia was not required to gather wood or water or to do any work. She slept much. The young people and children catered to her every whim. She was revered by the entire village.

Night after night, her stories continued. Each time, Taran sat by Fern to translate. Metia remembered the beginnings of settlement on this world and had heard Hannah's stories first hand. She enjoyed talking about the past and readily answered questions. Of course, she had no memory of Moses and Rila, but she had known their children Abraham and Martha well.

"My mother Hannah was only a baby when her father Moses was sent away, so she spent little time with him while he lived. She knew him mostly through the teachings he and Rila gave their children after they shed their bodies. Moses was a powerful man, physically as well as psychically. Rila fell in love with him the moment she met him, but it was some time before he paid much attention to her. At first, he spent his time and energy trying to find a way to escape. He could wrashiru but, I'm sorry to say, our own people bound him to the thortle world with forces stronger than chains."

Preventing someone from wrashiru? Fern was surprised. How? Was this the reason she hadn't been able to return to Earth? Had she been bound here by some force?

Metia looked at Fern, as though she'd heard her thought, and said, "There are some who have the ability to control others, and Moses was powerless against them. We do not practice such arts here, thus many of you do not know it is possible. And there were other things done on that world which we consider to be evil and do not teach our young."

She returned her attention to the group. "Of course, after Moses fell in love with Rila, he was bound by love alone to the fate of our people. Rila was a handsome woman, dark of hair, skin like this one," she pointed at Fern. "Her eyes this color." She held up her necklace. The gem stone caught the firelight and glowed with a pale, bluish light. "Hannah's skin was like polished wood and her hair and eyes were black. It was Hannah who told me most of what I know about our people's early days here."

One morning, Fern sat with Andli and Tala under the awning in front of their house, working on a new tunic for Tala. Andli was weaving. Tala was spinning yarn into course thread, and Fern spun it into finished thread. Rina joined them. She was carving intricate designs on beads. Metia, who had been sitting with the other weka at their house, crossed the sameg to join them. In unison, the women said, "Salut," and slid over to make room for her.

"Salut," Metia replied. Donal and Ara, who had been husking nuts on the sameg, joined them. They said little but continued their work, keeping their eyes on Metia in reverent silence. Metia rubbed her knuckles and said, "I used to be a weaver, but my hands are now tired."

Tala handed a finished ball of yarn to Fern, who placed it in her basket. Metia reached for the basket. "Bitti? May I have some?"

Fern nodded.

Metia took out a ball of fine cord which Fern had spun. Rina handed Metia her knife and the weka measured a length of cord, cut it off, and handed the basket back to Fern. "Tekuyate." She then picked up a few of Rina's beads and began to string a necklace.

Rina began to sing and the others joined in. This was a song Fern loved. It happened to be one Hannah had composed.

After the song ended, Andli asked, "Metia, do you remember when Hannah wrote this?"

"No. She may have written it before I was born. One of my earliest memories is of her singing that song to me."

An image flashed into Fern's mind—a woman singing to a baby. Fern saw the image from the mother's perspective, not the child's, and wondered why. She wanted Metia to tell more about the past but wasn't comfortable enough to speak Human Talk in front of so many people, even though they were family.

Did Metia read her mind? She held up the string of beads and said, "Our people made jewelry even before they came here. I have no memories of the thortle world but I heard stories from those who lived there. They made jewelry out of scraps of broken dishes and things like that." She glanced at the sameg where two toddlers played with their dolls. "They made dolls and other toys from castoff garments and anything else they could lay their hands on. They had to make their own tools. They were very clever. They had to be. The thortles didn't give them much. Oh, they supplied them with food and clothing, but nothing else. Their work seldom required tools, but if it did, they could not take them back to the sameg."

"Sameg?" Fern said. Did she misunderstand Metia? Or was the weka confusing the thortle world with this one?

"Yes. The common area in their part of the hive was called sameg. We brought that word with us when we came here. It is a word that holds pleasant memories because it was the center of our social life. Even on that world, we would gather every day to sing and dance and tell stories."

Metia raised her eyes to the sky as though searching for memories. "No one knows when our people first did these things. On the thortle world, there was much idleness. Psychic work cannot be performed for long periods of time, and there was nothing else to do. Our people had no materials to create art or record literature, so they would sing and dance. New captives brought their music and stories with them. Some tales were true, and some were myth. If their stories made sense to our people, we would retain them and retell them, generation after generation. New stories bolstered our spirits. Retelling them gave us a sense of community. But some captives were so traumatized they wouldn't talk about the past."

"Didn't new captives speak different languages?" Donal asked.

"Of course. They had to learn Human Talk and their stories had to be translated. Much of what they told us, we couldn't relate to, because it was so foreign to our understanding. Our people had no experience with animals or mountains or seas. We didn't retell the tales that made no sense to us. Much lore that may have been meaningful on this world was lost that way. Even so, we brought a rich culture here with us."

Ara said, "I've been told life on that world was boring."

"Yes. The work was not hard or time consuming. New captives, especially, were bored. Most of them were used to working long days, and idleness did not sit well with them. A few came from leisure classes, and they were used to being entertained when they were idle. We combined these needs, to be busy and to be entertained, and learned to entertain ourselves. Some captives came with physical skills like dancing and yoga and sports. They helped keep our bodies healthy. But some physical things we were unable to do, because there was not enough open space. Others involved fighting, but we didn't dare show aggressiveness on the thortle world, so those skills were lost. Here, such behavior is unnecessary anyway." She shook her head.

"One good thing arose from boredom—we learned to control our minds and bodies. The thortles could see what we did, but they couldn't see into our minds, so we had a whole universe to ourselves that they couldn't enter. We learned mental skills that the thortles didn't know we had, and we learned to control our procreation and to maintain our physical health."

Metia took off her necklace. "This poor old thing needs to be re-strung." She grasped the string in both hands and snapped it. Fern marveled at her strength. Some of the beads dropped on her lap. Without being asked, Tala rushed to the fire pit and returned with a bowl for the beads. Metia smiled at her and stripped the rest of the beads from the old string. She then tested Fern's cord and looked into her eyes with a gaze as penetrating as Tira's but as warm as Andli's. "This should last beyond my lifetime," she said and began to thread her beads onto it.

She went on. "The thortles taught our people no skills other than those required for their jobs. Moses told his children Martha and Abra-ham about the work he had done on Earth, but they had no way to put his teachings into practice on the thortle world. When they came here, they needed the skills to build and make things, but because they lacked experience, their hands were clumsy. It took generations to master the skills we have today." She plucked at her tunic and said, "When I was a child, such finery was unknown. My parents went naked at first and slept on piles of leaves until they could figure out how to make cloth."

A gentle breeze blew the aroma of baking skri their way. "I remember my first taste of bread—not skri, only a pancake. Before we learned to bake, even on a flat stone, we had only gruel made from crushed nuts and herbs. I don't recall how our people learned to make it, but Hannah said that on the thortle world, soup was brought out in large pots and spooned into bowls. So much of what we do here was influenced by that former life." Metia looked down at her necklace and said, "I'm too busy talking to pay attention. This will never do." She removed the beads from the cord.

Instead of resuming work on her necklace, Metia silently stared at the bowl of beads. Fern thought she'd fallen asleep but her eyes were open, as though she'd entered her own world. With a finger, she stirred the beads.

When Metia lifted her head again, Tala asked, "Is it true that Abraham and Anli's children died on the thortle world and were born again here?"

"Yes, that is true. I remember them well. Anli gave birth to them again here. Wosan was older than me and Horil was about my age. We used to play together. I remember Rala's birth. Because they were too young to wrashiru, their lives were ended so they could come to us as a new babies."

She chuckled. "I suppose the thortles didn't understand what was happening. Some of their slaves disappeared and couldn't be found, and these children died of grief. At least, that's what the people told the thortles. They didn't know what to do about it. Even their threats were not enough to prevent these things from happening." She paused and strung a bead on the cord.

"Rala and her brothers had complete memories of their lives on the thortle world. That's how I know so much about it. They would tell me stories. When they passed on, they allowed the curtain between the worlds to fall. They may be with us now, or waiting to join us again, but they are not likely to bring their old memories with them."

Fern didn't pick up on any anger or dread on Metia's part when she spoke about the thortles. When the weka finished talking, Fern managed to put together the words to say, "You don't seem to fear the thortles."

"Pooh," Metia said. "What does an old woman like me have to be afraid of?" She picked up her cord and tried to add another bead but kept missing the hole.

Ara scooted closer to Metia and said, "Would you like me to do this for you?"

"Child, your eyes and hands are still young and more suited for this work." She gave the bowl and string to Ara and chose the next bead.

Her eyes and hands were old, but she hadn't lost her sense of color and form. She chose each bead with care and handed it to Ara.

Rina said, "Feel free to use some of my beads, too."

"Tekuyate. Some of my beads are broken or worn out. It's good to have fresh ones to add." The beads followed a pattern of color and size, until half the cord had been threaded. Then Metia picked up her pale blue bead and said, "Now it's time for this one." She looked at Fern. "It once belonged to Hannah."

Unaccountably, Fern felt a thrill vibrate through her and she had to blink away tears.

After Ara added the blue bead to the necklace, Metia said, "I'll let you finish. Just follow the design I started."

Metia moved on to another household. Fern wished she could go with her, but Metia had many descendants and everyone wanted a share of her time. Fern marveled how well she had understood Metia. She didn't even need a translator. It reminded her of how she and Ansil could comprehend each other when they spoke in different languages. She sighed. She missed Ansil. And Tira—she was missing out on Metia's visit. Fern looked at Rina and Andli. Was Tira able to tune in to what Metia told them? She wished she had the right words to ask.

CHAPTER 14
HANNAH'S STORY

Another night on the sameg, Metia continued her stories.

"When they first came here, Moses was happy to breathe fresh air again, but Rila had never been outdoors. She had spent her life in rooms with boundaries—walls and ceilings. Here, there were no boundaries. This in itself was unsettling. Even though the land and sea stretched to the horizons, at first she took comfort in the thought that these were the limits to what the eye could see. Then she looked up into the sky. It went on forever. She was so frightened, she fell to the ground." A child tittered, as though she found Rila's reaction amusing.

"Her love and trust in Moses saved her. He held her in his embrace until she recovered." Metia paused.

"After a while, she grew thirsty. 'What shall we drink?' she asked. Moses had never seen a sea before, but he knew it was water, so he tasted it. It was salty and they could drink only a little. They walked along the shore until they came to a river. Moses tasted its water and it was sweet, so they drank. Then Rila said, 'I'm hungry. What shall we eat?' Moses looked around and found leaves and roots and tasted them. He gave her the ones that were good to eat."

Metia looked at the sky. The large moon hadn't risen yet and the small one was obscured by trees. Only stars were visible. "This night reminds me. It was such a time as this that Moses and Rila arrived here. Both moons were new. When it grew dark, Rila was very much afraid because she had never seen such darkness. You see, on the thortle world, in the hives, there was no day or night. The lights were always on. Moses told her about the sun and how it went to bed at night. The night was very long and it grew cold. Moses and Rila were both naked and she had never been this cold before. The next day, he built a shelter thatched with branches because he knew this would be warmer than sleeping in the open."

Metia looked skyward again. "That night when the sun went down, two slender crescent moons appeared in the sky, and Moses marveled. The world he came from had only one moon. He took this for a good omen, a promise that his people would flourish here. Night after night, as the moonlight increased, so did their hopes. They contacted their children on the thortle world and told them they had found paradise. They planned to prepare a home so their family could join them."

Metia shook her head. "I've never understood why we don't celebrate the two new moons. That's when our First Parents came here. Would someone bring me a cup of tea? Telling stories is dry work." Several of her descendants jumped up to prepare tea. When she tasted it, she said, "Someone sweetened this for me. Tekuyate." She set the cup down.

"Moses' skin was black because his ancestors lived in the tropics, but Rila was unused to the sun. Her face and shoulders became red and painful and her skin began to blister and peel. She was afraid her body was dying, but Moses knew it was only sunburn. He made a hat to shade her face and a cape of leaves for her shoulders. But Rila was used to clothes, so she asked, 'What shall we wear?' In his other life, Moses had picked..." Metia looked at Fern. As the word "cotton" popped into Fern's mind, Metia said, "Cotton. Moses looked for a plant that made cotton but could not find one. Then he found other plants that had fibers which could be made into cloth, but he didn't live long enough to make any."

Although they'd heard the story many times before, the audience hung on Metia's words. "Moses became sick. He could no longer eat or drink. He languished in his disappointment. Their escape from slavery to a better life was a failure. Rila could do nothing to help him. She watched him die, but his spirit stayed with her."

Metia sipped her tea. "Rila had never seen a dead person before, and when Moses' body began to decay, she asked his spirit what she should do. He told her how to bury the body. After she did this, she left the sea and went into the forest, looking for food. She found a tree with little fruits. 'What are these?' she asked Moses's spirit. 'Nuts,' he told her. She tasted them but they were bitter. He told her to soak them in water until they softened and the bitterness left. These satisfied her hunger better than herbs and roots. If they were soaked long enough, they would sprout, and then they were sweet. One day she found one that had had sprouted on the ground, so she ate it." A few of the children gasped.

"Rila became sick, much like Moses had. Did the sprout poison her? Moses didn't know, but the tree said to her, 'You have eaten my child. Now you shall not live.' Rila told the tree how sorry she was, but still, she could no longer eat or drink. She dug a hole and covered herself with leaves before she died." Metia closed her eyes and was silent for a moment.

"After this, Rila's spirit communed with the trees and plants and learned what her children must do to live here. Moses communed with the air, water, and stones and learned other things they must do. They taught all these to their children. One thing they taught us was to ask permission and give thanks for what this world provides us."

Rina said, "I always wondered why Rila lived longer than Moses."

"Rila had a gift that Moses lacked. She discovered how to alter her physical body to adapt to the chemistry of this world, as you do when you wrashiru between here and Earth. Unfortunately, she didn't learn it soon enough, and so she died, but her spirit taught her descendants how to change their body chemistry."

One of the children said, "I thought she died because she ate the baby nut tree."

Metia smiled. "I don't know if that story is true, or whether it was something made up to impress you children. I think it's more likely that the nut tree just asked her not to eat its sprouts."

Fern had taken the old stories at face value, believing them to be accounts of actual happenings. So these people had their folk tales, too? On reflection, a nut tree cursing Rila, dooming her to death because she ate its baby, didn't fit with Fern's experiences of the natural world. During her early days here, she had violated protocol a few times with no more consequence than the feeling that a plant was displeased with her carelessness.

Another night, Metia finished telling Hannah's story. "Hannah followed her sister and brother here. When she woke, she lay naked on the ground and something was poking in her back. It hurt. She rolled over and discovered it was sticks. She had seen them in visions but didn't know they could cause pain."

Fern closed her eyes and thought about lying naked on the forest floor. She felt twigs jabbing her in the back.

Metia went on. "She looked around and her eyes saw trees and vegetation for the first time in her life. She thought it was all so beautiful, but when she stepped out from under the trees and looked up at the sky, it was so immense, she became dizzy and, like her mother, fell to the ground. After she recovered, she got up and walked on the beach. The sand was not firm like the floors she'd known, and it shifted beneath her feet."

Fern felt a momentary wave of nausea. When she looked up at the stars, it went away.

"Hannah felt unsteady, at the mercy of these strange conditions. Rila spoke to her and assured her she was safe. When Hannah went down to the sea, it roared and came rushing at her as though it would devour her, then it would turn and run away. It was some time before she had the courage to approach it."

The children laughed. Fern had a vague memory of going to the beach when she was very small, running from the waves, screaming, her parents laughing at her. Or was she laughing with them? Hannah's memory seemed so real.

"When the afternoon grew hot, sweat began to pour from Hannah's body. She had never perspired like this before—it was cool in the thortle hives. She thought her body was leaking and that she would die. Moses spoke to her and explained what was happening. She knew he spoke the truth, but these new experiences were strange and frightening. Some of those who came after her were so traumatized, even with Hannah and her family to guide them, they wrashirued right back."

"What happened to them?" someone asked.

"I don't know. Perhaps they perished, because there was no one on the thortle world to support their transitions back to the physical life there. The ones who stayed here were very brave and did not succumb to their fears."

Her listeners nodded in assent.

"When our people came here, they had to do everything for themselves and that was a great change. On that other world, they had been fed and clothed and even their living space was cleaned for them. Here, when they were hungry, they had to feed themselves. Rila influenced many edible plants to grow larger, but neither Hannah nor any of her companions had ever fixed a meal. On the thortle world, food was provided ready to eat, so now they had to learn what to gather and how to prepare it. The spirits of Rila and Moses guided them. Moses told them how food on Earth was grown in rows in great fields, but the plants here said they didn't want to live like that. That's why we plant things where they naturally grow."

Metia gestured at the fire. "At first, they had no way to cook until Martha discovered she could make fire. This was another experience new to them. On the world they left, they were protected—nothing in their environment was hazardous or painful. When some of them tried to touch the fire, they got burned."

Again, a child laughed.

"The first time it rained, the people rejoiced. Water falling from the sky—what a miracle! But afterward they were wet and cold and miserable. After this, they learned to make shelters and eventually houses. Martha's mate, Tanil, learned he could shield people from the elements. He was delighted to be able to provide that comfort, but he used the power too much. He exhausted himself and nearly died. Over time, they discovered many powers that had been latent because there was no use for them on the thortle world."

Fern wondered what those powers might be, but she didn't want to interrupt Metia.

"Hannah told me all these things. She became a leader among the people even though she was the youngest of our First Parents' children. Martha and Abraham and their mates had young children to care for, but Hannah didn't mate until after the second Full Moons. She explored the world by foot and ethenos and guided her people to good places to live and find food. At first they lived near a volcano. Hannah had a premonition it was going to erupt. She warned the people and guided them to safety."

That sounded familiar to Fern. Had she heard this before? Yes, it had been part of "The Tale of Moses and Rila" that Tiril had recited before he left for Earth.

Later, Fern lay in bed thinking about Metia's story and how Hannah had reacted to the new things she'd encountered here. She could relate to Hannah's experience, arriving naked on a strange world. Unlike Hannah, she'd been given food, clothing, and shelter when she first came. Hannah and her brother and sister suffered deprivation until they learned how to provide these things for themselves. At least Hannah had her siblings with her. Fern missed her sisters.

That night, she dreamed of them. She was riding a school bus. Her sisters sat in the seat in front of her, talking to their friends. Their grandmother met them at the bus stop and, on the way to the house, the girls chatted about their day at school. Fern hung on every word. Once inside, Grandma gave the girls a snack and they started their homework. The younger one fell asleep and Grandma laid her on her bed. Fern lay down by the sleeping child until she, too, nodded off. When she woke, back on the unnamed world, she knew it had been an etheric projection and her sisters were okay.

* * *

Fern thought Metia would stay with them for the rest of her life. But when the large moon was full again, she had Hansa cut her hair short and gave her the silver tresses. Hansa said. "I will use this to make something beautiful for your descendants."

Fern felt through the breast of her tunic for the little pouch she wore on a string and thought of the medallion it contained, made with a lock of her mother's hair. She seldom took it out but kept it close to her heart. She recalled how Hansa had cut Tiril's hair before he left for Earth. Hansa had made their family a decorative piece that they had hung in the doorway of their house. No one thought to bring it with them when they evacuated, but it was nonessential and could be replaced. Someday, Tiril would come home.

That night on the sameg, Metia said, "Our people will slowly increase in numbers and our ways will change. It is inevitable. I cannot tell you all that the future holds, but I can tell you things that must not be forgotten. The old stories must be remembered and retold in perpetuity. They are lessons in wisdom and must never be lost."

She surveyed her audience and seemed to catch the eye of each and every one in turn. "And there is something even more important you must never forget. Our First Parents searched the universe for this world." She lifted her arm and gestured around, at the mountains gleaming in the moonlight, the river that shone like silver, and the trees that muted the night.

Then she reached up and traced the arc of the sky. "There are many worlds around the suns you see and suns you don't see. But very few support life such as ours. You must never forget the miracle you have here. You must never take it for granted. You must always remember that it is sacred, and you must always give thanks for what it bestows on you, even when faced with death and destruction." She closed her eyes and seemed to fall asleep, but no one disturbed her or the mood she'd cast.

Then she opened her eyes, looked around, and announced, "Tomorrow morning, I will leave you and return to the wilderness."

The older people showed no surprise, but many of the younger ones expressed dismay. Although she should have anticipated this, Fern was stunned. She turned to Taran. "Is it safe for her to go off alone?"

"It is her choice," he answered.

"But she's so old and fragile. She might get hurt and die."

"That, too, is her choice."

Without thinking of the magnitude of her offer, Fern went to Metia. "I'll go with you."

Metia rose and took Fern's hands in her own. "No. I am going to join my mate. You, child, have a different road to take. You must stay here for now. There are people who need you." Metia squeezed her hands. "Now I must rest." She left the sameg and went to the house where she had been staying.

Fern was puzzled. Was Metia able to see her future? But why would people need her? She had few skills other than spinning and weaving. Wouldn't it be more important to accompany this ancient woman into the wilderness, to take care of her when she could go no further? But Metia had declined her offer.

In the morning, the village tried to shower Metia with gifts—a new blanket, food, jewelry. "You would weigh me down so much, how could I walk?" She took only the tunic Tala had given her, a new hat, a blanket, and a pouch full of skri. Of the jewelry, she accepted only the necklace Ara had completed with beads Rina had carved and cord Fern had spun. Then she was off, into the forest, alone. In her heart, Fern knew she was not to return.

CHAPTER 15
TIRA

The months sped by. Fern's spirits had been high while Metia was there, but her departure had been a let-down. Although the ancient one's visit had been but a brief interlude in Fern's life, she felt like she'd known Metia forever. Why did she feel such a connection with this woman? The barrier she'd erected around her mind to protect her privacy had not kept Metia out. Now she missed her.

Fern continued her explorations and formal education. Visitation with her family on Earth became almost routine. She watched the older sister start middle school.

At Thanksgiving, her timing was perfect to join the family for dinner. To her surprise, Tiril had been invited. He knew she was there. When no one was looking, he grinned at her, but he didn't mention her presence. After Grandpa gave the blessing, Tiril said, "I really appreciate your inviting me to dinner."

"Well, we couldn't let you spend the day alone," Grandma said. "It's too bad you couldn't go home for Thanksgiving, but I understand how it is."

Tiril filled his plate with vegetables. Her grandfather said, "Have some turkey. You're not some kind of vegetarian, are you?"

"Well, I used to be. I'm not so strict about it now, but I still go light on the meat. And you have so much good food, I won't go away hungry."

"If you do, it's your own fault."

Despite her grandfather's gruff words, Fern could tell he liked Tiril. When Grandma began to serve pie, Grandpa looked at the clock and said, "That game's about to start. I'll eat mine in the living room. Terry, are you gonna watch it with me?"

"Sure. But I'll help with the dishes first."

Grandma waved him off. "No, you go watch the game. The girls will help me."

Tiril looked at the girls and asked, "Aren't you watching it, too?"

"No. It's boooring."

Fern didn't stay for the game, either. She left with the satisfaction that her family was doing well, and she was glad they liked Tiril.

When she visited on Christmas Eve, the house was quiet, the tree piled with gifts. Three stockings hung on a bookcase. Was one for her? She didn't think they'd hang one for Tiril. She went to her sisters' bedroom and wished them Merry Christmas. She planned to drop in the next day, but tried too hard and couldn't get through.

A few weeks later, she found her grandparents making plans for their annual trip to the cemetery. She chose not to accompany them.

* * *

Preparations for the Feast of the Full Moons caught Fern by surprise. It didn't seem possible they'd been in their new village almost a year and a half, Earth time, or that Tira and Ansil had been gone nearly a year. The families with babies, the last to return from the village by the sea, had joined them by now.

Her little niece Dorba was a toddler now, and she and Fern became good friends. When Sela joined Fern and Andli at their work, Dorba's antics reminded Fern of Simbi at that age, but Dorba was more mischievous. She tried to "help" Fern spin and undid several of her balls of thread.

Rufan joined them. He was extracting seeds from the little "pine" cones for sweet cakes. Dorba climbed into his lap, wanting to help, and spilled his bowl of seeds, Fern took a break from work to play with her. Sela and Rufan smiled at Fern with appreciation.

On this night of the Full Moons, food was less abundant than at Fern's first celebration. The nuts were still growing larger, but other food plants were not yet as plentiful. They didn't pass out sweets at sunset, but at midnight. When the rim of the small moon touched the larger, music and dancing ceased and cookies and cakes were distributed. Fern watched both moons reach the apex, the small moon fitting into the ring of the larger almost perfectly. She secretly thought of this festivity as special. After three more turns of the small moon, she would become seventeen in Earth years.

That night, she danced with every man and boy in the village. When she danced with Rufan, her hair came undone. After the dance ended, it fell around her shoulders in golden ripples. Both she and Rufan laughed. Fern bent to retrieve her beads and fasteners, but Rufan said, "Let me."

When he gave them to her, his hand touched hers and she felt a pulse of energy pass between them. "Tekuyate," she said and looked up at him. His smile was so warm it shivered through her.

"I need to rest." She retreated as far from him and Sela as she could.

The next day, Sela and Dorba joined Fern's household for a late breakfast. Sela asked Fern what was wrong.

Fern realized she was projecting her discomfort but didn't know how to explain it, so she said, "I'm just tired from last night." When Rufan brought some lenitrus and skri for his wife and child, Fern excused herself to go to the latrine.

Sela met her on the way back. "Fern, please don't feel uncomfortable with us. We won't pressure you, but Rufan and I would welcome you into our household."

So. It was out. Fern looked at the ground. "Sela, I like you and Rufan very much, but I'm not ready."

"Of course. You're still very young. Let's remain friends, but remember you are always welcome in our home."

"Tekuyate."

Sela hugged her. After this, when Rufan smiled at her, it was as a big brother smiling at his little sister. When in her dark moods, Fern would seethe with resentment that she had been considered as a second wife only, even though she knew these people made no such distinctions.

* * *

Shortly after Fern turned seventeen, Tira returned, walking with a small group from the village by the sea. They carried salt, seeds of plants that had yet to grow in this part of the mountains, and incidentals needed by the mountain villagers, as well as news of the sea people. Fern gave Tira the necklace Ansil had made which she had kept for her. Instead of moving back into their bedroom, Tira slept on the sameg. "I've grown used to this," she said.

Tira seemed to have matured. Despite the long walk, her cheeks were full. When Fern helped Andli set up a loom to make Tira a new tunic, she noticed Tira's breasts were fuller as well, and her hips wider. She looked like a woman, not the adolescent who had left for the sea.

One day, Fern climbed to the ridge where she found Tira looking out to sea. "Ansil said he would sail to where he could see this ridge, but we're too far away to see his boat."

A few days later, Fern returned to the ridge by herself. She thought about Ansil and his sailboat and remembered how much fun they'd had sailing together. An unsettled feeling washed over her. Her mouth was dry and she wished she'd brought water. There were no springs up here. She retreated to the shade of an erguvon tree and watched the gleaming blue in the distance darken to a swirling gray. That must be a storm, she thought.

On her descent to the valley, she gathered firewood and lenitrus, but her thoughts kept returning to her observations on the ridge. Was the sea village threatened by another hurricane? No, this storm had formed too quickly. It must have been a squall. How much warning did sailors have of these?

She hadn't quite reached the lake when Ansil appeared before her. At first she was delighted to see him. But he was fully clothed and dripping wet. He couldn't have come by wrashiru.

"I'm sorry, Fern," he said. "It was an accident. Estut miryit. There was nothing I could do."

She reached out but was unable to touch him.

"I'm sorry, Fern. Esmilu tefi. I won't leave you again, as long as you need me."

But then he was gone.

Fern dropped her wood and ran to the village. Tira was weeping in Andli's arms. Fern reached out to comfort her, but Tira sobbed, "He must have had a premonition. That's why he wanted to start a child so soon."

No wonder Tira needed a new tunic!

Fern rushed to her grove, took refuge in her library, and immersed herself in a cheap murder mystery. All other thoughts were kept at bay until she glanced at the chair where Ansil used to sit. Ansil! She threw the book at the chair, then picked up another book and threw it. But the library couldn't support such strong emotion. It dissolved around her. She found herself in the miaven grove where Andli waited with reddened eyes. "Oh, Fern, you have suffered another loss."

At first, Fern resisted her embrace, then collapsed against her. "How could they do this to me?"

Andli hugged her more tightly.

"How could he tell me he loves me and then get her...."

"But, Fern, he loves you both."

She shook her head. "That's not how it's supposed to be."

"But that's our way. Come. You and Tira need one another."

Fern pulled away and shouted in English, "I hate Tira!" Then she remembered that Andli was Tira's mother. "Estut miryit. But I don't want to see Tira right now."

"I understand. I'll let you be alone for now, but don't isolate yourself. Healing will come."

Fern bit her lips and nodded.

Andli headed toward the village, probably to comfort Tira.

Fern ran into the woods. Unconsciously, she skirted the lake and stumbled across the river. This grief nearly rivaled that of losing her family. When she stopped to catch her breath, she began to cry. But she didn't want to cry. Blindly, she rushed up the path to the ridge, banging her feet and elbows against roots and stones. The pain felt good. She found herself looking out to sea. The storm had passed, but not the one in her heart. She peered down the cliff. If she leaped—would it hurt as much as this?

Suddenly, she realized she wasn't alone. "Get out of my head, you asshole!" she shouted in English.

She heard him retreat, chuckling.

"It's not funny!" she cried.

"I'm only laughing because I had not heard that word before."

"Then I hope you know what it means."

He chuckled again.

What was she doing—arguing with a person who wasn't there? She bent her head and let grief weigh down her heart. She felt his presence, his sadness, his love and compassion. She almost felt an arm across her shoulders and irately shrugged it off.

"Are you more angry with me for getting myself killed or for getting Tira with child?"

She almost laughed at the first part of his question, but was enraged by the second. "You are a two-timing bastard!" Again, in English.

"From your perspective, it should be Tira making that accusation, not you. You are the 'other woman,' not she."

"What do you mean?"

"From birth, Tira and I knew we'd be allowed to mate. We were fond of each other as children and loved one another as we grew older. Then you came along. I loved you, too, and we would also be allowed to mate. It is a rare individual on this world who is so doubly blessed. Tira and I hoped that, in time, you would join our household. Now, unfortunately, that won't happen."

She stifled a sob. "Tira said you had a premonition you might die."

"I wasn't gifted with clear foresight, but somehow I knew we shouldn't delay starting a child. We'd already decided that Tira would return to her parents while I prepared a house for us. We were to live by the sea, for a time anyway."

"So that's why she walked home."

"Yes. We didn't want to take any chances with our baby."

Both were silent for a while. "Will you be reborn as the baby?"

He laughed again. "And be my own father? No. An entity is waiting. I'll be reborn later, when you no longer need me."

She cried again. She did need him. She had missed him. She almost wished he could have given her a child, too.

"You aren't ready for marriage yet, Fern. Especially marriage as it is here."

True, but that didn't lessen the pain. She continued to weep, letting her tears flush out resentment, disappointment, sorrow.

Evening approached. The sky darkened as she descended from the ridge. Ansil remained silent, but she felt his presence. The mountain cast a shadow over the path and the moons were not high enough for her to see. He guided her way. As she reached the lake, he said, "Fern, please take care of Tira for me. And our baby."

The baby. Despite her anger and distress, her heart reached out to the baby.

When she reached the village, all was quiet. Tira slept on the sameg. Fern tiptoed into her room, gathered her bedding, and spread it on the sameg by Tira. She put an arm around her sister and fell asleep.

To Fern's relief, Ansil didn't stay "in her head" all the time, only when she summoned him, or if he had something important to tell her. When he was with her, Fern could close her eyes and sense his presence. With her eyes open, it was as though he stood behind her. She could hear him as clearly as if he were there.

Fern came to understand how much Ansil meant to Tira and how grievous was her loss. She tried not to burden Tira with her own grief, but try though she might, the sting of envy and perceived betrayal continued to fester.

Still, she stood by Tira, who was healthy and required no special care, but who mourned deeply. For the first time in their life together, Fern and Tira became nearly inseparable. Fulfilling her promise to Ansil to take care of her, Fern nearly hovered over Tira. As her belly grew, Tira went on with her usual routine and laughed at Fern's entreaties to be careful, not lift so much, and other precautions Fern remembered from her life on Earth.

Fern and Andli assisted in preparations for the baby. Tira's new tunic was made to open in the front so she could nurse. Andli made two of these. Fern concentrated on things the baby would need. As she spun and wove, she poured blessings for the child into her work.

One day, Tira said, "You know, I was not able to see my future with Ansil, although I could see it with our baby. I didn't know what that meant, only that the future was uncertain. I'm glad I didn't foresee his death. That would have ruined our happiness together."

Tira never mentioned being in contact with Ansil. Fern was reluctant to ask her, in case she wasn't. She didn't want to hurt Tira's feelings, so she asked Ansil, "Do you talk to Tira like you do me?"

"No. She needs to move on with her life."

"And I don't?"

"Are you ready for me to leave you?"

"No, not really."

She had many questions. "What was it like when you died? Was it painful? Were you scared?"

"It wasn't painful—it happened too fast. I didn't have time to be scared. I saw the storm coming, so I headed for shore. Then the wind started to whip around from all directions. I was taking down the sail when an unexpected gust flipped the boat over."

"I thought you were a good swimmer."

"I am—was. Maybe I got hit in the head. I remember being in the water, then hovering above it. Before I knew it, it was all over, and there was no going back. I didn't have time to wrashiru. Afterwards, I felt mostly regret, and a sense of irresponsibility."

"Yes, it was irresponsible of you." Fern thought back to her one experience with wrashiru. "When I came here to escape death, I wasn't prepared for wrashiru, either. In fact, I had no idea what was happening, or that it was even possible. But you've wrashirued before. Why couldn't you this time?"

"I can't explain that any more than I can explain why you could."

"So, what is it like there? Wherever you are—do others stick around?"

"Yes and no. They watch over their loved ones and are able to help, but usually they don't stay as intimately involved as I am. There's a level of being that I only peeked at this time because I chose to stay with you. I've been there between other lives. I don't know how to describe it except to say that on the other side of life is love."

"Is it Heaven?"

"I suppose you could call it that."

"Is there such a thing as Hell?"

"Only if we make it for ourselves."

Why were his answers always so nebulous?

* * *

Aldan, one of Fern's old suitors, had mated with Hansa and now they had a son, Janil. Tira began to spend time with Hansa. They would sit together, Hansa doing craft work and Tira husking nuts. Tira also helped Hansa with Janil. To Fern, this made sense. Hansa was a young mother and Tira soon would be. Aldan often joined the young women, and the three began to take meals together. In the evening, they sat together on the sameg. Pregnant women didn't stop dancing until they were close to giving birth. Fern noticed Tira now danced with Aldan more than with other men and with Hansa almost to the exclusion of other women.

One afternoon, as casually as if announcing the color of a baby blanket, Tira said to Fern and Andli that she was going to move in with Hansa and Aldan. At first, Fern thought she misunderstood. She glanced at Andli, who only nodded and smiled.

Fern asked in English, "What did you say?"

"I'll be joining Hansa and Aldan's household. Not as a mate, at least not until after the baby's born. But it's important that my baby have a family from the start."

"But you do have a family. We are your family."

Tira shook her head. "On Earth, a woman in my situation would stay with her parents if she didn't have her own home, but things are different here. Aldan is not closely related to me, so he's a potential mate. My baby will have a father and two mothers when she's born."

Fern dropped what she was doing, stood abruptly, and ran to her grove —blindsided by yet another betrayal. After sticking by Tira all this time, trying to take good care of her, Tira had turned her back on her, exchanging Fern's undying loyalty for a new family situation.

Once she thrashed through her feelings, Fern did her best to put on a good front. For the sake of the baby, she helped Tira move her belongings into Hansa and Aldan's home.

That night, Fern couldn't bear to sleep on the sameg by herself, and moving back into her sisters' room didn't feel right, so she took her blanket to her grove. Ansil joined her.

"Do you know about Tira's new arrangement?" she asked.

"Of course."

"And you approve?"

"Why wouldn't I? Hansa and Aldan will be kind to Tira and the baby, and Tira will need a mate. Unfortunately, I can no longer fill that need for her."

"It seems like I'm always the last to know these things."

She felt as though he laid a warm arm across her shoulders. She wished he had real arms to hold her, a real shoulder to cry on, but all he had to offer was his presence. "I tried to take good care of Tira for you, and now she's chosen someone else, and I'm all alone again!"

"You have me."

"But you're not real."

He chuckled.

"Why do you think everything's so funny?"

He stifled his laugh. "From my perspective, 'All the slings and arrows of outrageous fortune' appear trivial, like you would view a child's troubles."

"So, I'm a child to you?"

"Estut miryit. I didn't mean to trivialize your feelings."

Slings and arrows—what did he know of such things? "Isn't that Shakespeare?"

"Hamlet. Tiril went to a play and let me watch. From here, language is no barrier. Who knows, after I'm reborn, I may study Earth."

Tiril. Fern looked up at the stars. Where in the universe was he? When would he be back? She knew the futility of searching the stars for Earth's sun. Yet Ansil went to a play with Tiril, just as easily as she enjoyed performances on the sameg. And Ansil could enjoy them with her. For a fleeting moment, the proximity of distance, in both the material and the immaterial worlds, settled into her mind. Things Taran had told her, "Space is not linear. All places are one, except in the conscious mind, which defines space." Wrashiru was not really traveling from one location to another, but stepping between folds of space. Because Taran didn't experience the universe as linear, he was not able to locate Earth's sun. "Since all space is one," he'd said "Earth is just next door, so to speak."

But she was in no mood for metaphysics. "Ansil, please leave me alone now." She nursed her misery until she fell asleep.

CHAPTER 16
RAMBLING

To indicate readiness for marriage, young people moved out of their families' homes to the sameg. Fern had done this to be with Tira, but the young men took it as a signal to pay special attention to her. Although she didn't welcome their advances, it didn't feel right to move back into the family home. Most nights, unless it rained, Fern slept in her grove. No one said anything. They were used to her eccentricities.

Once satisfied Hansa and Aldan were taking good care of Tira, Fern started to wander off and spend nights in the forest. She made herself a new backpack to carry her blanket, comb, and some skri. She began to ramble further afield, sometimes for days. As long as she doubled up on her chores at home, this seemed acceptable. When it rained, she'd hunker under brush or an outcropping. No one put an umbrella over her, but she occasionally sensed someone flashing through her mind, checking on her.

One day she struck out inland, to get as far from the sea as possible. She crossed the hills that sheltered their little valley and climbed a mountain beyond. When she reached the top, she thrilled at the view of the mountains and valleys before her. Below her, a rocky outcrop promised an even wider panorama. As she descended, she discovered she wasn't alone. Taran sat on the ledge in meditation. How did he get here so fast? He'd been in the village when she left. Suspecting this was his private spot, she began to retreat.

"You may approach," he said.

"Estut miryit. I won't bother you here again."

He nodded and stood beside her. "It is beautiful, isn't it?"

"Very."

After a few moments' silence, he said, "I have endeavored all my life to understand what attracts humans to mountains. It's not the view alone. On Earth, we visited a parkway that ran along the crest of a mountain range. We stopped at every point of interest and read the signage that told about the history of the place. The climate was so harsh and wind-blown, the trees were stunted, yet people had lived there. There was evidence of Native American camps, and later white settlers tried to homestead on those mountain tops, although life was easier in the valleys. They weren't very successful. The ground was too stony and the growing season too short. They probably starved. Later, the government bought the land to make the parkway, which put it to good use. But it amazed me that people would choose to live there. Something about the heights attracted them. I feel it myself."

"Me, too," she murmured.

He half smiled. "If I'd had my way, we would have built our new village on a mountain top instead of in a valley. It wouldn't be practical, of course, too far to carry water, too little food and firewood. As a young man, I tried to live by the sea, but the mountains constantly called me." After a silence, Taran turned to her. "It's time for me to return to my duties, and for you to resume your adventure."

Fern descended into the valley and up the next mountain ridge. She had explored this area by ethenos, but the experience of walking and climbing was different. That afternoon, during a rainstorm, she sheltered under an ancient erguvon whose canopy was so thick the ground remained dry. After bathing in a stream that evening, she returned to the tree for the night.

She sat in stillness. Instead of retreating into her mind, she became aware of the sounds of the night—the distant brook, the hint of wind in the trees, but nothing else. On Earth, she would hear a chorus of insects, frogs, creatures of the forest. In her miaven grove, she could hear the voices of the village and swimmers in the lake, but here it was quiet. She relaxed into the silence.

Her consciousness stretched out into the surrounding woodlands. On Earth, she would worry about bugs, or in a wilderness like this, predators. Here, she had always felt safe. Even her first day on this world, before she'd learned there was no animal life, she'd felt no threat. She missed birds and other denizens of the Earth, but she had become so accustomed to the silence, she seldom took note of their absence.

When the clouds cleared, she stepped from underneath the tree's branches to look at the stars. The moons' light reflected off the mountains. What were the names of these mountains?

When she returned to the village, she asked Taran. "I understand why you don't give a name to this planet, but what about things like mountains and rivers?"

"No, we haven't named them."

"Why?"

Taran took a few minutes to think. "I suppose it's because in our history we were unaware of places having names. Moses might have named such things, had he lived long enough."

"So, there's no reason they can't have names? It wouldn't alert the thortles?"

"No, I see no reason why it should." He smiled. "Do you propose to name them?"

"May I? I won't give names to this planet or its sun."

"Yes, that would be fine."

And so in her wanderings, Fern put much thought into naming the physical features of the world. The mountain where Taran went to be alone was easy—Mt. Taran. Then one beside it she named Mt. Rina. The river that flowed through their valley she called River Andli, and the valley itself, Doran Valley.

On nights away from home, with no one to make music for her, Fern would sing to herself and gaze at the stars. One pair of stars she had watched for years. She'd first noticed them shortly before her first Full Moons and had traced their slow progress across the heavens until they were no longer visible at night. By the time they appeared again, she was keeping her calendar. She had rejoiced—they marked the planet's year around the sun. One was a blue giant and the other smaller, but no less bright, and pinkish. She named them after her parents. Two other pink stars reminded her of her little sisters, so she gave them their names.

She watched the planets in their wanderings. When another appeared as a morning star, she named it Tira. As two others came into view, she called them Tala and Ara. She would have to find something fitting for Jorsil and Donal.

When Fern pointed out their namesake planets to Tala and Ara, they gazed at them in awe. Tira woke early to enjoy her morning star before the sun rose. She said, "I never thought of naming things. Thank you, Fern. Somehow, I feel a stronger connection to this world."

* * *

As Tira's pregnancy progressed, Fern read about childbirth, in Earth books, of course, and learned about complications she'd never dreamed of. She wasn't aware of any maternal deaths among these people, but death itself was not unavoidable. One afternoon Ansil interrupted her, unbidden. "You need to go home. Our baby will be born soon."

Suddenly, Fern was seized by anxiety for Tira's safety. Had there been a reason for her to join another household? Now Ansil seemed to think Tira needed her, despite her lack of midwifery skills. She wished she could wrashiru.

Ansil chuckled. "You don't need to run. You have time to get there."

"Is she going to be all right?"

"Most likely. She's young and healthy and has wide hips, and our daughter does not want to be an orphan."

As Fern approached the village, she came across Tira, not writhing in a sickbed, but out in the woods collecting kindling. Tira paused every so often to relax and breathe slowly. Fern insisted on carrying the wood back to the sameg.

After supper, Tira retired to her house with Hansa and Aldan. Their son was sent to his grandparents, and family members paid short visits to her throughout the evening. The music and dancing that night was muted and soothing. Fern tried to stay with Tira but grew sleepy. Andli sent her to bed, promising to wake her before the baby came. She slept fitfully on the sameg, aware of the expectant grandparents changing shifts throughout the night. Finally, Rina woke her. Tira appeared to be in little pain, but from time to time she would go into a trance and allow her body to work.

As the stars faded and the eastern sky glowed pink and blue, Fern felt an incredible happiness that brought her to tears. She knew Ansil was present. Tira groaned and bore down, and soon a little cry was heard. Tira drew the child to her breast and said, "Sita." Tira looked beyond Fern and, smiling through tears, she held up her little daughter. Fern looked behind her. She saw no one, but felt joy beaming from that quarter.

Hansa took the baby while Andli tended to Tira. Once the afterbirth was delivered. Rina took it from the house and returned with warm water. She and Andli helped Tira wash and change clothes. Then Hansa handed Tira the baby and combed her hair. When Tira walked outside, the entire village greeted her with applause. Fern thought Tira looked like a little goddess, presenting the people with a miracle.

Tira sat under the awning with Hansa and Aldan. Andli brought Tira a cup of tea and Aldan held Sita while she drank it. When the couple left for breakfast, Tira asked Fern to sit with her. "Ansil was there," she whispered.

"I know. He's been with me since he died."

Tira didn't say, "I know," as Fern expected, but, "I'm glad. I asked him to look after you."

Fern laughed. "He asked *me* to look after *you!*"

"And you have." She handed the baby to Fern. "This is your child also, sister."

Fern didn't know what to say. She was given the honor of holding the newborn even before the grandparents did. As she cradled little Sita against her, the baby rooted and found Fern's breast. Startled, she looked at Tira and they both laughed. Tira took Sita back and nursed her. After the baby was satisfied, Rina brought breakfast to Tira and held her grandchild so the new mother could eat.

Fern peered into Tira's dish. "What is that? If I didn't know better, I'd say it was liver and onions."

Tira said, "This may seem disgusting to you, but since we have no meat here, we find that both mother and baby fare better if the placenta is eaten."

Fern stared at her.

"Mammals on Earth eat theirs, even humans in some cultures." She laughed at Fern's face and said, "You haven't had breakfast yet. Go get some vegetables."

To her surprise, Fern still had an appetite.

That afternoon, Ansil visited her in the miaven grove. "Congratulations," she said, "you have a healthy baby girl."

"She is wonderful, isn't she?"

Fern sighed. "I wish you'd stayed around, in the flesh, I mean, so you could be a daddy to her."

"I will return in the flesh someday." He paused. Fern imagined she heard a sigh, then a catch in his throat when he said, "And she does have a daddy."

"I hope Hansa and Aldan don't treat her differently from Janil."

"You underestimate us. Don't Earth people have a saying, 'It takes a village to raise a child?' Our very survival, as a people, has depended on our taking care of one another."

* * *

Fern resumed her ramblings. Whenever she rested, she took refuge in her library and visited her sisters. After Sita was born, she found them sleeping and whispered, "Did you know you are aunties now? Our sister here has a new baby. I wish you could see her."

Tira recovered quickly and resumed normal activity. Sometimes she asked Fern to hold Sita while she did chores or went for a swim. Fern loved holding the little one, but admitted she wasn't ready for one of her own. Tira and Hansa nursed each other's babies and Fern could see the advantages of a group marriage.

Fern's thoughts turned more and more to the weka who walked about the wilderness. That life called her. One day while Tira ate lunch, Fern held the sleeping Sita. No sooner had Tira set down her bowl than the baby stretched and began to root. After Fern handed Sita to Tira, her gaze drifted to the mountains beyond the village. She turned back to find Tira watching her.

"You're restless."

Fern nodded.

"Then go do what you must do." Tira's eyes shifted to the horizon. "It'll be many years before I'll be free to explore the planet. By then I'll be old. Perhaps what we need are young eyes to discover what lies out there."

Fern's heart sailed. Thus released, she resumed her wanderings, going further and further into the forest, for many days at a time.

* * *

Two days into the wilderness, Fern ran low on food, but she wasn't ready to go home. She was following a river uphill, and so far she had discovered two waterfalls. She wanted to find the river's source. There was plenty of lenitrus and occasionally she found nut trees, but raw nuts weren't very tasty. She wished she could build a fire to roast them but she lacked the skill. Why not sprout them? She wrapped several in wet leaves and stored them in the bottom of her backpack. The problem was, she had no way to isolate the sprouts from the rest of her belongings, and her blanket became damp. Rather than turn back, she put up with the inconvenience.

Every turn of the river brought new wonders: breathtaking vistas, serene glades, more waterfalls. The way became steeper. She encountered new plants that looked like they might be edible. She summoned Ansil. "What do you know about these?"

"I'm not familiar with them. Why don't you collect a few and ask Doran when you get back home?"

Finally, she reached the mountain lake which gave birth to the river. She called the river Jorsil, after her brother who had journeyed to the sea to be with his love, Tana, and named the lake after her. Although the water was cold, she went swimming, then warmed herself on a sunbaked boulder by the shore where she camped for the night.

Still not satisfied, Fern climbed one of the peaks that cradled the lake. Here she was rewarded with a magnificent view. Forested mountains spread out before her like rippling waves on the sea. They beckoned to her, but it was time to head home.

She'd been gone five days. Perhaps there was a quicker route back. Fern went into meditation and from there to ethenos. She rose above the terrain and directed her consciousness towards the village. The river twisted among the hills, but from the air she found a straighter path.

After struggling through the forest for a day and a half, she came to a cliff too steep to descend. She used ethenos to find a way down. After this, she stayed closer to the ground when she plotted shorter routes. She arrived at the village nine days after she had left.

Everyone was happy to see her, but no one acted worried. She knew they'd been checking on her. She gave Doran the plants she'd collected. After examining them, meditating, and tasting a few, he told her which were safe to eat. "Next time, bring some seeds back," he said. "Maybe we can grow them here."

Diligently, she carried enough wood and water to make up for the days she'd missed. Before she set out on her next excursion, Rina helped her fashion a watertight pouch for sprouting nuts.

* * *

In subsequent ramblings Fern, collected more plants for Doran and seeds of those he deemed beneficial. She became very familiar with the surrounding territory. She was surprised at how little the adults, who had approved the site for the village, knew about their neighborhood. When she reported her findings, they appreciated the information. She mentioned this to Tira.

"Our people were confined for so many generations before coming here, perhaps this wide open planet is still too overwhelming for us to fully appreciate. We seem to like small, cozy spaces, like small houses and villages."

"I've never noticed anyone being afraid of the wilderness."

"No, we're not afraid, it's just so vast. We travel from one village to the other, but other than the weka, we don't explore."

"Ansil liked to explore the sea."

"Yes, he did." Tira lowered her head.

Fern felt a wave of sadness. "I'm sorry."

"Don't be. You and he are alike in that way—curious about what lies beyond the horizon."

Fern's ramblings built strength and stamina but left little time for leisure. When she was away, she missed lessons with Taran. As her physical abilities increased, she noticed her psychic gifts diminish. She had no trouble accessing her library, but ethenos became more difficult. Her communication with Ansil remained unhindered, but it became harder to check on her sisters. She missed Thanksgiving. One rainy night, sheltering under a bush, she asked Ansil what was happening to her.

"I have no answer. Tiril tells me that children on Earth who have psychic abilities tend to lose them as they grow older. He thought it was because adults don't encourage them. They even stifle them. But you've been encouraged, and no one here would stifle your powers."

Was another door closing? While she'd made no progress at wrashiru, she'd never given up hope of returning to Earth. Did this loss of abilities mean she'd never be able to? But what had she done to prepare to go home? She'd been so busy exploring the planet and worrying about Tira she'd neglected her studies. She knew without asking, she'd missed another Christmas. She had been here four years. Her classmates back home had only one more semester before graduation, and she hadn't finished eleventh grade.

When she discussed her concerns with Taran, he said, "Don't give up on yourself. I knew of adults on Earth who never showed psychic ability, yet learned to develop it later in life. Perhaps you have other lessons you need to learn first."

"Like what? I feel more lost inside myself than I do out in the forest."

"That may be your answer. Your needs are different. We explore within ourselves and focus on home and family. Only after our grandchildren are grown do we venture out into the wider world. On Earth, most young people pursue education and careers before they settle down to start families. That may be the rhythm of your life."

"Escaping into the wild is hardly education or a career."

"Look back into your history. Hasn't it been for some?"

Yes, in the past, men made careers of exploring the Earth. Few women were mentioned in those stories, but the men didn't travel alone. One of Fern's childhood fantasies had been to be an explorer. Now was her chance. As she journeyed into new territory, Fern learned more about the geology, hydrology, and flora of the land. At night in her library, she searched for explanations in books from Earth and realized that this was indeed education.

One evening, she sat on a rocky ledge to enjoy the sunset and recalled what her father had told her about her ancestry. Her European forebears had crossed the ocean to what they thought was an unexplored continent. Some may have watched a sunset like this and felt the call to venture on.

But eons before their wagons rambled westward, her Native American ancestors had come from Asia to spread across two truly unexplored continents, living much as the people here did. An emotion she could not contain welled up in Fern. It was in her blood. She was the daughter of pioneers and explorers.

She remembered her father's words so long ago, in another time and place, the night they sat on the beach watching the launch of the space shuttle, "There is the future. Your children and grandchildren will populate the stars." She also remembered her mother's words the night before she died, "I was not going to miss my chance to see a new planet, even though I couldn't tell anyone back home about it." The emotion in Fern spilled out as grateful tears. At last, life had a purpose.

All the time she had spent here, feeling out of place, without purpose or direction, yearning to return to Earth, something had kept her back. Maybe this was why she was born, to explore, to help settle, this new world.

CHAPTER 17
THE TREK

When Fern returned to the village and announced her decision to go "walking," no one objected. She took her time to prepare. She traded her nice tunic for Tira's old one. Andli insisted she take another old tunic for a change of clothes. She did as much spinning as possible to help Andli, and she made herself new sandals and moccasins. Rina gave her a waterproof, resin-coated cloth to keep things dry in her backpack, a few needles, and a knife. She took an extra water bottle. There was barely room in the basket for skri.

She decided not to take the little pouch that contained her most cherished treasures: the medallion of her mother's hair, the miaven flower from the tree on her mother's grave, and her little egg-shaped rock. She entrusted them to Andli, and to Tira, the necklace Ansil had made her. Although these had comforted her on jaunts, she didn't want to risk losing them. She debated whether to take her erguvon stick and decided to leave it. She drew a replica of it in her library, complete with sixty marks for the number of times the small moon had been full since her arrival, and she pledged to keep up with time on the virtual one.

Atla, the fire maker, gave her a small pottery box with an ember of fire and instructed her on how to use and maintain it. The last thing she did was have Hansa cut her hair so that she wouldn't be burdened by its daily care. Rina and Andli were visibly distressed to see those golden locks shorn off. Andli watched with tears in her eyes but Rina walked away. Fern assured both that it would grow back. She gave the hair to

Hansa, whose eyes shone as she ran her fingers through it. "I will make you something very special for your return," she said.

"Make something for Andli and Rina. I always have it on me."

That night, the small moon was full. Fern etched one last mark on her erguvon stick and made a mental note to make a line on the "paper" one in her library. When she danced on the sameg, her partners found her short hair a novelty and couldn't keep their fingers out of it.

Fern planned to set out the next morning but found excuses to delay. She emptied and repacked her backpack, adding incidentals and as much skri as would fit. She said good-byes more than once, assuring everyone that she wouldn't be alone because she'd have Ansil for company. Finally Ansil said, "You can't put this off forever."

She gave her family members one last hug. Ara clung to her with tears. Fern hid hers. "I'll be back, I promise."

With a whole world to explore, Fern chose to follow River Andli upstream from the lake, the one direction she hadn't traversed in her wanderings. For days, she followed it uphill until it became a trickle seeping from the mountainside. She climbed the mountain and surveyed the vast unnamed land before her. She summoned Ansil. "Which way should I go?"

"Which way is most intriguing?"

She chose a direction. She ate from the forest, rationing her skri and collecting what nuts she could find. When the skri ran out, she built a fire to make pancakes. She went barefoot as much as possible, saving her footwear for stony ground. Before the small moon was full again, her sandals fell apart anyway, so when she stopped to cook, she made a new pair. She tried to save her moccasins, which were harder to replace. One evening while bathing her battered feet in a stream, Ansil said, "What are you waiting for? Your moccasins are no use in your backpack."

Even when she tied her hat on with a cord, it would find a way to get blown off, and she was constantly snagging it on branches. The right materials for hats weren't readily available and weaving a new one was time consuming, so she finally did without. The fabric of her clothing was tough, but not indestructible, and she was glad she'd brought needle and thread for mending.

One night Fern lay on her back studying the faces of the moons. The large moon was just past full. "Ansil, did I ever tell you I wanted to be an astronaut when I was a kid? That was before I became afraid of the stars."

"But you're no longer afraid."

"No, thank goodness. Did you know Earth's astronauts walked on our moon? That might not seem a big deal to you, but it was for us. I used to fantasize what it would be like."

"There's no air."

"No, they wore space suits. You know, I could have gone there by ethenos when I was visiting Earth. I wouldn't have needed a space suit."

"Maybe one day you'll regain your ability and go back."

"I hope so. I'll be sure to visit these moons, too."

A few days later, from the crest of a mountain, she spotted smoke. Her first thought was forest fire. Suppressing panic, she scanned the terrain for the best escape.

"Relax," Ansil said. "It's only a campfire."

Campfire? That meant people. She hoped to find them before they moved on. Descending the mountain quickly proved difficult. She tried a likely shortcut which failed to live up to its promise. Eventually, she found a creek that rippled down into the dell where she'd spotted the fire. The scent of baking skri guided her to the camp of three weka, a woman and two men, who acted as though they expected her.

The woman was Roni, grandmother of Lila and Rogan's mate, Risa, who had been in Italy when Fern was at the sea village. As a young woman, Roni visited Italy during the turmoil following World War II. She posed as a refugee from Romania until she learned Italian. She had brought the word "barca" into Human Talk.

"Why did you go there at such a time?" Fern asked. "I thought you all went as tourists. There must have been peaceful places on Earth to visit."

Roni closed her eyes and took a deep breath. "My soul was in turmoil. I was haunted by nightmares from a former life on the thortle world, and wartime gave me the opportunity to deal with my feelings." She smiled. "Besides, I also had dim memories of a life in Italy and wanted to return."

"It must have taken a lot of courage," Fern said, "to go by yourself, not knowing the language or customs."

"Yes, but I wasn't alone. People all around me were displaced. Much courage was needed by everyone in those days, and they helped me work through my troubles."

Fern stayed with them several days, exchanging stories. Roni told Fern about Italy and Fern told them about Florida. Roni had much advice for Fern. "You are becoming fluent in Human Talk, but remember to always practice your English. That's a skill you don't want to lose."

Fern lent them her strength and skills, and they fed her well. The nuts in this valley were plump and bountiful. They taught Fern how to build a temporary oven to bake skri and loaded her backpack with it before she moved on.

* * *

Fern came across one other couple on her travels. Late one afternoon, she struggled up a mountain and rested on a ledge just below the summit. Once her weariness lifted, she looked for the best path to the top.

Out of the corner of her eye, she caught a face grinning at her and nearly lost her balance. She clutched the rock she'd been climbing and inched around until she came face to face with a desiccated skull. Beside it was another, a more delicate one. She took several deep breaths before approaching them.

The cool, dry mountain air had preserved the bodies in a mummified state. Both were wore tattered tunics, but the smaller one's still had hints of color. The pattern looked familiar. Fern extended a finger as though to touch it, but held back. Hadn't she helped Andli make it? Yes, it had been intended for her sister Tala. On the sunken chest hung a necklace Fern recognized—made by people of the mountain village, strung on cord Fern herself had spun, given to Metia, daughter of Hannah, granddaughter of Moses and Rila, First Parents of this world. And so, a chapter of living history was closed.

Fern sank to her knees, buried her face in her hands, and let the tears flow. Intertwined with her grief was joy and admiration. Metia's purpose was firm when she left their village, alone, to join her mate. She had declined Fern's offer to accompany her, and she had carried out her plan.

Fern hadn't intended to spend the night on this mountain top, where it was cold and there was no wood for a fire. She'd come only to scope out her next direction, but she felt compelled to stay. She set her backpack on the ledge and climbed to the apex where she surveyed her realm. In the distance rose taller, steeper peaks. One snow-covered mountain gleamed in the sunlight. She named it the White Mountain. Below her ran a silver ribbon which she knew must flow eventually to the sea. She summoned Ansil. "I just have to share this with someone."

"You are not the first human to have seen this."

"No, but I'm the first Earthling."

"We, too, are children of the Earth."

"But I was born there."

"True. In all their years of travel, this was the farthest Metia and Tenin went. They wanted to go further, but he died, and she chose not to go on without him."

"Have other weka gone beyond here?"

"No. The farther you go, and the higher you climb, the colder it gets. The weka have explored it by ethenos and wrashiru, but not by walking."

She looked down the steep slope she had scaled. Then she looked at the other sides of the mountain. It had been a difficult ascent for her, and she wondered how Metia had managed it. "She must have been highly motivated to climb up here when she was dying," Fern said.

"Yes, she was 'highly' motivated," Ansil quipped. "But she had ways of climbing you haven't achieved."

"She's wearing her clothes, so she couldn't have wrashirued."

"There are other ways," was all he'd say.

Fern descended to the ledge to eat, wrapped her blanket around her, and returned to watch the sun set. The small moon nestled in the western sky. The White Mountain turned purple before it faded into darkness. The stars came out. When the large moon rose, just past full, its light transformed the distant peak into a vision out of a fairy tale. The wind rose and blew through Fern's blanket. She made her way down to the more sheltered area where the remains of Metia and her mate looked always to the east.

Fern slipped her spare tunic over her clothes and huddled under her blanket. She took out her ember pot and held it in her hands. She dared not open the container lest the little ember burn itself out, but the thought of it provided warmth. Her strange companions gave her comfort. She sat beside Metia and spoke to her, knowing her spirit no longer inhabited those bones.

"After you left us, Tira came home. She had mated with Ansil, and when I found out, I was so angry. I loved him and wanted him for myself. But then he died, and now he keeps me company. Tira had him in life, and now I have him in death. Isn't that ironic?" Talking seemed to hold back the chill of the night. She told Metia about Tira's beautiful baby and her new family.

"I admire you and Tenin. You didn't take other mates. You were faithful to each other to the end. I wish I could find the kind of love you had."

Fern must have dozed off. She woke when she heard a voice, "I have waited for you to come." A puff of wind stirred the rags beside her.

Something besides wind stirred in Fern that night. Something from her white ancestors remembered the excitement of a new land few white people had seen. And something more ancient, from her red ancestors, a land that no human had walked before. For the first time in all her years on this world, Fern felt that she was a part of it, that it was hers, that she belonged.

She felt a warm mantle settle around her and heard the words, "This is how you can shield yourself from cold. You can do this without me. When the sun rises, go forth and continue my quest." It wasn't Ansil speaking. Had she dozed off again?

She could barely wait until it was light enough to travel. To keep her blood flowing, she got up and walked about the ledge, but she no longer felt cold. She looked at the stars. By now she'd learned to tell direction by their positions. The White Mountain lay to the south, so that's where she decided to go.

Long before dawn, the snowy mountain caught the light's first rays and glowed against the dark blue sky. Fern's blood thrilled. The pinnacle in the distance turned pink, then silver. Finally the sun rose so she could see to walk.

Fern pondered whether to bury the bodies. But Metia had not buried Tenin, and she had left her body beside his, so this must have been their choice. Before she took her leave, she named the mountain Lovers' Peak. Then she descended in the direction of the White Mountain.

As the day warmed, Fern took off her extra tunic. When she slipped it over her head, something rattled against her neck. She grasped her chest and, to utter surprise, found a string of beads—the necklace Metia had worn! How did it get there? She hadn't touched Metia, let alone the necklace. She fingered the pale blue bead which had once belonged to Hannah. She looked up at the mountain and knew that Metia wanted her to have it, but how it had been borne from Metia's neck to hers would remain a mystery.

Fern reached the river that afternoon. She named it Weka River in honor of Metia and Tenin. It was too deep to wade and she didn't dare swim lest her ember get wet and be extinguished. She had to follow Weka River upstream for many days until she found a place shallow enough to ford.

Food became scarce. She had traveled beyond where weka had sown nut trees or influenced existing ones to produce fuller nuts. The lenitrus she was familiar with became sparse and she was unfamiliar with new plants that grew here. Occasionally, she'd taste one and observe its effect on her. Some were edible but others induced vomiting. The morning after one such purge, when she belted her tunic, she had to tie it tighter. She was losing weight.

Each night, she visited her library and recorded her new findings in a notebook. She drew maps, to the best of her ability, and labeled the mountains and rivers she'd named. She sketched new plants she found and described their properties.

After she forded Weka River, Fern crossed the next ridge to a small valley. Here, she was delighted to find a waterfall that fed a pool suitable for swimming. The water was comfortably warm. There must be a hot spring upstream, she thought. In the pool, she found a rock that was hollowed out to a little cup which fit nicely in her hand. She thanked the mountain which had shed the rock and the waterfall for shaping it. Here she camped for several days. Nut trees grew in these woods, so she built an oven. She searched until she found a cylindrical rock whose end fit perfectly inside the cup. Equipped with mortar and pestle, she collected nuts, ground them, and made skri. It was so pleasant to go to sleep each night with a full belly. She named this stream Friendly River.

* * *

When the small moon was waxing for the sixth time since she set out, Fern knew it was close to her birthday. How she wished she could visit her sisters and grandparents! It had been so long. She had no choice but to make the best of it. The evening was pleasant, without rain. Fern camped by a river whose water was sweet with minerals. She built a cheery fire and baked pancakes. After eating, she went to her library. The TV was still there, but it hadn't worked in a long time. On a whim, she pushed the button anyway. To her surprise, it came on.

In her grandparents' kitchen, Grandma was removing birthday candles from a blackberry cobbler. Then she cut it into pieces and dished it out. "It's hard to believe Fern would have been eighteen today." She wiped a tear.

"It's okay," the youngest said. "Fern likes blackberries."

"Blackberries?" Fern recognized that voice. She was seeing through Tiril's eyes!

"Do you like blackberries?" the other sister asked.

"I've never had them before."

"What? How could you never have them?"

The girls topped the servings with ice cream and handed one to Tiril. He took a bite. Fern's stomach growled. She wished she could taste it. When Tiril laid down his spoon, Grandma asked, "Well?"

"Delicious. Do they always have so many seeds?"

"City boy! City boy!" the girls taunted. Fern had to laugh.

"Where do you get them?" Tiril asked between bites.

"We pick them."

"Where?"

Grandpa spoke up. "Son, if you're going to help us eat our food, you're going to help us gather it. When we get done eating, you can help with the dishes, then I'm taking you to our blackberry patch."

"Can we go, too?" the girls chimed.

"We'll all go," Grandma said. "I need more if I'm going to make jelly."

The TV picture faded. Fern was reluctant to lose the connection but was filled with gratitude for the brief glimpse. Tiril acted like one of the family. Her sisters spoke of her in the present tense. Had he told them about her? But her grandmother was still grieving. Surely he wouldn't tell the children and not the adults.

Yes, Fern thought in satisfaction, I'm eighteen now. On Earth, she'd be an adult. What was her status here? She wasn't really sure.

CHAPTER 18
MT. FRUSTRATION

A branch caught a small rent in Fern's tunic and ripped it open. Back in the village, Andli was quick to catch minor tears, but Fern tended to let them go. When she stopped to rest, she examined the hole. The fabric was so worn it needed more than a few stitches and she was nearly out of thread. After searching unsuccessfully for reeds by the small river she was following, she found a clump of tall herbs that were too stringy to eat.

Maybe they were suitable for cloth. She picked several that had gone to seed and extracted enough fibers to spin coarse thread to reweave the gap. Although as far as she knew, the fiber bore no resemblance to flax, she named the plant "linen." She collected seeds and promised to spread them, planting a few by the river and putting the rest in her backpack to carry home.

Fern followed Linen River, as she named it, upstream. Linen grew plentifully in this valley. As she traveled, she gathered stalks, soaked them when she stopped for the night, and spun thread once the fibers were ready. She stored balls of thread in her backpack until she had enough.

Then she camped for several days. She cut four straight, smooth sticks to make a loom and wove scraps of cloth for mending. She also made socks to wear under her sandals. When her last needle broke, Ansil advised her how to make new ones from the tough twigs of an erguvon tree.

Her first attempts were clumsy. With practice, she was able to whittle fine needles, but when she tried to pierce a hole for the eye, she usually broke it. Ansil told her to look closely at the grain for clues to where the wood was tough enough. Her next challenge, once she successfully made an eye, was to smooth out the tiny hollow space so her thread wouldn't snag. Eventually, she produced serviceable needles, if not as fine as those Rina made.

Spending time in one place, spinning and weaving, Fern felt lonely. Ansil was someone to talk to but she yearned for flesh and blood companionship. Ansil suggested that someone could wrashiru to her, but she declined. Wrashiru had its risks and wasn't done for trivial reasons. Instead, she thought about Andli while she worked. Sometimes, she was sure she felt her presence.

She still couldn't project to Earth and missed visiting her sisters and grandparents. Ansil assured her he was in touch with Tiril, who reported that all was well with her loved ones. He related stories from Tiril about what the girls were doing. She was missing their growing up.

After she resumed walking, she collected nuts when she found them, and whenever she came to a place where no nut trees grew, she'd bury a few in the leaf litter. She came across another warm stream and followed it to a hot spring. Here, she camped for a few days, using the scalding water to make tea in her stone cup. Downstream where the water was cooler, she bathed in a pool, her body soaking up the minerals. Even so, she continued to lose weight.

Fern steered always toward the White Mountain, but one day she crested a ridge to find a smoking volcano between her and her goal. If she could still do ethenos, she could survey the area from above to find the best way around it, but the gift still eluded her. Ansil was no help. When she asked him for a promising course, he said, "I don't see things as you do. From my prospective, there are no barriers between you and the White Mountain."

She named the volcano Mt. Frustration. She studied the lay of the land and decided that skirting it to the southeast would be the best route.

There appeared to be more vegetation in that direction, and that meant food and water.

But the volcano fields were more extensive than she realized, and they were a veritable desert. She tried to stay under the shade of trees, but found her path crossed by wide rocky areas. She veered farther and farther to the east, away from the White Mountain. There were many hot springs and some flows were too hot to cross, so she had to follow them downstream, further from her goal. She was able to make tea from her supply of dried herbs, but vegetation became more unfamiliar and her supply of nuts ran low. She cut her rations in half. Whenever she stopped for the night, she would meditate on her body to check for healing needs. The scarcity of food made this imperative. Her menses ceased due to weight loss.

* * *

Both moons were waxing. When Fern consulted her calendar, she knew the Feast of the Full Moons was approaching. She had nothing to make sweet cakes with, but she had enough nuts for a pancake. She folded the tastiest herbs she could find into the batter and baked it. At least she had a treat to celebrate with. That day she rested as much as possible in anticipation of the festivity.

More than ever, she missed the companionship of the people of the village. That night, she walked along the river, singing, the moons lighting her path. She imagined she had company, other than Ansil, walking and singing with her. She thought about Tiril. When would he return from Earth? Did he miss the Full Moons celebrations or did the many holidays there satisfy him?

At midnight, she came to a small clearing where she could see the sky unimpeded. Here she rested to eat her pancake. When the rim of the small moon touched the large one, she summoned Ansil. "You're the only company I have."

"Maybe I can help you with ethenos," he said. She let him enter her mind and, with his guidance, visited the mountain village for a too-brief moment. Her mouth watered when sweet cakes were passed around.

Tira handed a cookie to Sita and said, "This is your first Full Moons. And my thirteenth."

And my fourth, thought Fern.

To her surprise, Sita stood up and toddled over to Rina with her cookie. Then Fern was back in the wilderness, with only Ansil's voice for company. She nibbled on her pancake. "Have I really been gone so long?"

"You keep track of time."

"Do you visit Sita?"

"Of course. She's the 'light of my life', or would be if I were alive."

She was missing the baby's growing up. At times like this, Fern questioned the wisdom of going on this trek.

* * *

When she ran low on nuts, Fern looked for seeds with high oil content for extra calories. Occasionally, Ansil advised her on the edibility of a plant, but there were many he was unfamiliar with.

As her hunger increased, she began to sample more things that looked inviting. Some were too woody to eat. Some didn't satisfy hunger, and others had pharmacopeic effects. A few of these calmed her to the point that she'd sleep all day. Others gave her energy. Some deadened pain.

She had discovered a natural drug store. The people of this world healed with their minds and used herbs to supplement their medicine, but this new knowledge could come in handy. She named each new herb for its effects, collected a small store, and dried them. If a plant had seeds, she collected some. Every night she went to her library and recorded her findings in her journal.

Mt. Frustration lived up to its name, looming ever larger and hiding the White Mountain from view. Was there no way around it? Her socks wore thin, her sandals came apart, and the rocky terrain cut and bruised her feet. She veered further east to a river valley where the ground was softer.

Nuts were so scarce she no longer dared to plant any. She wrapped a few in moist leaves and carried them in her backpack until they sprouted, then ate no more than one a day. One morning, having found no nut trees in the valley, she ate a sprout for breakfast and climbed the next ridge. In the glen below, a river ran into a dense forest to the left. Off to her right, Mt. Frustration smugly hid all but the very tip of the White Mountain. Perhaps she'd find nut trees in this valley. As she descended the slope, she scanned the tree tops but didn't see any.

This river was narrow but too deep to ford. When she reached it, she asked Ansil. "Which way should I go?"

"Do you have any choice but to go upstream?"

"That's away from the White Mountain. Will I ever reach it?"

He didn't answer.

That afternoon, Fern spotted what looked like nut trees on the opposite bank. She had to go further upstream to ford the channel but what she found was a new variety of tree, with no nuts. She climbed the ridge on that side of the river. As she neared the top, she thought she smelled smoke. Were there people here? Her hopes were dashed when she came to the charred remains of a forest which stretched as far as she could see. She summoned Ansil. "I wonder what happened? Did a volcano set this on fire?"

"Possibly, or lightening."

Something white lay on the ground. Fern brushed away the ashes and found a root that had been baked tender by the fire. "Is it edible?"

After a moment, Ansil answered, "I'm not familiar with it, but I don't think it'll harm you."

First she thanked the mountain and the forest for the gift, then she thanked the fire for baking it. When she bit into it, her mouth puckered as though she'd tasted an unripe persimmon. A mouthful of water helped. In caution, she waited to see what else that one bite would do.

She poked among the ashes until she found more and filled her backpack. There was no water on the ridge, so if the tubers were edible, she'd need more than she had in her bamboo. She could see a river in the valley below but only blackened tree trunks, no living vegetation, so she returned the way she'd come.

By the time she reached the water, she was satisfied the root had no ill effects, so she washed and ate the rest of it. Once she got beyond the puckeriness, the taste was bland, reminding her of boiled potatoes, so she called them potatoes and named the river Tater River. Since everything on the ridge had burned, she wasn't sure what plant they came from. She began to dig under unfamiliar herbs but couldn't find the right one.

Fern reserved her unsprouted nuts and ate potatoes until they ran out. She wondered how much longer she could go on like this. She had to find a reliable source of food. A few days later she climbed another mountainside, plucked a leaf from an unfamiliar vine to see if it was edible, and accidentally uprooted it. Attached to the roots were more than a half dozen potatoes. After conferring with the vine, she took the larger ones and replanted the rest.

Finding no more nuts, potatoes became her staple food. Unfortunately, they grew only in high places away from water and were too tough to eat raw. Sometimes she built a fire near where she found them, but she required water to eat them. She continued to follow Tater River, climbing when she needed more potatoes, descending to bake and eat them. The constant up and down was exhausting. The potatoes didn't satisfy her dietary needs as well as nuts did, and she continued to grow thinner.

She began to pay more attention to creeks that emptied into the river and followed them upstream to their sources. This was a better plan. The springs were closer to where the potatoes grew. But a diet of potatoes and lenitrus wasn't enough, so she decided to leave the watershed of Tater River to search for nuts. At the top of the ridge, she gathered as many potatoes as she could carry and camped for the night by the next stream, where she roasted them all and dined on lenitrus.

However, in her salad were a handful of small oval leaves that she thought were lesper, a familiar plant. Instead, they were a look-alike that contained a powerful tranquilizer. Before she put an ember from the fire into her little pot, she fell asleep and woke to drenching rain. Although she scrambled to protect the fire, she was too late. It had been extinguished. She broke down in tears. She had only a few days' supply of baked potatoes and no way to roast more.

Ansil came to her. "I'm sorry I didn't alert you. My focus was elsewhere."

Fern felt a twinge of betrayal. If only Ansil had warned her the rain was coming. She knew it was really her own fault, but couldn't she depend on him anymore? Even his companionship was faltering.

How could she start a fire? When she was a child, she'd tried rubbing two sticks together, but of course nothing came of it. She went to her library and consulted a scouting book. The next day, once things had dried out, she tried the method in the book but couldn't make it work. Maybe she lacked the right materials. She thought about going to Mt. Frustration to get fire, but it was so far away, she'd likely starve first.

Ansil said, "Would you like me to ask someone to come to you?" At first she welcomed the idea of having company. She thought about Alta, the fire maker, but Alta didn't wrashiru. "Can the fire maker of the sea village wrashiru?"

"Unfortunately, no."

"Is there anyone else who can make fire?"

"No one who can wrashiru."

Fern shook her head. "Only if someone could bring food, and they can't. They'd only starve with me." She lay on the ground and thought about giving up, letting her spirit depart. She imagined her body being absorbed by the soil beneath her.

"You will not starve, Fern. Just follow the water."

She could indulge in despair only so long. Neither body nor spirit were ready to give up. Fern dragged herself to her feet and went on, downstream, away from the White Mountain. She followed the rivulet until it flowed into another, then that one into a small river, and that river to a larger one. But she found no nut trees. She ate what she could, trying new things. Some sustained her, others added to her pharmacopeia. Her only hope was to reach the sea, where she was confident she'd find food. But she didn't know how far it was.

CHAPTER 19
BREAKTHROUGH

One afternoon, Fern slipped on a muddy bank and wrenched her right leg. Immediately, it went numb. When she tried to get up, it collapsed beneath her. She felt along the bones, desperately praying nothing was broken. The long bones seemed intact, but when she touched her knee, the nerves came alive and she writhed in agony. Movement made it worse. She forced herself to lie still, moaning out her anguish.

Once she mastered herself by deep breathing, she sat up and felt her foot. Touching her right ankle set off more waves of pain. She breathed deeply again, trying to meditate. Her heart raced. She thought of Ansil, but what could he do? Her mind reached out for Andli and felt a mantle of comfort settle about her. She was able to sit quietly for a while, gently massaging her leg, then the knee and ankle. Even gentle touch hurt terribly.

Calm yielded to panic. What if she couldn't walk? How could she reach safety? Was this the end? She would die here by this as yet un-named river. Why name it now? No one would know what she called it. She thought of the knowledge she'd accumulated on her journey, the herbs and seeds in her backpack that no one would benefit from, and her spirit rebelled. No! Death was unacceptable. She'd get back somehow, if she had to crawl. Or swim. She wished Andli were here, but Andli didn't wrashiru.

The pain faded to discomfort. She looked around. A dense grove of young trees surrounded her. She pulled herself up with one, but couldn't put weight on her right leg. She tossed her backpack down the slope, reached for the next tree, then the next, and hobbled from one to another.

One sapling she leaned on gave way with her weight, uprooted, and fell over. She rode its trunk to the ground slowly enough to protect her injured leg, then looked at the poor little tree in dismay. She apologized and thought of setting it back up, restoring its roots to the soil, but it had snapped in half and its life was over. Her eyes traveled along the shaft. About four feet from the break, the trunk made a Y. Apparently, at some time the top had broken off and two dominant branches each tried to grow into a new crown. She realized she hadn't killed the tree, after all. It had sacrificed itself for her. She thanked the tree profusely, broke off the branches above the Y, and fashioned herself a crutch.

Now she was able to make her way down to the stream. She gathered vegetation as she went, not for food, but for healing. She filled her water bottle and chose a comfortable place to spread her blanket. From her backpack, she chose seeds that she knew had a pain-relieving ingredient. She crushed them with her mortar and pestle and swallowed the bitter paste. Then she scraped the mud off her legs, crushed the leaves she'd collected, folded them into the mud, and plastered her knee and ankle. She covered the poultice with the remains of her socks, then lay back to rest, thinking how Doran and Andli would be proud of her.

Only now did she summon Ansil. "Do you have any other suggestions?"

"Would you like a healer to wrashiru to you?"

Fern thought. "I think I've done all a healer could do. It was almost like Andli was here advising me."

"She was."

Fortunately, the night was warm and dry. Fern dreamed of gentle fingers running up and down her leg, absorbing the pain. The fingers settled on her knee, touching places too painful to touch herself. She felt them knit the tiny fibers in her knee. She relaxed. The fingers moved down to her ankle and foot, knitting, caressing. Her dream ended in a wave of gratitude, and she fell into a profound sleep.

When she woke, the sun was up and the pain was gone. Gingerly, she crept to the water and bathed. Her leg felt sore only when she put pressure on it. She trimmed the ends of the crutch, smoothed the Y, and padded it with a ragged sock. Again she thanked the tree. She was now able to make her way downstream, pausing frequently to rest, practicing her healing meditation each time. She found a clump of ahnti and, although she couldn't make a proper tea, she put a few leaves in her bamboo, confident the necessary elements would seep into the water.

When walking became too painful, she stopped for the night and took a sedative. In the morning, she recalled no dreams but was able to use the crutch as a walking stick. By the fourth day, she dispensed with it entirely. She laid it on the riverbank, almost reverently, and said, "Tekuy-ate. You have served me well. I'll name this the River of Gratitude."

As she followed the river, Fern sensed a presence, not of Ansil or her friends far away, but of something here in the valley. She looked at the trees shading her path and the water singing in the river and recognized she was among friends.

Late one the afternoon, Fern heard a reverberation and found herself at the confluence of two rivers. The soil here was rich and bountiful with edible plants. She camped for the night but didn't sleep well due to a late thunderstorm and lack of good shelter. In the morning, she counted her nuts—only four left. All were in some stage of sprouting. She ate one and debated what to do with the others. They wouldn't keep long once they sprouted. "Ansil, what should I do?"

"Why don't you go for a swim?"

"Why, do I smell bad?"

"You probably do, but I can't tell."

She waded into the River of Gratitude. The water, warm and soothing, washed away the night's filth and fatigue. She floated on her back and let sunshine filtering through the leaves caress her skin. The water seemed to soak into her pores and flow through her bloodstream. The stream carried her like a fallen leaf, turning, turning until it merged with the larger river, whose current swept her into the vegetation on the opposite bank. Reluctantly, she extracted herself and found the bottom with her feet.

Was that a flower beneath the water? Diving under, she found a bed of ostrica! She plucked one and it immediately closed into a tight nut. After gathering a few more she returned to where she'd left her things. She thanked the river for the oyster flowers and asked the ostrica for permission to eat them. Then she asked Ansil to open them for her.

After a few minutes, he said, "I cannot. My focus on this world is turning and my powers are diminishing. You'll have to open them yourself."

Dismayed, she sat and concentrated on the oysters, but they wouldn't open. She carried one back into the water, but it wouldn't open there, either. She tried crushing one between rocks, but either it was too tough, or she was too weak. If she had fire, perhaps she could roast them, but she didn't have fire.

Finally, she set them down and went in search of food on land. She found some lenitrus and ate her fill, but it didn't satisfy her hunger. She looked at the ostrica she'd gathered. Food, but she couldn't eat it.

She picked up the last three nut sprouts and held them in her hands. When would she find another source of sustenance? She was hungry enough to devour all three, but then what? Starvation would only be delayed, not avoided. She looked around at the woodland. This looked like the kind of place nut trees liked to grow. The ones that had nourished her on her long trek came to mind. Many had been planted by the weka, but she was the first person to come to this valley. Wouldn't it be nice for those who came later to find nut trees?

Fern closed her eyes and listened to the wind in the trees and the sounds of the river. There were no birds chirping, no insects or frogs or squirrels. She raised her eyes and looked about. Such a pleasant place, anyway. "I wish I could come back here someday." Hunger threatened to consume her. "Ansil, what should I do?"

"That's for you to decide."

Still she hesitated, waiting for the salad to digest, hoping her hunger would ease. As she sat on the ground holding the sprouts, she felt the rich bottomland soil beneath her and almost sensed tendrils growing out from her legs, reaching into the soil, rooting her to the spot. The breeze gently dried her skin and she could feel the air enter her pores and fill her lungs. Sunlight slipped among the branches and warmed her.

With a sigh, she rose to her feet, went among the trees, and buried the nuts in three places among the leaf litter. On her knees before the last one, she silently blessed them and asked them to grow well here. She imagined a trio of little voices expressing their happiness. She felt, rather than heard, a deeper voice welcoming her, accepting her as one of its own. She felt completely at peace.

When she returned to the river bank, she sat and cradled an oyster in her hands. If she couldn't open them, she should put them back in the water where she found them. She closed her eyes and imagined what life must be like for an oyster flower living in the river. The ostrica in her mind opened like a lotus. Pop! She looked down at her hands—the one she held had opened! Gratefully, she savored it. "Thank you, Ansil."

"I didn't do it. You did."

But how? She picked up another and thought about putting it in the water. Nothing happened. She imagined it living in the water, spreading its petals to the mineral-rich current. Pop—it opened. It was so simple! All she had to do was to think like an ostrica. She feasted, then rested, satisfied in both body and soul.

Before evening, she made herself a shelter and gathered more ostrica. "How did they get here?" she wondered. "I thought they only grew near the sea."

"This place must have been near the sea at one time," Ansil said.

She remembered Doran's explanation years ago of how earthquakes could cause downhill places to go uphill. She camped here for a few days, dined on oysters, made new sandals, and mended her body as well as her belongings.

One evening, emerging from her library, she thought she smelled salt air. A wave of nostalgia washed over her. She closed her eyes and recalled the salty breeze from the Atlantic Ocean. The pleasant memory of her visit at the village of the sea people rose in her mind. She imagined she sat on the shore of the sea. Out in the water, fire exploded into the sky and the wind carried the smell of brimstone. She sprang to her feet but the ground beneath undulated, throwing her off balance. She fell into herself and woke from the vision.

She was safe, in a little forested valley between two rivers. She'd witnessed part of the history of this place, of the upheaval that had removed it from the sea but allowed the oyster flowers to flourish far from their original home.

* * *

The small moon had passed full three times since the Feast of the Full Moons. Fern estimated it must be Thanksgiving. Sadly, she was unable to project herself to be with her family. "Ansil, is Tiril still in contact with my sisters?"

"Yes, and he's been invited to eat Thanksgiving dinner with them again."

"Ask him to tell them I said hello and I love them. Wait—what was I thinking? Tell *him* I said hello."

"Should I tell him you love him?"

"Sure." When was Tiril coming home?

Ansil told her the ostrica didn't keep well, so before she left camp, Fern gathered enough to last one day. Then she followed the Oyster River, as she named it, downhill toward the sea, eating well, until Oyster River spilled into a larger one which had no ostrica beds. Fern was tempted to go back upstream, but something compelled her to continue her course toward the sea.

CHAPTER 20
CAPTURE

One morning, Fern found a new plant whose leaves reminded her of a dandelion, so she gave it that name. "Ansil, are you familiar with this?"

It seemed to take forever before he replied. "No. I have not seen that plant before."

"Can you give me any advice?"

"Take a tiny bite and see what you think."

She sampled a morsel. The flavor was bitter-sweet. Before moving on, she took note of where and how it grew so she could find more if it proved edible. Hours later, when that nibble produced no adverse reaction, she ate a whole leaf. It actually soothed her hungry stomach. She wanted more, but stopped herself, just in case.

In the heat of the afternoon, thunder boomed in the distance. Fern found an overhanging rock near the river where she could shelter from rain. As she climbed the bank to the outcropping, she started to feel dizzy. *It must be the "dandelion!"* She tried to purge herself, but it was already digested. She set down her backpack and returned to the river to drink and fill her water bottle. Her disorientation intensified as she struggled back up to the overhang. She gripped the ground and crawled into the cleft, where she spread her blanket and tried to make herself comfortable.

What had she done? Was this plant lethal? Ansil had been no help. If she could mentally connect with Doran—but if she could, she would have done that before she ate the leaf. If he was unfamiliar with the plant, even he might not know of an antidote. She regretted not letting him into her mind more. If she had, he could have advised her many times on this journey.

Fern sat on her blanket and tried to meditate, to reach out to Doran. Mounting fear and panic prevented any such connection. She struggled to remain calm, knowing this was her best chance for survival. She attempted a healing meditation, imagining the cells in her body expelling the toxins, but she couldn't concentrate and became increasingly disoriented.

She began to fall over, and her head banged against the rock. All she could do was lie still and pray her body could take care of itself. Consciousness drained from her. She slipped into a dream. Unlike her ordinary dreams, this one was eerily real.

* * *

She stood on a sunny hillside meadow where wildflowers of many colors grew among the grasses. How long had it had been since she'd seen so many flowers? Fern could name only a few of them, but she breathed in their scents. Beyond the fragrance of the blossoms, she detected the earthy aroma of the soil. A butterfly landed on a daisy. Rejoicing, she began to gather a bouquet, dancing from one flower to another.

It was then that she noticed the color of her hands. They were no longer golden tan, but light brown. She lifted a sleeve. Her arm, too, was brown but not tanned. And what was she wearing? Not a tunic, but a dress, or robe of sorts, that fell to her feet. And shoes. She kicked them off and looked at her feet. They, too, were brown. The rocks and stems on the ground hurt, as though the soles of her feet had lost their toughness from years of going barefoot. Her free hand explored her head and found it covered by a scarf, which she loosened and let drop to her shoulders.

She caught a movement out of the corner of her eye. When she spun around, she saw nothing but the meadow and surrounding hills and woodlands. *What a strange dream.* A shadow glided across the meadow. She looked up to see whether it was a large bird or a small cloud.

That's when the dream morphed into nightmare. The clear blue sky pixilated. The fragments folded in on one another, the colors darkening as they fell, until they turned black and threatened to consume her. She averted her eyes from that terrible sky, crouched to the ground, threw her arms over her head, and tried to sink into the soil.

Something lifted her. Her feet left the ground. The flowers fell from her hand and the scarf from her shoulders. She shed her clothing, then her senses.

When Fern woke, the dream had not ended. It had merely begun. She lay on a pallet on the floor of a small, dimly lit room, covered by a blanket. Beneath it, she was naked. She lifted the blanket and looked at her body.

Instead of the young woman she'd grown into, she found the body of an adolescent girl. The breasts were small, the nipples no longer pale but a rich mocha. Further down, instead of red-gold pubic hair, she saw black down. When she tried to sit up, her hair pulled and she had to lift her hips to free it. She reached back to grab her hair, which had grown well below her waist. Not blonde—it was black!

Fern was surprised by the depth of shame and embarrassment that engulfed her. A previous experience came to mind, so many years ago but never forgotten, of waking naked in her mother's arms after their escape from the fire. This time, she lacked the comfort of her mother's embrace.

The heart within the chest pounded, tears washed from the eyes, and every breath released pitiful moans. Fern tried to shield herself from the confusion and terror that gripped this body. She struggled to separate the self she knew from the girl who inhabited it, but they seemed to be one entity. Years of mental training helped her dissociate her mind to some extent. She looked about the room. It was circular and, except for the pallet, it was empty. She could see no source of light, not even a door.

She stood up and pulled the blanket around her. Fern had never had a dream this real, or an etheric experience in which she had taken another body. Another personality wrestled for control, circling the room, banging on the wall, looking in vain for a door, then broke a fingernail trying to claw her way out. Fern tried to suppress the other, her confusion tinged with curiosity

The girl's emotional distress proved stronger than Fern's mind control. As captive in the body as in the room, Fern floundered in despair. She called for Ansil, but he failed to answer. Aloud, she cried out for Andli, Taran, Rina, Doran—all in vain. She collapsed to the pallet and clutched the blanket more tightly. In desperation, she shouted for Tira.

The wall opened to admit a middle-aged woman. Her brown hair framed a kind, if sad, face. There was something familiar about her, although Fern knew she had never seen her before. The wall closed behind her. The girl pulled the blanket up to her chin and the woman spoke to her in words she couldn't understand, but which had a hint of familiarity. Then words spilled out of the young girl's mouth which were entirely foreign to Fern.

The woman put her hand on her chest, looked into the girl's eyes, and said, "ForTaNin." Fern realized the woman was introducing herself and urged the girl whose body she inhabited to do the same. The girl put her hand on her chest and said, "Miri."

ForTaNin continued to talk in her strange language. Fern listened intently and caught snatches of words and phrases which sounded disturbingly familiar. Miri somehow got the message that this woman would take care of her. She began to cry again. ForTaNin sat beside her and laid a comforting arm around her shoulders while Miri wept.

Eventually, the sobbing subsided. The door slid open and someone handed ForTaNin a small bowl which contained a brown liquid. She tilted it to her lips and took a sip, then handed it to Miri, indicating she should drink. The girl hesitated, but Fern doubted it was anything harmful. Finally, Miri clutched the blanket around her and drank. The draught was more gelatinous than liquid and had a sweet, earthy taste. Almost immediately, it imparted a feeling of well-being.

The door reopened and ForTaNin exchanged the bowl for a small pile of cloth. Fern now took note of what the woman wore. She was dressed in pants that reached just below her knees and a shirt with sleeves that barely covered her elbows. The fabric was bright green with a small pattern of many colors.

Miri blushed to see a woman dressed like a man. The clothing in For-TaNin's hands was similar, but the background was red. Miri protested and hid her eyes behind the blanket. Surely she was not expected to dress so immodestly. But she offered no resistance when the woman pulled the shirt over her head and threaded her arms through the sleeves as though she were dressing an infant. ForTaNin took away the blanket and had Miri step into the pants. Finally, she slipped some soft shoes onto the girl's feet.

The door opened and ForTaNin stepped out into a larger room where there were several people, all dressed in similar colorful pants and shirts. When Miri realized some of these were men, she shrank back. ForT-aNin took her hand to lead her through the door, but Miri objected. She couldn't go out among those strangers—those men—with her skin exposed like this. She picked up the blanket and draped it over her head and around her body, covering as much as she could. Only then would she step across the threshold.

ForTaNin led her around the room, but both Fern and Miri were too overcome to pay attention to what the woman tried to show them. The room was round, with a domed ceiling, and glaringly white. On the wall in one area were shiny silver shapes totally unfamiliar to Miri but which Fern suspected were plumbing fixtures. There was no furniture, only several pallets lining the walls. Miri kept her head down and carefully made no eye contact with any of the men, but she couldn't help glancing at their bodies and those of the immodestly clad women. She was fascinated by the colors of the clothing. The people themselves were also of many colors. One young man had golden hair and one woman was very dark, with black, wooly hair.

Fern suspected ForTaNin was introducing Miri to the other people, but she didn't understand the language. She caught a few words, but not enough for full comprehension. Finally, with an even sadder expression and a tone of apology, ForTaNin said something to Miri and disappeared through a door, leaving Miri in the care of a strange woman. Although the woman smiled and acted friendly, Miri turned away and, unable to find the door to the room where she'd been, sat against the wall on a pallet and pulled the blanket over her head.

While Miri peered out from the edge of the blanket, trying to understand what had happened to her, Fern puzzled over finding herself in another's body. She retained all the memories of Fern but seemed to have added the memories of the girl Miri—of a life that must have been on Earth, of people who were dear to her, parents, brothers, and sisters. Miri began to cry quietly, hiding behind her blanket.

Poor Miri. She had unaccountably been snatched from all that was familiar and thrown, naked and alone, into this strange place. This was the second time Fern had been snatched from home to the unfamiliar. At least she had kept her own body the first time, and her mother was with her for a while. Miri had no one. Fern tried to comfort her. She tried to summon Ansil, but he failed to answer. She wished she could contact Taran. Perhaps he could explain this.

Miri heard a rustle of activity and looked up to see a door slide open and admit a small man with gray hair. Voices rose in greeting as he smiled and spoke to everyone. Miri huddled beneath her blanket again.

Fern felt a presence. Miri looked up and found the old man gazing into her eyes with a grave expression, no longer smiling. Fern knew she'd never met him before, but she felt she knew him, and he made Miri feel safe.

He sat facing her and gently held her hands. Without words, he let her understand that her life had changed forever and there was nothing anyone could do about it. Although he offered no hope that she would ever return home to her loved ones, he assured her that no one here would harm her, and that she was among those who would be her friends. He spoke his name to her, "ElSoDan." She nodded and said, "Miri."

ElSoDan took Miri's hand and helped her to her feet. He led her to a part of the wall where she could see a faint line indicating a door. In the center was a small red area with a yellow and orange design. He pointed to her sleeve and she saw that it was the same pattern as on her clothes. When he touched the spot on the door, it opened to reveal her room. "Thank you," she said in her language. With a little bow, ElSoDan left her alone. She lay on the bed and cried herself to sleep.

While Miri slept, Fern dreamed. Or had she come back to herself? It was hard to tell. She was in the forest again, sitting at a campfire. It was night and there was no moonlight. Ansil sat across from her.

"What happened?" she asked.

"I don't know. I wasn't privy to your thoughts."

"That 'dandelion' must be a psychedelic drug. I'm not dead, am I?"

He laughed and shook his head.

She told him about her experience.

"What do *you* think happened?" he asked.

She shuddered. "I think I dreamed about the thortle world. But why was I in another body?"

"Perhaps if you explore it more you'll find out."

As the scene faded, she remembered she had lost her fire some time ago and hadn't seen Ansil since he died.

* * *

Miri woke when the door opened to admit ForTaNin, who beckoned Miri to accompany her. Miri grabbed the blanket. People gathered in the middle of the room around a cart which held a large pot of porridge. Miri was hungry. ForTaNin tugged at her arm and led her to one of the shiny protuberances on the wall. When ForTaNin turned a lever, water came out. She bent over and showed Miri how to drink from it. Then she washed her hands and insisted Miri do the same.

Miri understood why she had to wash when they returned to the food. There were no spoons. The thick porridge was scooped into bowls, and the people ate it with their hands. Although Miri was appalled, she was hungry, and there was nothing else she could do. As they finished eating, everyone washed their hands again.

After Miri ate, she felt urgency in the lower part of her body and wondered how to ask ForTaNin where the privy was. She looked around the room. Near the water place, a woman pulled down her pants and squatted on the floor. Others stood nearby, women and men alike, but none averted their eyes. Miri did, long enough for the woman to finish, then she glanced up to see her wash her hands. When the yellow-haired man lowered his pants to urinate, Miri turned her back.

Fern felt Miri's distress. She was also amused, remembering her own reactions when she was new to her adopted world.

Miri licked the porridge from her hands but didn't venture near the water place. ElSoDan entered the room. He stood silently before Miri and she understood that she could now wash. He accompanied her to the water place. After she'd washed, both the woman she'd seen relieving herself and the yellow-haired man approached Miri.

Fern caught the words, "Estut miryit."

Miri seemed to understand this was an apology. She didn't want to look the man in the eye, especially because she'd seen him indecent, but she couldn't help herself. He had the most beautiful eyes she'd ever seen, as blue as the sky.

Then the women stood in a semicircle around the place with their backs to Miri and the men went to the other side of the room, also facing away. Using gestures, ForTaNin showed Miri how to use the latrine, which was a hole in the floor through which the waste fell. Afterward, she showed Miri how to rinse around the hole to clean the area.

After Miri washed her hands, a door slid open. Even Fern, who had an idea of where she was and thought she knew what to expect, was totally unprepared for what happened next. Something came through the open door.

Before Fern's mind could register what she saw, Miri threw herself into a frenzy of hysterics, shrinking into her blanket, gripping it about her head, as though it could save her. Only when Miri fell to the floor, shaking, and dropped the blanket, could Fern see through Miri's eyes.

A sight from a horror film loomed over her—the face of a giant insect, huge eyes rotating on short eye stalks, mandibles opening and closing, emitting metallic sounds. Then worse—an arm with the hydraulic motion of a spider's leg reached toward her. A claw clutched the blanket and snatched it away. Fern's mental training failed her. She screamed, losing all rationality. Then the claw touched her arm. Miri fainted, and Fern with her.

They came to in the arms of ForTaNin. The creature had stepped back and ElSoDan was talking to it. Although his face looked serene and his voice was calm, Fern could feel anger emanating from him. ForTaNin held Miri closely, rocking her and humming softly until she stopped shaking.

ElSoDan came to Miri and mentally assured her that the beast would not harm her. They helped her stand up and, holding her arms out, turned her around slowly while the demon examined her. Then it turned and left the room. When Miri saw many legs moving underneath the robe it wore, she vomited.

CHAPTER 21
MEMORIES OF THE THORTLE WORLD

Fern woke sobbing. It took several minutes before she realized where she was and that she was safe. She huddled under the rocky ledge in the morning sun. She could sense Ansil's presence but could no longer see him. Other than nausea, the effects of the drug seemed to have passed, but terror and sorrow still shook her. She was unable to talk for a long time.

When she tried to tell Ansil about the experience, she was thrown back into horror and confusion. She chewed on an ahnti leaf to compose herself so she could go on.

"Why would I have a dream like that? Do you think it was a flashback to a former life?" She took several deep breaths. "Is it possible I once lived on the thortle world? That girl Miri…was that me?"

"It's very likely."

Fern took a sip of water. She tried to hold back tears, but the ahnti, wise medicine that it was, released them anyway. Once she was calm, Fern recalled a conversation she'd had with Lila. "ElSoDan—wasn't that Taran's name in a previous life?"

"Yes. Perhaps you'll remember more and all will become clear."

"I don't want to remember more! Now I understand why you all don't like to talk about it." She couldn't bring herself to say the words "the thortle world." Her earlier image of the thortles, from Tira's descriptions, had in no way prepared her for the impact of that encounter. The feeling of dread she'd experienced during her last months on Earth hung over her, heavier than ever. "Now I understand why I was so terrified of the stars. I was afraid of going back there again." She was careful not to gather "dandelion" again, or anything that resembled it.

As Fern made her way downriver that day, she tried to put the memories of Miri out of her mind, but they kept crowding in. She picked only vegetables she knew were edible and grazed as she walked, but found no nuts or oysters. She thought about climbing over one of the ridges flanking this valley but lacked the energy. Besides, she despaired of finding nuts in neighboring valleys. She hoped to reach the sea, where she might find ostrica, before she succumbed to starvation. She wondered what it felt like to starve to death. Was it painful? Maybe she'd just drift away.

Did some dandelion residue remain in her body? In the heat of the afternoon, when she stopped to rest and meditate, she found herself back in Miri's world.

* * *

Confined to her little room and the large common room, neither of which had windows, Miri couldn't tell day from night. Though the light was sometimes muted, it was never dark.

When one of those demons came into the large room, Miri cringed, warily watching its movements. Through Miri's eyes, Fern watched with cagy fascination. Taller than any man, the thing had a large ant-like head, no visible ears, and eyes set on protuberances that swiveled to give it a view in all directions. And the mouth! The "jaw," always in motion, worked sideways, producing metallic noises that shivered through Miri's nerves. Hard bodied like an insect, its movements were the creepy motion of a spider. For Fern, Tira's description—a cockroach as big as she —was benign by comparison.

Most of its body was covered by a richly colorful robe, but beneath the fringe, eight legs were visible, feet shod in shiny slippers. On its "chest" was a metallic breast plate, blazoned with boldly colored symbols. Each of its four "arms" ended with three pair of jointed opposing "fingers" which showed astonishing dexterity.

Outwardly, the other people showed no fear of the beast, but vibrations Fern received from them were of hyper-vigilance tinged with hate. She wondered how anyone could get used to such an abomination.

Another kind of creature sometimes came in. In no way was it as frightening, but Miri was alarmed the first time she saw one. It scuttled in on all fours like a friendly dog, its body soft and furry, with a cat-like face. It sought attention from the people and, when it spotted Miri, it galloped over to her and rubbed against her thigh. Miri shrieked when it touched her, but the animal turned on its back and almost purred. Its upturned feet resembled hands. Someone called and it crossed the room to lap up food that had spilled on the floor. Later, more of them came in, carrying rags, brushes, and small containers, and proceeded to clean the rooms.

Eventually Miri learned the ways of these people. ForTaNin began to teach her the language. The large room was called the sameg. She told Miri that the creatures had a name for her, JinKaJin, which was a number. ForTaNin said that among the people she could continue to be known as Miri, but to the creatures, and in their presence, she would have to answer to JinKaJin.

* * *

Fern came out of the trance, still shuddering from the appearance of the thortle but amused by the memory of the cleaning creatures. How many kinds of captives did the thortles have? She wondered what world the cleaners came from. Fragments of Miri's memories told her that she liked them, treated them like pets.

She summoned Ansil and told him about the vision. She said, "Now I understand why I had so much trouble learning Human Talk. The first time I learned the language, I was emotionally shattered."

"That could explain it," he said.

Although Fern was very careful of what she ate, she continued to experience hallucinations the dandelion had triggered. These came when she was at her weakest, in the hot afternoons or early evenings when she most needed rest. She couldn't forego sleep or meditation, so she learned to accept them and watch Miri's life play out in her mind.

* * *

Miri once had a brother with whom she was so close they knew each other's minds and could talk without words. They never told anyone else about this. ElSoDan reminded her of this brother because they could communicate in the same way. He tried to explain to Miri what had happened to her. He told her they were no longer on Earth and put a picture into her mind of a large metal building flying through the sky. She couldn't believe this. It wasn't possible. Fern knew ElSoDan was telling the truth, but such a thing was beyond the girl's comprehension.

Miri hoped to find a way to escape, to get back home. She watched the door through which people and creatures came and went. It had a black and white symbol but when Miri touched that spot, nothing happened. Since she couldn't open the door, she waited for an opportunity to slip through it. When she finally got her chance, the room she entered was full of demons. Miri rushed back into the sameg before the door closed again.

One day, the yellow-haired man took Miri by the hand. She was uncomfortable with this familiarity, but ForTaNin told her to go with him, that he wouldn't harm her. He led her through the door with the black and white symbol and into another room full of huge objects made of metal. To Miri, these were strange and unfamiliar, but Fern recognized them as some sort of machinery.

The man showed Miri around the room and tried to tell her what the things were and what their purpose was. Fern understood, better than Miri did, that this was communications equipment. Miri was ashamed to be alone with the yellow-haired man, but he made no inappropriate advances. He sat down on a rug in front of a bright square and motioned for her to sit beside him.

On the square were shapes Miri had never before seen. Fern recognized the written language of the thortles. The man looked intently at the square, then leaned back and indicated that Miri should do the same. That made her dizzy. The man reached for her hand and she held onto him to steady herself. The square seemed to draw her into itself and she couldn't look away.

Fern became aware of another mind touching Miri's. Miri was frightened, and Fern recoiled from the contact. She withdrew into herself and let the other mind assure Miri it was all right. After a while, the mind released Miri. The yellow-haired man squeezed her hand and the square went blank. The man smiled and said, "You did well."

One of the demons came into the room and the man stood up to talk to it. After the creature left, the yellow-haired man took Miri back to the sameg.

ForTaNin explained to Miri what happened. She had been chosen for her ability to talk without words. Everyone had work to do. ForTaNin's job was to teach Miri the language. The yellow-haired man's job was to teach Miri how to communicate with others far away. Once she was properly trained, Miri's job would be to send and receive messages with her mind. "I will teach you to read the symbols, then you will be able to do your job. It's not hard work." Fern realized Miri was illiterate.

Neither Miri nor Fern were sure what ElSoDan's job was, but everyone seemed to hold him in high esteem. He was absent for long periods of time, but Miri didn't know where he went. One day, amid a loud cry of alarm, ElSoDan suddenly materialized. Everyone crowded around him. He appeared to be naked except for a red loincloth.

With horror, Fern saw it was not cloth but blood and guts spilling out of his abdomen. He held his belly with both hands and Miri felt energy sucked from her as he struggled to master his body. Then he shook his head and, with a sad smile, he looked at his friends and died.

"What happened?" Miri asked ForTaNin. "Did the creatures do this?"

ForTaNin shook her head. No, not their creatures, some other kind. The cleaners came to remove the body and clean up the blood.

Miri retreated to her room to cry. She sensed a presence and ElSoDan spoke into her mind. He told her his job was to carry messages in person, but this message had not been well received. Someone or something had taken a weapon and slashed his belly open. He'd tried to escape but didn't have enough warning. Now he was at peace, he said, and he would see her again in another lifetime.

Fern returned to herself, grieving for ElSoDan. Once her tears dried, she told Ansil, "It appears ElSoDan could wrashiru, but it didn't save his life. It's a shame. I liked him." Miri's grief for ElSoDan lingered. He was a friend, a teacher, someone she trusted completely.

The next day, as Fern walked along the river, she found herself still mourning for ElSoDan. She stopped and shook her head. The man had lived long ago. He was not real to Fern like he had been to Miri. Why did she miss him so? She recalled ElSoDan's message to Miri, that he would see her again, in another lifetime.

"Taran!"

Ansil's replay was tinged with amusement. "What?"

"ElSoDan—I haven't lost him! He's still with me. Now he's Taran." She wished she could reassure Miri. If she went back to that world again, she would try. Now she understood why she had trusted Taran from the beginning. But why did Miri trust him so? Fern let her imagination regress in time. She found no memories, only a certitude that Miri had known ElSoDan/Taran in a previous life. She was glad Miri had his friendship and guidance for the short time she did. It was a comfort to her.

Later, after more thought, she asked Ansil, "I wonder how they got Miri on their spaceship? Her experience was similar to what I remember when I wrashirued here, but not exactly. Hers was more unpleasant."

"They probably used forced wrashiru."

"Forced?"

"We don't do it, but I understand it was done on the thortle world. On their ships."

"How? I mean, if you all couldn't get me back to Earth, how could they get Miri to leave?"

"There were things done by our people on the thortle world that we don't do here."

She remembered Metia saying as much. "I wonder who forced Miri? ForTaNin?"

"I can't answer that. I don't know Miri's mind."

That night, when Fern visited her library, she imagined the long, carpeted hallway as usual, but halfway down she saw a doorway she'd never noticed before. She went in and found another library. When she opened a book, it turned into a screen with writing in Human Talk. "Ansil, what's this?"

"This is the common library of our world. Here, you'll find our literature, translations from other languages, and some writings brought here from the thortle world."

She was able to make out the meaning of a few words. "Miri was illiterate. She had no idea what those symbols were." Fern looked at the writing again and was surprised that, with some effort, she could read it. She recognized the "Song of Moses and Rila" that Tiril had recited in English so long ago, but this was in Human Talk, and she could not only read, but understand it. "Miri must have learned to read," she said. "And tapping into her memory, her knowledge has somehow come into mine."

Fern scanned the shelves and found a collection of Hannah's poetry as well as books by people she'd heard of only in stories. There were even works by Taran. Discovery of this new source of reading material sustained Fern for several nights.

But in her waking hours she struggled to stay alive. She felt herself weakening and had to stop more frequently to rest. At such times, she'd take refuge in one library or the other.

By now, Fern was able to roughly correlate her days with those on Earth, but without being able to project herself there, she couldn't be certain. After studying the calendar in her library, she summoned Ansil. "It must be close to Christmas."

"I believe so."

"Does Tiril have any news of my family?"

"No. He has finished college and is coming home."

"He's coming home?" When would she be able to see him? If she could reach the sea alive, she would find food. Then she could follow the shore to the sea village. Perhaps she'd find him there. But it was such a long way.

Starvation and weakness hindered her concentration and made it difficult to read. At such times, Miri's memories would intrude.

* * *

There was too much idle time for Miri's comfort. She had been used to working many hours every day, but here, only a small part of each day was spent in work. All their needs were furnished and they didn't even have to clean up after themselves. Miri's fingers ached for handiwork, but no materials were available.

Most people sat around talking every day and occasionally they'd burst out in song. One time, a woman began drumming on a dish the cleaners had overlooked. A couple got up and began to dance. Others joined them. The yellow-haired man smiled and extended a hand to Miri, but she shook her head and retreated to her room.

The yellow-haired man taught Miri to record messages she received by pushing little buttons. The content of the communications confused her. She didn't know some of the words and when she asked him, the yellow-haired man said she didn't need to know what they meant. Her job was only to send and receive them. Eventually, Miri was able to distinguish among the minds she communicated with. One told her his name was JonRilJin.

Miri asked ForTaNin about the strange words. She explained that they were in a great machine traveling among the stars, on their way to another world, the one where the creatures lived. The next time she exchanged messages with JonRilJin, she asked him about this. Yes, he said, he lived on the creature's world and she was coming to him. Now she had no choice but to believe. Miri lost hope of ever going home or seeing her family again. There was no word in the new language for home.

Out of curiosity, Fern tried to learn as much about the spaceship as she could, but she was limited by Miri's memories.

Although Miri had her own bedroom, others slept in the sameg. The first time she found ForTaNin sleeping on a pallet by her door, she asked why she didn't have her own room. ForTaNin told her that only women of childbearing age had their own rooms.

One day, the yellow haired man came into Miri's room. He sat on her pallet and talked softly. She wouldn't let him touch her. More than ever, she was afraid to be alone with him, but when they were in the message room together, he treated her like a sister.

Fern was curious to see how this played out. The man was handsome, and nice, and Miri was attracted to him. But she didn't want to mate with him. He came into her room many times and Miri understood what he wanted, but she wouldn't let him touch her. She tried to get ForTaNin to move into her room with her, but the older woman shook her head and said the creatures wouldn't approve. Fern was relieved the man didn't force his affections on Miri.

Fern told Ansil, "I'm learning a lot about myself from Miri. Some of my hang-ups were carried over from her life. Like my siderophobia, and my resistance to learning Human Talk. My modesty, too, I guess. One thing that I don't understand, though, is why I only want guys who are unavailable to me. When I first came here, all the boys in the village, except Tiril, were attracted to me. And in the village by the sea, all of them except you, but I didn't want any of them. I only wanted the ones I couldn't have. Look at that blonde man. I don't even remember his name. He was good looking, and nice, but Miri didn't want him. Why?"

"Fern, don't forget, I was available."

"But I couldn't share a husband with Tira. Maybe there's something from a life before Miri that affected us both. Will I ever know?"

He had no answer.

CHAPTER 22
RESCUE

By now, Fern's clothing was unwearable, so she walked naked, wearing only Metia's necklace. She thought about putting it in her backpack for safe-keeping, but the blue stone hanging against her heart gave her comfort. She'd mended her blanket so many times it looked like a ragged patchwork quilt. When the sun was high she'd throw it over her shoulders to protect herself from sunburn. She'd lost so much weight, her bones began to show. She kept walking because it was her only choice. Even reading in her library had become too much effort. She found peace only in meditation.

She told Ansil, "When I'm meditating, it's so pleasant, I want to stay there all the time. I'm tempted to just slip from this world to the next. Would I find you there?"

"Perhaps, but there's no guarantee we'd be in the same house."

She sighed. No, she wasn't ready to abandon herself to that realm. She had unfinished business. She thought about her little sisters. Despite the impossible separation, she still felt responsible for them. Also everyone on this world who loved her and would miss her. She had a responsibility to them, if only to carry her knowledge and seeds back to them. She hoped to live long enough to return.

For so long, Fern had found barely enough food to sustain her. She no longer felt hunger, only a vague plea from the tissues of her body. There came a morning when she was so weak her backpack was too heavy to carry. She thought about discarding it, but that would end the fragile connection she held to life and hope. She set aside her mortar and pestle and thought of keeping only what she considered most essential. But first, she must rest. She'd had the long night to sleep, but perhaps a little nap would help. Would she die in her sleep?

Ansil said, "No, Fern, you are not going to die yet. You have a long life ahead." So she rolled herself up in her blanket and lay down.

This sleep proved unusually refreshing. She dreamed she had skri. She lifted the biscuit to her mouth. At first, it had no taste, but she chewed anyway. As her taste buds awakened, she savored it and wanted more. Another appeared in her hand and she ate that, too. When she woke, her belly felt full and her strength had returned. She loaded her backpack and went on.

That day, when she stopped for rest in the heat of the afternoon, her stomach growled and demanded to be fed. She recognized this sensation —hunger—as a healthy feeling. She ate what lenitrus she could find and lay down for a nap. The dream came again. She ate two skri and a third came into her hand. Again, she woke with a full belly, but to her amazement, she still held a biscuit. "I guess I'm still dreaming."

"You're not dreaming," Ansil said.

She laughed and dove into the river, emerging refreshed. She banged her knee on a stone and knew for certain she was awake. When she returned to collect her belongings, the skri was still there! She picked it up, turned it in her hands, and tasted it.

"How is this possible?"

Ansil chuckled. "Do you remember how, when you brought your mother here, everyone marveled, because none of us had been able to transport another person or an object?"

"Yes, but I haven't been able to do that since."

"It seems you are able to do many things when the need is great enough."

She examined the skri. "Where did this come from? Did I just conjure it up?"

"It came from the hearth of the mountain village. Don't worry, they can spare it."

"But how did it get here? I didn't wrashiru, did I?"

"No. Conjure would describe it better. Somehow, you brought it to yourself. This is something new to us."

"New to me, too," she muttered.

Fern ate the skri later that day, but she was unable to bring any more that night. Not until the following night, when she was desperately hungry, did she get more. She woke, not only with a full belly, but with three extra skri.

The next night she dreamed she was in the mountain village. Andli was there, as well as Taran and Rina and Doran. Tira approached with a little girl who held a basket of skri in her chubby arms. Sita? How old was she now? The child filled Fern's hands and she woke the next morning with more bread than would fit in her backpack. She was obliged to eat the extra before resuming her journey.

That night, Fern had another dream. The blonde man from Miri's memory said, "You must come with me."

ForTaNin rushed up in tears and hugged her. "Goodbye. I will not see you again in this life."

The yellow-haired man took Miri and a few other captives to a room she'd never seen before. He told them to stand against the wall and one by one he fastened a net across them. "What's happening?" someone asked.

"We are going to another place," he said. "Do not be alarmed. Nothing will harm you." He stood against the wall and drew a net across himself.

A short time later, Miri felt movement, then her body rose and her feet left the floor. Only the net kept her from floating. Miri panicked. Other captives screamed, cried, moaned, or whimpered. The yellow-haired man said, "It's all right. It won't hurt you."

Fern realized she was weightless! She wanted to release the net and enjoy the experience, but she had no control over Miri's actions. The yellow-haired man talked to them in a soothing voice and explained what was happening. Miri understood his words, but the concepts were too foreign. To Fern, many of his words were unfamiliar, but she understood they were going to a different place.

Finally, Miri felt herself falling. She began to panic again, but as soon as her feet touched the floor, she breathed with relief. The yellow-haired man released them from the restraints and led them into a smaller room where they were crowded together. After the door closed, Miri felt a sensation of falling, then everything stopped. When the door opened, they were somewhere else. Miri's eyes darted about. *What sorcery is this?*

The thortles had elevators, Fern thought.

The yellow-haired man said, "Follow me." They walked down a long passage to a door that opened to sunshine and open air. Miri drew the sweet air into her lungs, hoping against hope that she was back home. But, no, the trees that arched over the path were unfamiliar, with leaves more orange than green.

Soon, Miri's chest began to hurt and her head ached. She gasped for air. When they entered another building and the door closed behind them, Miri could breathe again. The man said, "This is the end of your journey. You'll find life here more pleasant than it was on the ship." He held Miri's hands, kissed her on the forehead, said goodbye, and left. Miri never saw him again.

When Fern woke from this dream, she knew this had been Miri's last breath of fresh air, that for the rest of her life she was kept indoors.

* * *

When she meditated during the heat of the following afternoon, Fern had a new experience. A hard knot deep within that held struggle and despair suddenly exploded into joy. It rose inside her, filling her being, until it could no longer be contained, and spilled out into the universe. More flooded in to become a stream of ecstasy that flowed through her. She basked in this new-found joy and held it in her heart when she emerged from her meditative state.

After this, she knew instinctively which plants were edible and which weren't. She also knew what parts—leaf, stem, seed, or root—were easier to digest. That was fortunate because her supply of skri ran low again, and she got no more.

One morning, a roaring began in her ears and increased as she walked. Was this a symptom of famine? She was sure the lenitrus she'd eaten was safe. She had no choice but to press on.

The river valley narrowed to a gorge and Fern recognized the sound of a waterfall. There was no room beside the river to walk through the gorge, so she climbed the precipice beside it. Halfway up, she had to rest. She fell asleep and Miri entered her dreams.

This dream, though brief, related many events in Miri's life.

In the new place were many rooms, much larger, with pillars that held up ceiling arches. There were also more people, including children. Miri had her own small room. The latrines and washing places were in a separate room, giving them more privacy. Here, they had spoons to eat with. Some had homemade musical instruments, and the children had toys.

A man with blue eyes and reddish brown hair approached Miri and introduced himself as JonRilJin, the man with whom she had exchanged messages. She liked him from the start. They often sat together in the sameg to talk. He always treated her with respect. One day when JonRilJin asked to come into her room, she let him. They sat and talked. As time went on, she let him hold her hand. Before long, she let him put his arm around her and, eventually, kiss her. After this, he brushed and braided her hair every day.

Finally, she let him mate with her. After that he slept in her room. She was ashamed they didn't have a proper marriage, but what could she do? There was no priest. Even so, she was happy with him.

Fern woke, her body infused with a warm sensation that lasted until hunger once more took over. Finally, a pleasant memory from Miri. She had found love. Fern wondered if she herself would ever find such love. She stretched, collected her belongings, and climbed to the top of the ridge.

From there, she looked down the valley and wondered how far it was to the sea. A hundred yards below, the water fell into dense forest. This side was steeper than the other, too sheer for her limited alpine skills. How was she to get down? She surveyed the ridge for a gentle decline.

She stumbled across potato vines and dug a few. Although she had no way to cook them, perhaps she'd find another way to render them edible. She grazed on lenitrus on her way down. It was nearly dark by the time she reached the river again.

Her path had taken her far downstream and the sound of the waterfall was faint. She was disappointed. She wanted to see it up close, but it was unwise to turn back. Not only was she exhausted, she was lightheaded from hunger. She sat against a tree and picked up one of the potatoes. What if she soaked it in water, or beat it to a pulp? There must be some way. She drifted off to sleep.

Fern woke with burning hands. She dropped the hot potato and rushed to the water to cool her palms. Then she retrieved the tuber. It was still quite warm. "What on Earth?" she said in English.

"You forget, you're not on Earth," Ansil said with a laugh. "You transported it to a fire to bake. You should have been more careful when you brought it back."

"So I can send things, not just receive them?"

"Apparently."

She checked the other potatoes. They were unchanged. She ate the baked one and hoped to get more skri in her dreams, but none came. However, at midday, and again the next evening when she went to sleep, she held a potato in her hands, protected by a corner of her blanket, and each time she woke with a baked potato.

The following morning, she woke with a raw potato in her hands and the smell of smoke in the air. Fire! A forest fire—but where? She jumped up but couldn't tell the direction of the wind. She listened but could only hear the river. The river. She could always take refuge there. She collected her things and, in her haste, tore her blanket.

She paused. Why was she in such a panic? It was the smoke. Where there's smoke there's fire. Fire had been responsible for the major losses in her life, but fire had also been a friend, and panic was counterproductive. She took several calming breaths and headed downriver.

Walking became easier. There was almost a path by the river. Around mid-morning, she smelled smoke again. She waded out into the water and saw a small column of smoke rising above the trees. Too small for a forest fire. Weka? Excitement overcame her anxiety.

In a little glen beside the river, Fern found a small hut, a campfire, and someone leaning over the fire. Not an old person, but a young man. He stood up and turned. His hair fell to his shoulders and he had a short beard. His eyes—green like the sea. Then she beheld that grin, the one she'd so often seen when checking on her little sisters on Earth. The grin softened to a smile, and she rushed into Tiril's arms.

Her initial joy was tinged by embarrassment when she remembered she was naked. The embarrassment was tempered by shame because she was also scrawny, scratched, and scarred, and here he was in the vigor of young manhood. Yet he seemed happy to see her, and if he noticed her disarray, he gave no indication.

"Don't worry," she heard Ansil say. "He'll fatten you up."

Tiril turned his head and grinned. "Ansil," he said, "you may leave us now."

Ansil chuckled, and that was the last Fern heard from him. She could feel his withdrawal and knew she would miss him. But he had been fading for some time, his focus turning from this world. She was grateful he had stayed with her long enough to deliver her into Tiril's arms. She laid her head against Tiril's chest and shed a tear. His arms tightened around her.

After a few minutes, she pulled her tattered blanket around her and sat down.

"Are you hungry?" Tiril picked up a small pancake from a flat stone by the fire and handed it to her.

"Tekuyate." She tore into it before she remembered her manners. Too many years in the wilderness with only a disembodied spirit for company. She tried to eat more daintily. Then, with a thousand questions in her mind, she asked, "How did you get here?"

"From the sea village, I came by boat to the mouth of the river this one joins. I would have come to you sooner, but you kept changing rivers."

"You knew where I was?"

He nodded. "Ansil helped."

"Why didn't you wrashiru?"

"I wanted to bring you some things that I couldn't make in the wild." He reached into the hut and brought out a new tunic and a comb.

The tunic was Andli's handiwork and the comb was Rina's. Fern gathered them to her heart. "Tekuyate," she said, not only to Tiril, but also to her mothers far away. "I'm so glad you're here. You've saved my life."

Tiril baked another pancake for her and wrapped lenitrus in it. "No, you would have made it to the sea by yourself, and you'd have found your way to the village of the sea people. But you would have suffered needlessly, and you've accomplished what you set out to learn."

Yes, she had accomplished much, but what had she set out to learn? She still wasn't sure, but she was definitely ready to go home. The lenitrus-wrapped pancake was delicious, more so because Tiril had fixed it for her. She looked up at him. "I am so glad to see you."

He smiled.

Fern went down to the river, bathed, combed out her hair, and put on the new tunic. When she returned, Tiril had a bed prepared for her in the hut, a proper bed, fragrant, soft, and deep, with clean bedding. As she nestled into the mattress, she heard soft music. Tiril was playing a flute. She slept the rest of the day.

She dreamed of JonRilJin. He and Miri mated for life and neither took other mates. Together they had three children. Then there was another boy, a captive. He came to them frightened and missing his family. Miri and JonRilJin took him in and tried to comfort him. He kept saying he wanted to go to namai. At first she didn't know what he meant. Finally, she understood—he wanted to go home. She told him this was his new namai. No, he told her. Not namai.

Fern woke with a bittersweet yearning. Miri's adopted son had brought the word namai into Human Talk. She'd always liked that word. It was so unthortle-like. Now she knew why. She shifted her body, releasing the soft scent of the bedding. Only then did she remember where she was. She got up and joined Tiril by the campfire. They snuggled into each other's arms and she said, "I want to go to namai."

CHAPTER 23
NEWS FROM EARTH

Fern told Tiril about her life as Miri.

"I always suspected you had a bond with us. It's because you had a life on the thortle world. That's why you came here when you wrashirued."

"Could you have been JonRilJin in a former life?"

"It's possible. I remember fragments of previous lives on the thortle world, but I have no recollection of that one." He added another stick to the fire. "Tell me about your adventures on this world."

When she told him about the White Mountain and how much she wanted to go there but couldn't, he promised, "One day, you and I will go there together. That will be quite an adventure!"

A thrill crept up her backbone. She told him about the waterfall up-river. "I could have reached it by going back upstream, but I kept running out of food and didn't think I could spare the time."

His face brightened. "I'd like to see it myself. Let's go there before we head back to the sea."

"Tell me about your adventures on Earth."

He sat back. "I lived with John and Alice Devoir at first. They're a mixed couple. She was born on Earth and, when he visited, he fell in love with her. Since she couldn't wrashiru, he stayed and they got married and raised a family. They helped me learn the ways of your culture."

"Was it hard?"

"Yes, it was quite an adjustment. Just riding in a car was unnerving—going so fast, and those huge machines hurtling towards me at the same rate of speed! The first time, I was so scared I huddled down in the back seat and closed my eyes. The Devoirs laughed at me." He laughed.

"I had to work to pay for college. Some jobs went against what I'd lived by all my life, like flipping hamburgers and mowing lawns. Then I got lucky and joined a band, so I could make a little money as a musician. My best job was at a summer camp in the mountains. Once I learned about the local plants and animals, nobody could top my understanding of the wilderness."

"I bet. What about my sisters and grandparents? How did you get to know them?"

"I put myself in a position to meet them. I chose a college in their area and joined their church."

"And you coached softball."

He nodded. "That was fun. Believe it or not, my experiences here with games helped. Although softball is a competitive sport, I emphasized cooperation within the team and urged them to give encouragement to their opponents. I made sure the girls were rewarded as much for positive attitudes as for performance. This endeared me to your family. And, of course, my team excelled. When your grandparents noticed me at church, our friendship blossomed. They knew I was living away from home, so they 'adopted' me, invited me over for meals, and such. I went by the name Terrell on Earth, and they called me Terry."

Fern closed her eyes. She wished she could have been there. In a way she had been, through Tiril. "How are my sisters doing?"

"When I first met them, they were still grieving deeply. Over the years, I watched them heal. Your grandparents struggled at first, trying to get used to caring for two young children, but your sisters are good people, and they've been a comfort to your grandparents."

They talked late into the night. "Your grandparents treated me almost like a son, and your sisters said I was like a big brother to them."

Fern's heart swelled and she began to cry. "Your involvement with them may have helped them heal."

"I think so. I really like your family. It was hard for me to say goodbye."

"I know." Fern reached for Tiril and they hugged. She shared his pain of parting, perhaps for a lifetime, from those he'd grown to love.

When she was ready to go to bed, Tiril made himself a pallet by the fire. "You sleep in the hut."

"Tekuyate." She wasn't quite ready for more intimacy.

The following day, Tiril wouldn't let Fern help with chores. He encouraged her to rest and take nourishment. He went foraging and brought back succulent leaves which she crushed and mixed with ahnti leaves to make a salve for her skin.

They baked the potatoes she'd brought. "These are new to me," he said. "Good tasting, but puckery."

"Drinking water helps. Someday, I hope to find a way to fix them that'll reduce the puckeriness."

Over lunch, he told her more about his life on Earth.

"I studied music in college and participated in the music program at church. I learned to play every instrument I could get my hands on. Here, we're limited because we don't use metal, but who knows? Someday that may change. Anyway, I have lots of good ideas and learned new pieces we can play here." He smiled with modest pride. "I also translated some of our songs into English and published them. I had to take credit for composing them because I couldn't reveal their true origin. They caught on pretty well and I think they'll find their way into Earth's culture."

His face sobered. "Another thing I studied was American History, particularly the slave years. I was trying to find records of our First Father. That was difficult. Moses was a common name and we don't know the names of his owners or relatives. We don't even know which state he lived in. But I was able to do a lot of leg work. Now I know where to look for records. I mean to track him down."

Tiril picked up her comb. "Let's see what I can do with your hair." He combed and plaited it much like Andli and Rina used to, tying off each braid with bits of thread. "I always wanted to do this. Even before I left for Earth."

When he finished, Fern took the comb from him. "Now it's my turn."

As she teased out a snarl, Tiril said, "Before I left, I told your grandparents who I really am and where I'm from—ouch!"

"I'm sorry. You surprised me." She combed more gently. "Well, go on. Did they think you were crazy?"

"At first. They thought I was joking. I left it alone for a few days until they brought it up again. They had noticed I was rather naïve about some things most college boys know, and other things didn't add up. For instance, I was proficient in ballroom dancing but ignorant about video games. I told them a brief history of our people, and they began to wonder if I was telling the truth after all."

Fern finished his hair. Tiril felt his head and said, "Tekuyate. It's been a long time since I've had a proper hair-do. Come, sit down." He held her hand. "Once your grandparents half-accepted my story, I told them about you. They were stunned. They said your sisters believed you were still alive. They thought the girls were just in denial, that they couldn't accept the fact that you were really gone." He paused. "They have a friend in law enforcement who helped them get the sheriff's and fire inspector's reports from the house fire. Only one set of remains had been found."

"My father's."

He nodded. "The officials weren't able to account for that. For some reason, they didn't release that information to the family or the newspaper."

Fern shivered. "I'd always wondered about that."

"I think the police searched for you and your mother elsewhere, but of course, they couldn't find you, or any evidence you'd survived. Her wedding ring was found in the ashes, so they closed the case."

"Of course. It couldn't come with her when she wrashirued. I wonder what they did with it?"

"Your grandparents have it, and your father's. Everything else was put in an urn and buried. There wasn't much. The fire was very hot. I visited the grave. They put all three names on the headstone."

"I know. I saw it." Fern closed her eyes and let sorrow drain through her tears. "So, did you tell my sisters?"

"Yes. Your grandparents and I sat down with them and told them." He laughed. "Funny thing, your sisters often accused me of being from another planet! Still, they were surprised to learn it was true. Yet they weren't surprised that you are still alive. They said you visited them in dreams and told them about your life here. They wanted to know if you would come back. I told them I didn't know, that you'd tried to but weren't able to wrashiru. They also asked if I would come back again."

Fern drew a deep breath. Would she have to endure another long separation from Tiril? "What did you say?"

"I told them that if I did, it would be with you." He put his arm around her. "I also told them that when I came back here, I would ask you to marry me." He kissed her.

Instead of answering, Fern asked, "What kind of marriage do you envision for us?"

"I lived on Earth long enough to appreciate your ways. I'll be happy with any kind of marriage you are happy with."

"One mate?"

"Of course."

She kissed him back.

They went swimming during the afternoon heat. Fern was shy at first and hesitated to take off her clothes until she remembered this was the man she loved.

They sat on the bank to let their skin dry. Fern told Tiril about the ostrica she'd found upstream.

"Yes, there are beds of them at the mouth of this river. When I encountered real oysters on Earth, I guess I expected them to be plants, too. When I tasted them, it was quite a surprise."

As she wriggled into her tunic, Tiril said, "Your skin is already starting to heal."

"Yes, but I'm out of salve."

"I'll go collect some more. You stay here and rest."

Instead, Fern gathered more fragrant leaves and remade the bed in the hut, making it wide enough for two.

* * *

After breakfast the next morning, they combed and plaited each other's hair. Tiril massaged Fern's skin with salve. Her body also absorbed the love that emanated from his fingertips. "I didn't realize how much I missed human touch," she said.

"That's why the weka travel in pairs or threes."

She massaged his body in return.

"Mmmm. On Earth, I had people all around me, but no one to do this."

"They have people who do it for a living."

"But it's not the same."

Later, while foraging, Fern asked, "How did you get into college without school records?"

"It's difficult but not impossible to forge documents. My records reflected that I was born at home and home schooled. Both are true, of course. Once I adjusted to your culture, I was able to blend in, get a driver's license, go to college, and so on." He drew a deep breath and smiled. "But it's so good to be home."

"I wonder what people think became of you. After all, you've literally disappeared off the face of the Earth."

"I told everyone I was joining the Peace Corps. They can write to me at the Devoirs' and maybe I'll answer them, until they get tired of writing and forget about me."

"How could they forget you? I couldn't."

Together, they fixed lunch. When Tiril poured pancake batter, he said, "This is the last of our nuts. There are nut trees near the coast, but that's days away. Where did you find the potatoes?"

"They grow on high ground." After they ate, Fern took Tiril up a ridge to dig potatoes. "We'll take some back to the sea village," she said.

"If they won't grow at sea level, I bet they'll grow in the mountains. I've thought about combining mashed potato with the ingredients for skri, to see how that turns out."

"We'll have to try it when we get more nuts."

"Speaking of food, how did you like meat?"

He made a sour face. "I didn't."

"Now, I saw you eating fried chicken at a church picnic, and you seemed to be enjoying yourself."

"Yes, but that was special chicken I took to the picnic. I knew no one would think anything about it if I were a vegetarian, but I tried to eat meat to experience the whole of life on Earth. At first my body didn't recognize it as food. After I got sick a few times, Alice started buying meat from a small farmer. It was more expensive, but his animals were well cared for and not traumatized when they were butchered. I could tolerate that better. I think the animals' emotional state affects their meat. That's what I took to the picnic. Most of the time I ate meat substitutes. There's such a variety of foods on Earth, I understand why you thought our diet was boring when you came here." He smiled. "Your grandmother's food agreed with me pretty well, probably because she puts love into her cooking. It makes a difference."

"Yes," Fern said. "She does enjoy cooking. I'd never thought about it that way, but it's more than just food preparation. It's the spirit of the cooking. It's in keeping with how we do things here."

"I found it overwhelming to give thanks to everything, like we do here. Your old culture is so complicated. To give thanks over something as simple as a bowl of breakfast cereal, there are so many plants and animals and human workers involved, it would take longer to give proper thanks than to eat it! I finally followed your grandparents' lead and gave thanks to God. That seemed to cover everything."

That evening, they relaxed by the campfire. "It feels good not to have to hurry all the time," Fern said.

"Yes, it does. Life on Earth is rush, rush, rush. It's no wonder the people aren't very healthy." He poked the fire. "By the way, this will interest you. Your mother had psychic abilities."

"My mother?"

"Yes. Your grandmother told me. Your grandfather was quite surprised—it was news to him. Your grandmother said that when your mother was small, she would see things that no one else could. She saw colors in the air around people. She'd say things like, 'That man has black around him. I don't like him,' or 'That lady's sick. She's got puke around her.' She was normally shy, but sometimes she'd go up to a stranger and tell them about the pretty colors around them."

"Really?"

He nodded. "Your grandmother discouraged her and she stopped talking about it."

Fern shook her head. "Mama said she thought I had psychic abilities, but she never told me she did."

"She didn't remember. It was suppressed at an early age. Another thing, your mother had an uncanny ability to 'find' things that no one else could. Her parents suspected she hid things just so she could find them. But occasionally it was something she had no access to."

"Like what?"

"Once at a family reunion, a cousin had accidentally left her child's seizure medicine at home. Everyone was in a panic because it was the weekend and no one knew how to get it replaced. They'd flown in, so they couldn't just drive home for it. Your mother asked the child's parents to look in the suitcase again, and there it was! After everybody went home, the cousin called your grandmother and told her she'd found the child's vitamins on the kitchen table. She usually packed them with the medication and didn't understand why she took one and not the other. Your grandmother remembered this, because she thought it was very odd."

Fern had always known her mother was an amazing woman, but she hadn't suspected how amazing. Were her mother's psychic abilities more powerful than her own?

Tiril went on, "In light of all this, I now wonder who brought whom here. And that may explain why you haven't been able to wrashiru."

"Huh? I thought I brought my mother. That's what everyone told me."

"That's what your mother told us. You were unconscious when they found you, but she was awake. She said she'd been in bed asleep and heard you call her, but she couldn't wake up. You were pulling on her in a panic. She smelled smoke and realized the house was on fire, but she couldn't move. When you collapsed, she thought it was all over. The next thing she knew, both of you were here. She told us you had brought her, and with no evidence to the contrary, we accepted that."

Fern was stunned. "So she saved my life, not the other way around."

"Maternal protectiveness is one of the most powerful forces in the universe. What I think happened is that both of you combined your latent talents and accomplished it together. You have a strong inclination for protectiveness yourself. Both of you are amazing women."

CHAPTER 24
FULFILLMENT

Although Fern was happy with Tiril, she became restless. She'd grown accustomed to being always on the move. When the small moon was full again, they decided to visit the waterfall. While packing for the trip, Fern removed her collection of herbs and seeds from her backpack and stored them in the hut. There, she uncovered a cache of skri. "Where did this come from?" she asked. "Did you bring them with you?"

Tiril looked puzzled. "No, of course not. I ate what I brought long ago. You must have brought them."

"How do you figure that?"

"You don't remember procuring some from the mountain village?"

"Yes, but then I lost the ability and couldn't get more."

"Apparently you still can. These'll come in handy. We can get there faster if we don't have to climb to dig potatoes."

"But my mind throws up blocks against this sort of thing. I'm afraid I won't be able to get any more, now that I know I've done it."

"Yes, you will. I'll help you unlock your mind."

That evening, they sat together in a meditative state. Tiril accompanied Fern to the virtual corridor that led to her libraries. A third doorway appeared. Fern hesitated until she felt Tiril's presence beside her. Then she opened the door and they stepped through.

On a table in the center of the room, Fern found a display of "tools." One was in the image of a skri. She picked it up and tasted it. It seemed so real. She chewed and swallowed. As she ate it, she understood this represented her gift of procurement. Nearby was a bowl of tea. She sipped from it and found her ability to heal herself. She drank deeply and felt threads of mending weave through her body. Next was a set of wings. This puzzled her. She looked at Tiril. "Surely I can't fly."

He chuckled. "Not physically, but you can travel by ethenos."

Should she try them on? She only held them in her hands and closed her eyes. Her imagination soared and she knew she hadn't lost that power after all. When she laid down the wings, beside them appeared a leaf of ahnti. She stroked it and connected with her budding ability to commune with plants.

She picked up a pair of eye glasses, which held the gift of seeing into the future, but she laid them down with trepidation. Sometimes it was better not to know. There were a few other tools she could explore later, when she was ready. But something was missing. "I don't see anything that represents wrashiru."

"Neither do I."

She sighed. "So, whenever my mind blocks me from using an ability, all I have to do is come here to find it."

Tiril smiled and said, "Yes."

They made their way leisurely upstream, talking, singing, Tiril playing his flute. For the first time in many turns of the moons, Fern felt she could afford the luxury of pausing to enjoy her surroundings. Life was no longer a desperate search for food. She pointed out new plants she'd found and told Tiril about their properties and uses.

"Wow!" he said. "You've done more to expand our knowledge than anyone has since we first settled this planet. Can you remember everything?"

"No, it's too much to remember. I recorded everything in a journal in my library. I even sketched the plants and the seeds I collected."

"Doran will be impressed."

"When times were hard and I was afraid I was going to die, I worried that all this knowledge would be lost."

He hugged her. "We weren't going to let you die."

When they rested in the long afternoons and camped in the evenings, Tiril guided Fern through her mind, helping her unlock and sharpen her gifts. She was amazed at her mind's intricacies. She played with her talents and expanded them. She couldn't procure things frivolously, but they never ran out of skri.

After one session, tears filled Fern's eyes. "Do you realize you are the only person I've allowed complete access to my mind? Taran wasn't able to teach me everything he wanted to, because I wouldn't let him in. I let Andli in, only so she could keep me healthy. Sometimes Doran popped in to teach me something when I couldn't understand his words. Ansil helped me find my library, but that's all I'd let him do. I didn't trust him as much as I trust you."

Tiril took her hand. "I don't know what I've done to earn so much trust, but I feel honored."

She threw her arms around him. "I feel safe with you. You've been my link to my family. You *are* my family."

* * *

The waterfall was a magical place. Sunlight danced in the splashing water to create rainbows. Fern named it Rainbow Falls. When the moons rose, the waters gleamed like silver. At the feet of the cascade was a pool perfect for swimming. They found a small cave for shelter from rain. Tiril played tunes that mimicked the sounds of the waterfall.

One afternoon in her tool room, Fern picked up her wings and, using ethenos, mentally rose above their camp, followed the river upstream, and traced the long path to where she'd encountered Mt. Frustration. She confronted the fiery mountain. *You stood between me and my goal. You made me change my path.* But her new path had led to Tiril. *Perhaps I should thank you.*

Rising into the air, she drifted over the volcano and gazed into the mighty caldera churning with black fire. Safe from any harm, neverthe-less she quailed at its power. She imagined the intense heat that pierced to the bowels of the planet. She thought about the mountain village where she had entered this world and how it had been destroyed by such as this. That, too, had changed the course of her life, leading to Ansil.

The White Mountain shone in the distance. What had Ansil said? From his prospective there was no barrier between her and the White Mountain. Well, now there wasn't. She rose and skimmed the treetops. How wonderful it was to fly! Wrashiru would not show her the beautiful land that rolled beneath her. And there was so much to explore.

Time seemed not to matter. She soared over the White Mountain. She'd never seen so much ice and snow and was too overawed to explore it properly. Returning to what had been her closest approach to the mountain on foot, she traced her steps from there to the mountain village, and was astonished at the distance she had covered.

When she returned, she told Tiril about her experience. "In the past, when I explored Earth by ethenos, once I flew from New York City to St. Augustine. It's about a thousand miles. I can't measure miles here, but the distance from here to the mountain village seems about the same."

"That's as the crow flies. Figure in the uphill and down, zigzagging to follow rivers, can you imagine how far you walked?"

"Well, no wonder I lost so much weight! If I'd had any idea how far I'd gone, I probably would have turned back sooner."

"I envy you. I can wrashiru, but I can't do ethenos. It sounds like fun."

"I wonder if I could teach you? We'll have to try it someday."

That evening, Tiril mused, "I'm no philosopher like Taran, or botanist like Doran, but I made some observations about the plant life on Earth. Here, plants don't need to protect themselves from animals, so they lack defenses, like thorns." He used the English word. "We don't have fruits or flowers here like on Earth because, until we came, there was no reason for the plants to lure animals for pollination or to spread seeds. That may change. Plants are already responding to us. These ideas became apparent to me when your grandparents took me blackberry picking."

"Yes, I saw that conversation."

"They couldn't believe I'd lived in the country all my life but never had blackberries. So they took me down the road to an empty field where the berries grow."

Fern smiled in memory of romping there with her sisters while their grandparents picked blackberries. Popping warm berries into her mouth, crushing out the juices, the seeds gritting in her teeth.

He continued, "By the time we finished, I was so scratched and bleeding, your sisters laughed at me. But I did learn to maneuver around the thorns, and I made myself heal overnight. It was a good learning experience, in more ways than one. I had to celebrate it in song." He played a few bars on his flute, then sang, in English:

> Gleaming black in the Sun.
> I reach my hand around the thorns.
> A little tug—if ripe, it comes away.
> If not, let it ripen for another day.
>
> This bush now picked,
> More fingers black and red
> Reach out to me. I turn.
> More beckon.
>
> Have I not picked here?
> Have more now ripened
> In a moment's time?
> Or efforts rewarded—more revealed?
>
> My pail not full,
> My back begins to ache.
> My vision blurs from sweat.
> I must go home.
>
> But more waylay my path,
> And bush gives way to bush.
> Is there no end? I must
> Go home and tend my wounds.

How much is life like berry picking?
Thorns among the fruits to scratch.
And not all picked. Not time enough,
Before, subdued and tired,

We must go home,
Perhaps to bake a pie,
For sure to rest,
Remember, and renew.

"It had to be in English because Human Talk doesn't have all the words. Actually, your grandmother gave me some of the ideas. I was too proud to complain about getting tired, but she said when her back begins to ache, it's time to go home. Then she kept picking more berries on the way back to the car. I shared the song with them, and they liked it."

Fern gave him a wry smile. "Not a philosopher?"

"Not really. I would aspire to be a poet, but I lack the talent."

"You sell yourself too short."

"I think I'll stick to music." He played a few bars. "It was actually your grandfather who taught me the proper way to pick berries. I kept getting the half-ripe ones until he set me straight. He said to give them the slightest tug, and if they were ready, they'd fall into my hand. He was right. But he's not always a patient man."

Fern smiled wistfully. "I wish I'd been there."

With easy living and plenty of food, Fern filled out and her body healed. She became the picture of youthful health and beauty. Tiril delighted in fixing her hair. "I wish I had Ansil's talent for bead making," he said. "Then I could do it justice."

Ansil. She missed him. Neither had been able to contact him. Tiril assured her they'd encounter him again one day, in a new form.

Tiril finished her hair and gave her the comb so she could do his. She loved the feel of his silky dark hair. She tried to plait it in a different pattern every day.

While she worked on it, he said, "On Earth, I was overwhelmed by so many beautiful girls. Blondes like you, red heads, and of course brunettes. Blue eyes and brown eyes, many skin colors, so much variety. I was of an age when I should have enjoyed the pleasures of mating, but it was unwise for me to become involved with a woman unless I intended to remain on Earth and fulfill my responsibilities. We usually go as couples, or as children. Taran cautioned me about the challenges I'd face. He used Forsil as an example."

"Who?"

"John Devoir. He fell in love with Alice and couldn't leave her. So, if a girl pressed me for anything beyond friendship, I'd tell her I had a beautiful blonde waiting for me at home."

"But I wasn't waiting for you. I might have mated with Ansil, if he'd lived, even though he was already mated with Tira."

"I knew that. But it wouldn't have prevented you from mating with me as well."

Fern shook her head. Sometimes she wondered if she could have found happiness with Ansil and Tira, but would she have been able to live with two men? "Why didn't you go with Lila and Taran, like Tira did?"

"I had a different agenda. I wanted to do as much background research as I could before I left. I wanted to be prepared for the college experience, and to find Moses."

"But you were separated from your parents for years. Didn't you miss them?"

"Of course, I missed their physical presence, but I was in contact with them. And I had Rogan and Risa, and Tira's parents at the mountain village. Remember, our people have lived this way for millennia."

She nodded. "But the way I grew up still has a strong hold on me."

"Of course it does. And now I understand, having lived among your people."

She worked on his hair. "What about Hansa? When I first met you, I thought you were in love with her."

"I was sorely tempted. We've always been close. But I learned from my parents' experience not to fall in love with a close cousin, like Taran and Rina. Lila and Taran still love each other, but they can't agree on where to live, and they're happier apart. Hansa is like a sister to me."

So, her assumption that Tiril had been attracted to Hansa hadn't been wrong after all. "I wonder, if I hadn't come here, if I'd remained on Earth, do you think we would have met? Would you have fallen in love with me? Would you have married me and stayed there?"

He shrugged. "I can't answer that. It would have been a dilemma greater than the one Lila and Taran faced. And I'm not sure I'd be happy living on Earth for the rest of my life."

"Well, since I can't wrashiru, I've become resigned to living here for the rest of mine." She bent down and kissed his head. "And I think I'll be happy, as long as you are with me."

They honeymooned at Rainbow Falls with short excursions to surrounding mountains and forests. Both moons were waxing again. One day, while collecting lenitrus, Fern asked permission to pick from a wispis plant, but when she reached out to pluck a leaf, her hand was stopped by a wave of nausea. "I don't think I want any of this today," she said.

Tiril looked surprised. "You usually like wispis."

But she had no taste for it the next day, either, and found herself turning her nose up at other foods as days went by. One night, tender a lover though Tiril was, he hurt her breast. "They're sore," she said.

He cradled her and kissed her neck. "I think I know what's wrong with you. Or rather, what's right. And I think we should head home."

At first, she failed to catch his meaning. Then she focused inside herself and found new life stirring. "How can that be? I haven't had a cycle in a long time."

"Apparently, your body was ready."

She looked up at him. In the moonlight, his eyes danced with joy. She'd been so focused on her love for Tiril, she had given no thought to motherhood or her readiness for it. She snuggled closer and let his love envelop her. Yes, she was happy. Tiril wiped a tear from her cheek.

They returned to the hut, packed up the belongings they'd left, and made preparations for the journey home. "I'll miss this place," Fern said.

"Maybe we'll come back some day."

"Would this hut still be standing?"

Tiril grimaced. "Probably not. It's only a temporary shelter, and I'm not the skilled builder Ansil was."

They resumed a leisurely but purposeful journey downstream. River flowed into river. When they reached the sea, they spent several days snacking on ostrica.

They pulled Tiril's boat from among the trees where he'd left it. Fern hesitated. "I'm not sure I want to go by boat."

"I'm a good sailor."

"So was Ansil."

"But I'm more careful. We'll hug the shore and not challenge storms like he did."

She half feared seasickness, but the queasy stage of her pregnancy had passed. It was so pleasant to skim the shoreline and watch the mountains flow by. Sailing was faster than walking and less taxing. When the sun was high, or if a storm threatened, they'd beach the boat until it was safe to go on. Fern wondered how Tiril had managed to drag the boat on and off shore by himself, but she didn't ask.

While watching the waves, Fern reminisced about back home—the fish and dolphins and manatees. She surveyed the skies and thought about seagulls and pelicans.

She may have read Tiril's memories, or perhaps he read her thoughts. He said, "Now I understand why you miss birds. I love birds." He paused. "At first I was attracted to their music, but I learned I have an affinity for them. Unfortunately, it's wasted here. All the animal life on Earth is so fascinating."

"What about bugs?"

He made a face. "My apartment was infested with roaches. Initially, they intrigued me—all those little creatures scurrying around! But that didn't last. So I made a pact with them. I wouldn't spray them if they'd stay away from me and my stuff. I learned how to keep the mosquitoes away, too."

"Did you make a pact with them?"

"No. I altered my body chemistry slightly, so they weren't interested in biting me."

That night as they watched the moonlight play on the waves, Tiril said, "One regret I have is that I never got to hear the song of a nightingale. I read about them, and I heard a recording, but never had the opportunity to listen to a real one. I used to listen to birds and whistle back." He began to whistle, then picked up his flute and played. The tune was unusual, but vaguely familiar.

A memory flashed into Fern's mind, of sitting on her bed on Earth, listening to a mockingbird in the magnolia tree outside her window. The bird was concealed among the leaves where she couldn't see him. He sang for a long time. Tiril's tune imitated a mockingbird song.

The following morning was misty with no wind. Tiril paddled the boat into a current which carried them gently in the direction of the sea village. "This reminds me of some mornings on Earth, and of another bird." He sang in English:

> The morning was a' singing,
> Music danced from tree to tree,
> As a thousand little song birds
> Gaily trilled among the leaves.
>
> Then a song so soft and plaintive
> Drifted low among the rest.
> T'was a solitary mourning dove,
> That was, like a monk, brown dressed.

Then the call, oh, it was answered
By another 'cross the way.
Who-i-whoo-whoo-whoo then echoed
Through the morning and the day.

"Is that one of yours?"

"Yes. I wrote it for your sisters. Unfortunately, the mockingbird was beyond my talents."

Their course took them seaward. Fern watched the shore recede until only a thin line peeked above the horizon. Before they lost sight of land altogether, she asked, "Isn't it time to tack?"

Tiril shifted the tiller and set the sail. "Were you nervous?"

"I just don't think this is the right time to take chances."

As they approached the beach, a picture of pelicans skimming along the shore in a straight line flashed through Fern's mind.

Tiril said, "Speaking of birds, you know those statues of a monk people have in their yards?"

"I think it's St. Francis of Assisi. Patron saint of birds."

"Your grandmother has one in her flower garden."

Fern closed her eyes and pictured her grandmother's flowers, the sunshine, the bees and butterflies.

"I didn't want to show my ignorance to your grandma, so I went to a garden store and asked about the statue." He chuckled. "The clerk must have thought I grew up in a cave. She told me who he was. Naturally, I had to read up on this guy. He was the patron saint of animals and nature. Birds flocked to him, and he would preach to them. There were stories of him communicating with all kinds of animals—wolves, even bees."

He paused to adjust the sail and rudder. "Once a wolf was ravaging a village. The people wanted to kill it, but St. Francis tamed it, then it left them alone. Sometimes he could control nature, like diverting hailstorms from crops. In one village, after he saved their crops, the people resumed their evil ways, so the hailstorms returned. Another time, he was traveling by boat and they went through a storm. They couldn't use their sails, and the sailors had to row. That must have made them hungry, because they consumed all their food before the trip was over. St. Francis shared his food with them, and it multiplied, so there was more than enough to feed everyone. Sound familiar?"

"Like the loaves and fishes."

"Yeah. Apparently the Church had no problem with St. Francis sharing a miracle with Jesus. Once he preached at a little country church and the crowd helped themselves to the grapes in the vineyard. When the priest objected, St. Francis assured him they'd still get their usual amount of wine. What was left of the grapes was eventually harvested, and they produced almost twice as much wine as usual."

"Must have been a good year."

Tiril smiled. "There were other curious things. Did you know he was psychic?."

"Really?"

"The stories don't use that word. They call what he did miracles. He could read the minds of his brother monks. If he detected they were up to no good, he'd visit them in dreams and try to set them straight."

"How much of this do you suppose is true?"

"Well, the Catholic Church doesn't just take these stories at face value. They investigate. I'm sure there've been trumped up claims to sainthood over the centuries, but some of the stories ring true. My study of St. Francis led me to reading about other saints. Did you know there were some who could wrashiru?"

"No!"

"And some could levitate themselves, or objects."

Fern thought about things she had witnessed through the years but her mind had resisted believing. "So that's how people carried those heavy logs and stones to the sameg."

"This should really interest you. Some were able to procure food or money. Not for self-gain, but for the good of the community."

When that sank in, she laughed. "I'm certainly no saint!"

"Maybe, but many of the saints were certainly psychic. The money had probably been lost to begin with, and the food may have been sitting somewhere going to waste. What I got out of all this is that our people are not alone in the universe. These abilities have been known on Earth throughout the history of mankind."

"Wow."

"But it seems that how one's gifts were received by others depended on which side of the altar rail one sat on. Unfortunately, a lot of people who showed these talents were burned as witches. And poor St. Joan got both treatments. She was sainted, after she was declared a witch and burned at the stake."

"I'll have to read up on those saints."

Chapter 25
Going to Namai

Now that she could use ethenos again, Fern visited her sisters and marveled at how they'd grown. The first night, she found them asleep and told them Tiril had arrived safely and that they were now married and going to have a baby. She hoped they could still hear her.

The next time she visited, she caught a conversation the girls were having with their grandmother.

"I wonder if Fern will have a girl or a boy?" the youngest said.

Her sister added, "I wonder what she'll name it."

Grandma shook her head. "I can't picture Fern all grown up, and married. She'll make me a great-grandmother, and I can't even brag about it. No one would believe me."

The next day, Tiril and Fern came to the mouth of a wide river and sailed into a bay. The valley stretched inland for miles. He pointed out a distant rocky ridge that rose above the intervening hills. "On the other side of that is the mountain village."

"Can we go there from here?"

"It's possible, but the climb would be hard."

"I want to go home to have the baby." That beautiful, soft word, namai. As she said it, she realized what she meant by home—the mountain village.

"Of course, but we'll go to the sea village first."

That night, camped on the river bank, Fern mused, "It was near here that Ansil had his accident."

"Yes."

With a catch in her throat, "Did they ever find his body?"

"No." Tiril said, as nonchalantly as if a mere possession had been lost. "It probably washed out to sea."

"I was very angry with him for dying."

"So was I. He was a good brother, but foolhardy at times."

"I just don't understand how, with your psychic abilities, no one foresaw that, no one warned him. Tira seemed to think he had a premonition, and that's why they started a baby."

"Why didn't you ask Ansil?"

"I did, and he said he didn't see it coming."

"Well, psychic abilities aren't perfect. Like our physical senses. We often ignore what they tell us. As for seeing the future, it's better to dwell in the present. If you'd known you were going to lose both parents, but could do nothing to stop it, how would you have felt?"

"Miserable. And I'd have blamed myself for not preventing it." She shook her head. "I blamed myself, anyway. Knowing ahead of time would have made it worse."

The next morning she was anxious to get underway. By afternoon, they had reached the sea village.

The first person to greet Fern was Andli. They hugged and wept. Fern looked around for Tira, half expecting and fully hoping to see her, too.

Andli answered her thoughts, "Tira has a new son and waits for you in the mountain village." She looked at the necklace Fern wore. "Metia's?"

"Yes." Fern told her how she got it.

Andli smiled with approval and laid something in Fern's hand. "I brought you this."

It was her little pouch with the medallion, the miaven flower, and the egg-shaped pebble. She showed it to Tiril.

He picked up the little stone. "I remember this. You found it in the volcano fields and told me it was like a bird's egg. And you've kept it all this time!"

Another member of her mountain family was present. Jorsil stood nearby with his mate Tana, and between them stood a child whom Jorsil introduced as Sisa. The little girl wouldn't let Fern hug her, but gazed up at her in awe.

Tiril tapped her shoulder. His mother, Lila, stood by, waiting to greet her. Behind her, Rogan stood beside a woman who must be Risa, now home from Italy.

Lila threw her arms around Fern. "Daughter."

Fern melted into the arms of her child's grandmother.

A small house had been prepared for them. That night, the entire village gathered for supper in their honor. They were urged to tell of their adventures, especially Fern, who had walked further across this planet than anyone before. When she was tired of speaking, music and dancing took over. Tiril smiled. "Someday, I may compose a ballad about Brave Fern who set out alone to explore a strange new world."

"I wasn't alone. Ansil was with me."

"Oh, he doesn't count."

She imagined she heard Ansil chuckle, but it was only in her memory.

When they stood to say goodnight, the whole village sang them off to bed.

* * *

Fern shared half of her collection of herbs, seeds, and roots with the sea village. Andli was interested in the healing properties of plants Fern had discovered and said, "Doran will be very happy. I'm glad you recorded their growing habits for him."

"I'm going to leave one potato here. It may not grow at sea level, but I think they'll grow in the mountains."

"If anyone can get them to grow, Doran will."

Taran joined them and didn't hide the pride he took in his children's accomplishments. After what felt to Fern like a lengthy visit, they set off for the mountain village. Lila accompanied them. "I want to meet my grandson," she said.

With Fern's gift of procurement, they didn't have to carry much food. Instead, they filled their backpacks with items for the mountain village. In the evenings when they rested, Tiril talked about his experiences on Earth and his adjustment to life there.

"Despite my years of preparation, I discovered how little I knew, how little I understood." To Fern, he said, "I also got a taste of what you were up against when you first came here. I had a good command of English, but when I was immersed in the language, hearing and speaking it all the time, having to think in it, I found it emotionally exhausting. I had to spend more time in meditation and sleep."

He squeezed her hand. "I gained new respect for you. You were dropped onto our world with no warning or preparation, into a foreign language and customs, and at the same time you were grappling with the loss of your family. I realized what a strong person you are, and what an asset you are to our world. I'm glad I'm the lucky man who won your heart."

Fern blushed. "I used to feel like I was a failure, especially when I couldn't learn the language." She thought about Tira and all the years she had resented her because she felt inferior in comparison. Now, the tables were turned. Though her accomplishments had surpassed Tira's, she knew Tira wouldn't be jealous. Fern looked forward to a reunion with her sister and to rearing their children together.

Taran cleared his throat. "Fern, I owe you an apology for the way I tried to educate you. I attempted to teach you the same way I did my other children. I thought you would overcome your previous conditioning with little effort, but I was wrong. I didn't understand your needs, and for that I'm sorry."

She was almost too surprised to speak. "But you were right—I only had to unlock my mind. Once I did that, things became so much easier. Of course, it was the memory of my life on the thortle world that helped me unlock it."

Tiril told Taran what he'd learned about Fern's mother. This led to a discussion about Fern's former fear of the stars.

"One thing I forgot to tell you," he said to Fern, "your grandmother told me that your mother had nightmares when she was small, but once she stopped using psychic abilities, the nightmares stopped."

Taran shook his head. "Perhaps both of you were targeted by the thortles."

Fern shuddered. What if her mother had been kidnapped? Would she have been born on the thortle world? "Are you sure my sisters are safe?"

"I had no indication to the contrary," Tiril said. "They don't show strong psychic abilities. I guess that's a blessing."

"Yes," replied Fern. "A mixed blessing."

Knowing she'd soon be unable to do so, Fern slept on her belly as much as possible. One night, she found herself hugging the planet in her sleep. The world seemed to hug back and told her, "My child, I will nurture you all the days of your life."

"I will nurture you as well," she whispered.

"You already do, and for that I am grateful."

"But why do you afflict us with volcanoes and hurricanes?"

"My child, I cannot help it. That is part of me, the way I am. But I promise to warn you, so you can prepare for these things."

"Tekuyate," Fern found herself saying as she woke.

She shifted position. Tiril put his arms around her and she curled against him. When the baby moved inside her, she laid Tiril's hand against her belly.

He murmured with pleasure and pulled her closer. "Perhaps we should give him an Earth name," he whispered.

"Maybe we should let him choose his own name."

"Of course."

As they approached the mountain village, Fern wondered about her grove of miaven trees and whether they'd blossomed in her absence. At a turn of the path, she saw a splash of red and purple. She hurried ahead and found a miaven in full bloom. "Doran has been here!"

No one said anything. When they came to the cliff overlooking the valley, the woods before them sported color wherever miaven trees grew. Fern was too overcome to speak.

"Actually, this is your doing," Taran said. "Once the miaven trees understood how much we humans enjoy flowers, others began to bloom. See how they're starting to spread?"

Rina and Doran climbed up to meet them, accompanied by Tala and Ara, now grown as tall as Fern. With them was a young man she recognized, with a start, as her brother Donal. They lunched together and caught up on news before descending into the valley.

"Doran," Fern said, "do you think we can convince other plants to produce flowers?"

"I've given that some thought. I was waiting for you to come home so you could help me. You know more about flowers than I do."

Her heart leapt and her mind envisioned vines and trees and other plants putting out colorful bracts or even true petals.

"That's what I mean," he said.

She smiled. She didn't mind that he read her thought.

After they reached the valley, Tira met them, accompanied by Arlon, Fern's old suitor from the village by the sea. Tira carried a newborn in her arms and a little girl rode on Arlon's shoulders—Sita, Ansil's daughter. Arlon set her down. Sita kept her hands behind her back. Fern thought she was shy, until the child produced a bouquet of miaven blossoms and handed them to Fern. By habit, Fern sniffed them, but they had no scent. *That's something else we can work on.*

Tira put her son into Fern's arms and hugged her. "Sister, I am so happy you've returned home."

Fern began to cry. A tear fell onto the face of the sleeping infant who arched his back in protest. They all laughed. Tira took the baby back and said, "You'll stay with us until we build you a house. We could have built one for you, but we thought you'd like to have a hand in it."

"Tekuyate." She'd always wanted to design her own home. Memories of life on Earth stirred within her, thoughts of helping her father remodel their old farmhouse. "There are a few things I'd like to do differently." She looked at Tiril. "For one thing, I want a window, and shelves to put things on."

Tiril smiled. "And so you shall."

Sita grabbed Fern's free hand and led her to the sameg. Soon they were surrounded by women, men, and children anxious to greet them. Sita released Fern's hand, ran to the hearth, and grabbed a skri. The dream memory of the little girl handing her bread flashed through Fern's mind and she realized it had been Sita who'd sent her the skri. This child had been instrumental in saving her life. She and Sita had combined their talents to accomplish that, much as she and her mother had combined theirs to bring her here.

Fern sat down in front of Tira's house and laid the bouquet of flowers in her lap. Her gaze drifted around the village, to the surrounding mountains and forests. Namai at last.

With her great adventure now behind her, she was ready to pause and reflect while the child within her grew. She felt safe in the care of family and friends. Her thoughts briefly receded to another world, another time when she'd felt safe and cared for, another home, her family of origin. If she disregarded the early years which she didn't remember, she had by now spent over one third of her life here. Someday it would be half. As time went by, the percentage would increase and Earth would become only a childhood memory.

Sita interrupted Fern's musings and placed the skri in her hands. "Here you are, Auntie Fern."

Thereafter, she was called by the children, "Auntie Fern." To subsequent generations, she became known simply as "Ahnti."

GLOSSARY

Ahnti – plant with medicinal properties that resembles our resurrection fern

Barca – boat (Italian)

Bitti – please (German)

Erguvon – tree with heart-shaped leaves

Esmilu tefi – I love you

Estut miryit – I'm sorry

Ethenos – etheric, or astral, projection

Fan-flower – an edible flower that grows in the jungle

Human Talk – their language

Kirrib - soup

Lenitrus – salad greens

Miaven – a small, ornamental tree

Namai – home (Lithuanian for house, home, roof)

Ostrica – "oyster," a plant that lives in the water (Italian)

Salut – hello

Sameg – common area in the middle of the village

Skri – bread

Tekuyate – thank you

Thortles – captors, from whom the people escaped to this planet

Wispis – edible plant with frilly leaves, like our leaf lettuce

Weka – oldest generation living, great-great-grandparents

Wrashiru – transporting (Beam me up, Scotty!)

CAST OF CHARACTERS

Fern's adopted family:
  Parents: Andli, Taran, Rina, Doran
  Sisters: Tira, Tala, Ara
  Brothers: Jorsil, Donal
Extended family:
  Rufan, son of Andli and Autin (deceased)
  Sela, his wife, a weaver
  Dorba, their daughter
  Tiril, son of Taran and Lila
Elders and weka:
  Alta, Taran's mother, the fire maker
  Noba, Andli's mother, has the gift of Ethenos
  Bregan, Taran's grandfather, the wood splitter
  Motan, a chemist
  Metia, a weka, daughter of Hannah
  Roni, a weka Fern meets on her trek
Others from the mountain village:
  Simbi, Fern's toddler friend
  Farsa and Belan, Simbi's parents
  Hansa, Tiril's cousin
  Aldan, her mate
  Janil, their son
  Narvil, one of Fern's former suitors
  Darsan, a geologist
  Tirna, his student

Tandil, a small boy
Sea people:
    Ansil, young man Tira is in love with
    Lila, mother of Ansil and Tiril
    Rogan, her mate, father of Ansil
    Arlon, a boy who has visited Mexico
    Tana, a girl Jorsil is interested in
Ancestors who appear in stories:
    First Parents: Moses and Rila
    Martha, their daughter, the first fire maker
    Tanil, Martha's mate
    Abraham, son of Moses and Rila
    Anli, his wife
    Hannah, the youngest daughter of Moses and Rila
    Hartha, a poet, daughter of Martha and Tanil
    Wosan, Horil, and Rala, children of Abraham and Anli
On the thortle world:
    Miri, a girl who is captured from Earth
    JinKaJin, the number the thortles give Miri
    ForTaNin, a middle aged woman who teaches her
    ElSoDan, an elderly man with strong psychic powers
    JonRilJin, young man who becomes Miri's mate

TO THE READER

Thank you for reading *Quest for Namai*.

It has been my pleasure to take you on this journey. If you enjoyed reading this novel, please write a review on Amazon and Goodreads. Reviews help sell books, and sales nourish the writer, physically and creatively, so she can bring forth more stories.

To read more of my work, visit my website, https://marieqrogers.com/ and my Amazon page. I am available for readings and talks on topics related to my writing. You can contact me through my website.

May all your quests lead you safely back to namai.

About the Author

When not traveling, award-winning author Marie Q Rogers has nothing better to do than wander the woods of North Florida and think about curious things. Her musings have evolved into short stories, novels, and creative nonfiction posted on her website marieqrogers.com.